The Weeping Willow Sings

Billie Grable

BOOK PUBLISHERS NETWORK
Changing the World One Book at a Time

Book Publishers Network
P.O. Box 2256
Bothell • WA • 98041
Ph • 425-483-3040
www.bookpublishersnetwork.com

10 9 8 7 6 5 4 3 2 1
Printed in the United States of America

ISBN 978-1-940598-22-2
LCCN 2014930790

Editor: Julie Scandora and Amy Taricco
Cover Designer: Laura Zugzda
Typographer: Marsha Slomowitz

Author portrait: Matthew Brashears
http://www. brashearsphotography.com/

http://theweepingwillowsings.com/

To Mom, for teaching me how to sidestep reality and embrace that place in my heart where anything is possible.

And to Dad, for my stubborn drive and bossy disposition. I miss you.

ACKNOWLEDGMENTS

It's been said that a book is judged first by its cover. The cover on the first edition of *The Weeping Willow Sings* certainly had its critics. Some thought it was a children's book, and others simply didn't understand the meaning at all. Truth be told, I am the artist behind that creation. Having no experience in graphic design, I thought I could do the job. I have learned that developing a compelling cover is a job for a graphic designer—not an amateur artist like me.

The cover design on this second edition of *The Weeping Willow Sings* was created by Laura Zugzda. It provides the essence of the story—a weeping willow tree, an unfinished painting, and the ghost of a man who discovers that death didn't end his problems; it only made them harder to resolve.

Huge thanks goes to Sheryn Hara for providing her years of publishing experience to this project. And a special thanks to my first editor, Amy Logsdon Taricco, whose Catholic upbringing provided a special dimension to her edits. And to Julie Scandora, final editor and accomplished painter, who provided last-minute touches that only an artist can give.

I thank each and every person who has read *The Weeping Willow Sings*. I appreciate the private messages I've received on Facebook and in email and am humbled that my novel has touched so many lives.

ONE

———

Sunlight filtered through the studio window and dulled before touching the hardwood floor. The pressure points on John's forehead throbbed, and the corners of the room began to fade.

Half-finished paintings littered one side of his studio, each a desperate attempt to capture the fleeting memories of a tree house hidden in a willow tree.

Every time John tried to recreate the scene on canvas, each stroke became a defiant barrier between his childhood and the present—the most important memory remained lost in his mind.

John cleaned his paintbrushes with walnut oil and sat his latest canvas next in line. He analyzed each one, searching for the missing piece—a wrong shade or muted highlight, a branch too short or too long—any sign that the image hadn't vanished entirely.

Defeat overwhelmed him as he turned his attention to the paintings on the opposite wall. A family portrait had captured Maggie's enchantment, and Nora's beauty, before his frenzies darkened the circles under Nora's eyes.

A recent sketch Maggie had drawn of John sat next to the portrait. Her raw talent was undeniable. She had captured the twinkle that used to be present in John's smile.

When Maggie turned seven, they transformed her bedroom into a castle. Their synergy prompted one to complete the other's brushstroke, as walls became stone barricades, and the ceiling, a sky filled with stars.

He could not lose his ability to paint.

Fear showered the room as he mixed fresh colors on his palette. With shaking hand, he started over, and when he finished, he stepped back and scrutinized his work.

The only recognizable objects in his painting were turbulent gray storm clouds and black streaks of driving rain.

John paced the perimeter of the studio, then stopped, and gazed at the family portrait. The images stared back at him.

The paint softened around Nora's face and produced an angelic glow. When he looked into Nora's eyes, she smiled and whispered, *Just trust me, John.*

When John hit his lowest point, Nora was always there to bring him back, and she praised each painting he created.

"Your life is a gift," she would tell him. "Just look at your amazing talent. You have so much to give, to share. You do realize that, don't you, John?"

Yes, Nora would help him.

He rushed to the door and tried to open it. A man's voice boomed so loudly the windows in the back of the studio trembled.

We knew you'd come back.

John jerked his hand from the doorknob and whirled around.

"What do you want?"

Lightning crackled, and hysterical laughter shook the room. The family portrait grew larger in the distance. Nora smirked at John. The rain fell in sheets and puddled on the floor.

The sudden downpour ended. John leaned into the door. It froze against his back. He gasped and then rushed into the center of his studio.

He scanned each corner of the room once. Then again.

All clear.

He was alone.

The pools on the floor turned to steam and disappeared. When he looked at the portrait again, Nora appeared as solid as the canvas bearing her image.

It's time, John. She cannot help you.

The voice exploded inside his head, and he pressed his hands over his ears.

If he went to Nora now, they would convince her to send him away.

He could eliminate the oppression without Nora's intervention. He had shut the voices out in the psych ward. He'd do it again.

John knelt next to the easel and prayed. "God, our … my Father, you know my weakness. Give me strength to overcome the evil that threatens to take my mind from my body. I beg of you. Amen."

John leaned back on his knees and waited for the roar of God's thunder. His face grew colder with each passing second. The floor hardened and penetrated his calves, winding up his legs until disappointment stiffened his body.

He staggered to his writing table and collapsed in the chair. The air moved, and when he looked up, electrical wires dangled from the ceiling. He blinked and steadied himself against the desk and watched them disappear.

When he closed his eyes and envisioned the electric shock treatment imploding his mind, he saw Maggie.

Watching. Crying.

John turned to his desk, grabbed a notepad and pen from the top drawer, and began to write. The ink was black and bold against the white paper. The words felt right and offered momentary relief.

A sudden movement caught his attention. He peered out the window next to his desk. The July sun scorched the grass as Maggie ran across the backyard. Her long blond curls flowed freely in the wind; he could almost feel the silky strands between his fingers.

She deserves to be free, John. You've harmed her enough. You know what you must do.

The voice was soft and reassuring, and John's resistance dissolved. He loved Maggie too much. And Nora—she deserved more than the erratic existence they lived in.

John took a long, deep breath, allowing his final message to take shape in his mind before returning pen to paper.

* * *

Maggie could climb the apple tree with her eyes closed. The feel of the bark against her bare feet gave her a sense of power as she climbed. It was automatic—the way each foot knew which branch to step on, the way she felt light enough to fly as she moved closer to the top.

Halfway up, the branches trembled, and when she peered upward, her best friend, Becca, smirked down at her.

"What took you so long? I've been sitting here forever, and I practically have bark growing on my butt cheeks."

"Well Miss 'I'm so funny I could win *Last Comic Standing*,' I believe *ass* is the term you're looking for." Maggie swung her leg over the last branch and sat down.

"Nope. Butt cheeks is more accurate. Can you please tell me where you've been?" Becca's tacky pink top and faded black shorts made her look like she was the one forced to shop at Value Village or the Walmarché.

"I've been hiding. Mom's on another rampage. And Dad's giving her the silent treatment." Maggie's baggy camp shirt hid a teeshirt speckled with paint. It was the one she always wore when she painted with her dad. Maggie loved how she and her father could dissolve into an imaginary world when they picked up a palette and paintbrush. Those days had been less frequent lately, but Maggie wore the tee just in case Dad called a spur-of-the-moment painting session. After all, she wanted to be ready.

Maggie picked a green apple, took a huge bite, and pulled a saltshaker from her shirt pocket. Just when she started to sprinkle the apple with salt, her mother yelled from the back porch.

"Mary Margaret O'Brien, where are you? Get in here this minute and bring me the saltshaker."

The irritation in her mother's voice made Maggie angry. If Dad really were sick again, Mom wouldn't yell at her like that. Her voice would be soft and sad and sound like it was a million miles away.

Maggie chomped her teeth into her apple, thumbed her nose, and flipped the bird all at the same time. Becca sneezed and laughed so hard she doubled over and almost fell off the branch.

"Maggie, is that you laughing? You aren't in that tree, are you? Your father doesn't want you climbing the apple tree."

Becca's hand remained clamped over her mouth and Maggie kept quiet until she heard the back screen whack against the door jam.

"Geez, Mag, I almost peed my pants." Becca broke the silence as she wiped the tears out of her eyes.

Maggie hurled her apple toward the ground and threw her hands up in disgust. "God, I just hate her sometimes. She's such a liar. Dad has never told me I couldn't climb trees. Besides, the apple tree is the only place I can go to get away from *her*."

"But why would your mom lie?"

"Because. All moms lie. Especially mine. She keeps saying how sick Dad is, and I know for a fact that he's just frustrated about his latest painting."

"Whaaaat? I bet he's just getting depressed … again." Becca rolled her eyes and took a huge bite of her apple.

Maggie looked away and bit her bottom lip. Sure, he was depressed— he had schizoaffective bipolar disorder, to be exact. That, and post-traumatic stress from the Gulf War. Maggie had read and reread the doctor reports from all the times her dad ended up in the psych ward. And she'd done some research of her own on the Internet and proved two things: One, most artistic personalities were prone to some sort of depression, and two, as long as her dad took his meds, he would be fine.

She untangled her long blond curls and secured her hair with a scrunchie.

"All artists get depressed, Becca. It's a sign of their, well, their creative genius. Take Sonny on *General Hospital*. He has bipolar disorder in real life, and they actually wrote it into the plot."

"That had nothing to do with genius, Maggie. Hollywood just wants everyone to think he's normal, that's all. Besides, your dad isn't a soap star."

"Of course he isn't, dimwit. He's an artist. And FYI, when Dad was a kid, he spent all his time painting in a tree house his dad built for him in a willow tree. It had this sort of mini art studio with a hidden view of a valley, filled with tons of wildflowers and a pond." Maggie had heard the story so many times she had it memorized. "And when the wind blew at just the right speed, the willow's branches would *actually* sing."

"Yeah, well, where exactly is this willow tree? Maybe we could go there, and it could give us some singing lessons."

Becca grinned like a three-year-old, and Maggie wondered if her best friend was ever going to act like she was almost fifteen.

"Actually, I've never been to the willow tree. But Dad said we'd go there so I can paint in the tree house like he did."

Maggie had every intention of painting in that tree house. The only problem was some guy named Shane lived there, and it was obvious her dad hated him. But he promised that when he got rid of Shane—whatever that meant, she wasn't quite sure—he'd take her to paint in the tree house.

The screen door flew open again, and when her mother shrieked, "*NOOOW*, Maggie!" the *NOW* sounded slurred and confirmed the worst. Every time Dad got quiet, Mom started drinking. Great, here we go again.

"Are you going down there, Maggie?"

Becca tossed her apple core up in the air, and Maggie watched it ricochet off two branches before she said anything. "Yeah, but I'm not going near her, that's for sure. It sounds like she's already had too much wine."

"Yeah, I know, Maggie."

Maggie hated the I-know-exactly-what-you-mean sound in Becca's voice. Sometimes she wished she could keep her mouth shut and not tell her best friend all her personal business.

"Okay, whatever. I gotta go now, Becca."

Maggie climbed backward down the tree's trunk. When she reached the last branch, she wrapped her arms around it, swung once across the grass, and hit the ground running.

＊ ＊ ＊

A fruit fly circled the mound of apples nestled inside Nora's perfectly rolled piecrust. She thought about swatting the fly, but even that seemed too hard.

Nora shouldn't have agreed to John's release from the psych ward. But he seemed so, so … normal. And he'd been taking his pills, hadn't he? She should check. No, she reasoned, this time is different. He'll be just fine.

She rummaged inside the cupboard and pulled out the pack of cigarettes she'd hidden after she quit smoking. She poured a glass of wine. Maybe John just didn't feel good. That was entirely possible. Just because he was getting quiet again didn't mean …

Damn! Nora polished off her glass of wine and poured another. She should've quit the wine when she gave up cigarettes, but she couldn't tolerate John's downward spirals without it.

And now. She may as well be honest with herself. John's frenzied mood had started. He could disappear again. Never come home this time. If only John had heard the doctors. If only he would believe that shock treatments weren't necessary. If only she had told Maggie the truth about her father's condition. Maybe she wouldn't blame Nora when he disappeared again.

She grabbed a potato from the sink, peeled it, and then reached for another and another. She forced the peeler across the skin until all traces of dirty, brown flesh were gone.

She dumped the potatoes in a saucepan and shoved it under the faucet. She looked out the kitchen window and saw the branches in the apple tree shaking. Becca jumped off the lowest branch and disappeared over the fence.

The water streamed over the edge of the pan. Nora jerked the faucet off and reached for the saltshaker.

Damn her! Nora yanked the pot from the sink and water splashed across the floor. She slammed the saucepan on the stove and threw a roll of paper towels on the floor, stomping the entire roll until it was completely flat.

"Lord, dear God-I-can't-believe-you're-doing-this-to-me-again-John!" Nora tripped over the flattened roll and fell, landing next to the back door. When she looked up, Maggie was standing behind the screen.

The gold specks in Maggie's hazel eyes glowed like a cat backed into a corner. She trembled, her hands hidden and her elbows clamped to her side. Her sun-bronzed face flushed as she bit her bottom lip.

Nora leaned against the fridge to steady herself. The anger still raged in the pit of her stomach, and she swallowed hard as Maggie walked past the screen door.

"Didn't you hear me yelling? I'm cooking dinner, and I need the salt. Where were you? Why didn't you answer?"

"I must've been at Becca's. I would've answered, honest."

Nora wanted to scream at Maggie for lying, but the scared look on Maggie's face made her pause.

"Maggie, come here for a minute." Nora watched Maggie hesitate before she offered her the saltshaker.

"I … well … Becca and I were eating green apples. And they're always better with salt."

Maggie's face paled. A wave of guilt washed over Nora, and she forced a smile. "Peace offering, huh?"

"I'm sorry, Mom. I don't want to make you mad. And I don't want Dad to be sick anymore. He's all right, isn't he? I mean, he's not going back to the hospital again, is he?"

Nora sat down at the table and pulled her daughter close. Maggie smelled like tree bark and green apples and shook like a scared rabbit as she nestled her tiny frame into her mother's embrace.

Nora closed her eyes and wrapped her arms around her daughter. Dear God. I can't do this again. Please. Help him. Help me. Help us.

* * *

John wrote until an acceptance he'd never known calmed him. He reached into the bottom drawer of his desk and removed a hand-carved wooden paintbrush case.

He would give it to Maggie. But he couldn't leave his daughter an empty case. None of the brushes on his easel felt right; they didn't connect him to the art he shared with Maggie. He looked inside the bottom drawer of his desk, the place where he stuffed all those mementos that would seem like junk to anyone else. He found several brushes rubber-banded together, bristles smashed in disarray and covered with fluorescent paint, the ragged remnants of the day he and Maggie had splashed the stars all over her bedroom walls, the day when the line between make believe and real life had disappeared and everything was possible. They were perfect.

He folded Maggie's letter and tucked it underneath the brushes. Then he wrapped the container in brown paper and wrote her address on it. He held it in his hand and imagined her surprise when she opened it. He sealed it tight and tucked it inside his jacket.

He wrote Nora's name on an ivory envelope and slipped the note he'd written her inside. He placed it under their wedding picture in the top drawer. It wasn't difficult to tell Nora good-bye. She had her faith, and John was sure it would provide her comfort after he was gone.

John surveyed his studio one last time and then walked out and closed the door. His legs moved like petrified branches as he staggered into the living room. He lay down on the couch, and the fragrance from a fresh bouquet of garden roses lulled him to sleep.

When John woke, it was dark outside. Nora was putting away the last clean dish when he walked into the kitchen. He watched her close the oven drawer.

Nora turned, startled at first, and then went to him. The scent of her perfume and a hint of red wine surrounded John as her hand touched his shoulder.

Threads of gray mingled with her sun-streaked brown hair. Tiny lines etched her forehead and deepened her frown. Nonetheless, Nora was still a natural beauty. Her large blue eyes rimmed with thick brown lashes were still capable of melting his heart and changing his mind.

"Hungry? I have a plate ready to microwave. Your favorite, pot roast."

"No." John stared out the window and avoided eye contact.

"How about dessert? Apple pie with ice cream?" She looked up at him and tried to meet his gaze.

"Thanks, but I'm ..." The room felt crowded, and John heard someone snicker. He struggled to find the right thing to say because he knew what Nora—what they—could do to him.

"But you're exhausted from painting."

Nora looked down and wiped her hands across the front of her tank top. She ran her fingers down John's red plaid shirt, drawing small hearts around each button. He stiffened, and she turned and walked over to the counter.

"Let me know when you're hungry," Nora said, pouring a glass of wine and hesitating before facing him.

"I'm going upstairs to tell Maggie good night." John leaned against the doorway to strengthen his resolve. "Then I'm packing for the trip to the coast with Steve tomorrow." The statement came out as a challenge, and John readied himself for Nora's response.

"What trip?"

"With Steve. We're going to North Beach. Clam digging. Come on, Nora, I told you about it days ago."

"You're coming back, aren't you? I mean, are you sure you should drive?" A flush of color rose up her neck and she took a drink of her wine before speaking again. "I'll make a nice breakfast and pack a lunch in the morning."

"No. No lunch either. We'll eat at North Beach."

Nora hesitated before she spoke. "John, can we talk?"

"I'm tired, Nora." John turned to leave.

"The shock treatments."

John spun around and glared at her.

"They aren't going to do that—give you them. Dr. Roberts said the new medication you've been taking will help with the—"

"I know what they said. What they intend to do. You can't possibly know anything that went on, Nora." John watched her fidget with her wine glass. "How could you know? You weren't there."

Nora's shoulders drooped as she leaned against the kitchen counter. "Did you take your meds today, John?"

He glared at her and waited before he answered. When he spoke, a single word hissed from his lips. "Yes."

The lie forced Nora to steady herself against the counter and John to walk away.

The hardwood stairs echoed as John ascended to the second floor. He paused at the top and took a deep breath before walking into Maggie's bedroom.

A black light illuminated the fluorescent stars as they twinkled across the ceiling and down the castle walls. When John walked in, Maggie sat leaned against the window sill. She turned and smiled. She stretched her hand toward the sky and tried to touch the moon's gilded edge with her fingertips.

"How does the moon do that, Dad?"

"Do what, honey?"

"Look small enough to pick from the sky with your hand."

"Ah. That's one of life's greatest mysteries, Magpie."

John sighed as he sat on the edge of her bed. There was so much to explain. He wanted to tell her he'd be at her high school graduation. Walk her down the aisle when she married. That she'd always be his baby, even when she had babies of her own.

You know what you must do.

The voice oozed inside every fiber of John's body, and he had to wait a moment before speaking.

"Maggie, honey, I'm going clamming in the morning with Uncle Steve."

"When did this come up, Dad? I thought you weren't supposed to drive." Maggie sat up so fast John knew he'd have to choose his words carefully.

"We decided a couple of days ago. Don't worry so much, Magpie. I'm just fine." John stared out Maggie's bedroom window and hoped a breeze would come in and whoosh the fear out of her room.

"You were painting the willow again, weren't you, Dad?"

Her eyes flickered with worry. John's mind flashed to the unfinished canvases lining the studio wall. "I thought I had it right this time. It was like …"

"You were a kid again, inside the tree house painting the wildflowers in the meadow. And they danced, didn't they, Dad? And you knew that heaven was sending down every bit of warmth to make them safe so they could grow …"

"But they didn't. I can't. It's too late." John shuddered as a different voice echoed in his head.

That's right, John. It's time.

John stared at the floor as he rose to his feet.

"No, it's not!" Maggie's voice startled John, and he quickly scanned each corner of the room. She grasped his hands and moved closer to him. "I'm almost fifteen, and you promised to take me there. Let's go, Dad; let's go tomorrow."

If you take her there, you will destroy her. Just as they destroyed you.

John let go of Maggie's hand and moved away from the bed. "No. Not tomorrow, Magpie."

"But if we go together, you and me …"

He puzzled over her words. "You're right, honey; maybe someday you can go there and find what's missing. Promise me you'll go, Magpie."

"Of course, okay, but Dad …" Her eyes filled with tears.

"Everything is going to be fine now, Magpie. You'll be fine." John tucked Maggie under her covers and hoped she'd remember how much he loved her. He leaned down and kissed her forehead and cheeks and then the top of her nose.

Maggie leaned up and kissed John's eyelashes. "Butterfly kisses … Dad?"

"Yes, honey." His voice faltered as he spoke. The room grew smaller, and John prayed for the strength to tell his daughter good-bye.

"I love you, Dad." The moonlight played across her face, and his heart felt as if it would burst. He leaned down and kissed her again.

"I love you too, Magpie." John tilted his head to one side and smiled and then watched her close her eyes.

Maggie kept her eyes closed until her father left her room. She waited for a second and then sat up and whispered to the stars. "Dad's sick again. I don't want Uncle Steve to have to take care of him." She took a deep breath. "That settles it. I'm going with them."

She jumped out of bed and gathered clothes for the trip. She couldn't take much. The pickup would already be full with shovels, buckets, and coolers of ice.

She changed her clothes and then slipped back between the covers. The hands on the clock inched slowly, and when it struck midnight, Maggie crept out of bed.

She stuffed pillows beneath her bedspread, making sure it looked like she was snuggled underneath. She tiptoed downstairs and inside the garage. The truck's canopy door squeaked as she opened it. She waited until she was sure nobody heard it before climbing inside.

Maggie unraveled a sleeping bag and scooted all the way to the bottom. She hoped her Dad wouldn't be too upset when she jumped out of the truck and surprised him. After all, he loved the ocean almost as much as the willow tree. And once they had a good walk on the beach, she could convince him to go back home. And maybe she could persuade him to take her to paint in the tree house.

Just like he always promised he would.

TWO

———

John stepped out of his old pickup and left the keys in the ignition. He closed the door and ran his hand over the fender before heading toward the sea.

He spotted a large piece of driftwood. He sat down on its smooth gray edge and dug a deep hole in the sand. He pulled out the hand-carved wooden case from his jacket and made sure Maggie's name and address were protected before burying it. He smoothed the sand until it looked as though no one had been there and then walked toward the beach.

The morning breeze delivered no unwelcome voices. John closed his eyes and allowed the humbling roar of the ocean to fill his body. Acceptance fueled each step and guided him closer to the waves crashing against the shore.

The early morning sun touched his back as he removed his shoes and dug his toes into the wet sand. The roar of the ocean gave him comfort as he walked over the foam-covered sand into the cold saltwater.

The first wave hit John's ankles and swirled between his feet. He thought about looking back but knew he was finally alone. And he had finally beat them. He didn't allow the shock treatments to destroy him the way they destroyed his mother.

The second wave knocked against John's knees, and when it receded, he stumbled down a steep ledge. He gasped as he fell deep into the ocean. A cold burst of saltwater flooded his mouth. A sharp burning sensation ricocheted through his chest. He waved his arms and hammered his legs wildly against the current as his lungs filled with saltwater.

A weightless sensation took over, and images of Maggie whirled around him. Her voice framed each one like a thousand angels singing in concert as he accepted the union between his body and the sea.

* * *

Maggie woke up coughing. The ocean breeze hammered the sides of the truck canopy. She thought it was going to fly off and hurtle her into the waves.

She crept out of her sleeping bag and peered inside the cab. It was empty. Clam buckets served as an obstacle course as she pushed the canopy open with such a force she fell to the ground. The tracks from her dad's shoes were still visible in the sand. He couldn't have gone far, not without his gear.

She struggled to her feet and followed his footprints toward the beach. She should've worn tennis shoes instead of flip flops. Every time the sand covered the floppy heels, she stumbled. She pulled them off, tearing the thin bands away from the soles and ran barefoot across the sand.

The sun glowed so brightly it momentarily blinded her. She wished she had her sunglasses. She shielded her eyes and quickened her pace, keeping her focus on the footprints in front of her. Maggie glanced up just long enough to search the trail for any sign of her father as her bare feet sunk deeper into the sand.

Maggie rushed up the first sand dune and searched the deserted beach. A pair of shoes sat next to a brown jacket on the shore. She recognized the red Keds her dad called his "kid" shoes.

She scanned the sea and saw her father floating on the crest of a wave. She screamed at him. When he didn't respond, she sprinted into the water. A huge swell pulled her under, and the saltwater stung her eyes as she tried to touch the ocean floor. Her arms and legs flailed against the weight of the sea. She tried to hold her breath. Just when everything began to dim, she saw him.

Dad. Suspended in front of her, his arms stretched out. When his fingers touched hers, he pulled her into his arms. They glided like two fish through the bubbling tide. When she opened her mouth to thank him, water rushed in, and everything went black.

* * *

John fought the darkness and tried to connect to his surroundings. He couldn't understand how he had moved out of his body and ended up on the shore. The peace, that final feeling of—

Oh God, Maggie, drowning.

When John turned toward the ocean to save her, he saw Maggie crumpled on the sand. Her hair was matted to her face. Several small crabs were scurrying up her arm as if they'd found a new playground. Her legs were twitching violently on the sand.

He rushed over and tried to give her mouth-to-mouth, but he couldn't get a firm grasp, or he was just too weak to perform the task. He scanned the beach and saw an old man standing at the top of the closest sand dune.

John screamed at him, swinging his arms as wide as he could. He tried to run toward the man, but the sand sucked John into the ground. Adrenalin fueled him forward but he was frozen in place. His legs were cement cylinders, each foot unyielding to the other. When he looked down again, Maggie's lips were blue.

Help me! My daughter, I think she's dead!

The two men running towards him were getting close.

John tried to run, but his feet no longer touched the sand. The salty air hurled him forward and moved him so fast he couldn't stop.

No, please, I'm right here. John's feet skimmed above the sand, and just as they were about to collide, the first man ran right through him.

John felt the rush of the man's blood. The sharpness of his bones. The solid mass of his muscles sent John sailing backward. He stumbled, then turned, and watched the two men attempt to save his daughter.

"Get on your cell and get help, Henry. I'll stay right here with the girl." Lefty raised Maggie's head up and started giving her mouth-to-mouth.

Please, you have to save her.

Darkness surrounded John, and time slipped away. He sank into the shadows, free-falling into a thick black fog, his arms and legs paralyzed and crumpled into a fetal position. He tried to scream, but each time he opened his mouth, it filled with hot air, and his voice dried up. The fog swirled around him in slow motion. The heat burned his eyes. It seemed an eternity passed. Just before he gave in, he saw a flicker of light and heard a familiar voice.

"Please, mister, my father. You have to find him."

Maggie's plea brought John back to the beach. Two men in white jackets held a backboard stretcher. The two older men looked on as John crept between them and sat next to Maggie.

Her lips were no longer blue. Hints of pink had returned to her face, and tears cascaded down her cheeks. John watched Henry move the wet hair off Maggie's forehead.

"I know, honey. I saw him. We'll find him, don't you worry." Henry looked up at his partner as if he were seeking permission for something.

Lefty shook his head in a resolute *no* before speaking.

"You okay? We thought you were a goner. How'd you get here, young lady? Why in the world are you on this beach all by yourself?"

"My dad. He carried me out. I think he got pulled back in. Please …"

John twisted with the agony of her words.

"But Lefty …" Henry stammered, and Lefty punched him in the arm and motioned Henry to be quiet.

John moved as close to Lefty as he could and screamed in his ear. *Henry's right, Lefty, I'm right next to you. Henry's telling the truth. You must believe him!*

Lefty didn't flinch, just watched the paramedics wrap Maggie in a warm blanket and lift her onto the backboard. Henry turned and looked at John. He opened his mouth as if to say something to John, but Lefty grabbed hold of Henry's arm and pulled him away.

"The ambulance is waiting, Henry. Let's follow them to the hospital."

"But we can't leave yet. My dad."

John tried to speak, but his daughter's sobs forced him to his knees. The paramedics moved so fast, and John felt so weak, all he could do was watch them take her away. He tried to connect his feet to the wet sand, but he couldn't feel it beneath him or the coldness of the water as it splashed over his bare toes.

This can't be happening. He would wake up and be with Maggie at the hospital. He would even have the shock treatments.

He mustered his strength and walked toward the first sand dune. The wind stopped suddenly, and the sun's light intensified and scorched every thought from his mind. He turned back toward the sea, craving the wet saltwater.

A thick mist came out of nowhere and blanketed the shoreline. It swirled toward John, tossing and turning him until the dizziness forced him to the ground. His face plunged into the foam on the wet sand, and he could feel the bubbles as they popped against his face.

When he looked up, the dense layer of fog was gone. A man with shaggy brown hair, tattered clothes, and brown sandals stood at the water's edge. He had a ghostly aura. The thundering surf provided an eerie backdrop. The man's voice rose above it as he spoke.

"This is a selfish thing you have done, John O'Brien."

Selfish? He had just saved Maggie's life. There was nothing selfish about saving his daughter. How dare anyone pass judgment after he almost lost her!

"You were watching! My daughter almost drowned. Why didn't you help?"

The water swirled around the man's feet, and the movement threatened to spin John back into the darkness. It took every bit of his strength to look this man in the eye and give him a defiant stare.

The wind picked up, and a lone sea gull circled over the man's head. He reached up and touched the bird's wing and then motioned it on its way. He brushed away the hair that drifted across his face and rubbed his thumb against his chin as he met John's glare.

His eyes were splashed with a blue so intense it challenged the sky, their radiance so forceful it sucked the anger from John and left him helpless.

"The ocean took your body, John, but not your soul. Your deep connection to Maggie pulled you away from death just long enough for you to save her."

"I don't believe you." John reached down and punched his hand as hard as he could into a mound of seaweed. It left no impression. He took several steps forward and then quickly looked back. Not a single imprint appeared in the sand.

"Who are you? How do you know who I am?"

The man laughed. "None of that matters. Why I'm here does."

John kicked at a sand dollar, and when it didn't sway from its resting spot, he turned and gave the stranger his full attention.

"Are you … Jesus? Or an, an angel?"

The man laughed again. "I am here to deliver a message."

The wind whirled the dry sand toward the sea, and it passed through John as if he wasn't there. He took a breath, hoping it would end the uneasiness churning inside him, but the sand burned where his heart should have been and pushed him closer to the waves.

"You are dead, John O'Brien."

The man's body faded and swirled as he talked. His words thickened the blood flowing to John's heart.

"But I feel it. My body." John ran his hands over his shoulders and brushed the wet hair away from his forehead. He reached down and unbuttoned his shirt, then buttoned it up again.

"You have no body, John. Only the sensations of one." The man smirked but didn't stop talking. "You will continue to feel your body, John, and all the emotions you should have experienced during your short life. Emotions after death, John, are the greatest punishment of all."

The hair on the back of John's neck burned, and he could see sweat dripping off his hands. Panic strangled the words in his throat. When John looked at the man for help, the man's lips curled with laughter.

"Your love gave you the power temporarily to transcend death. It can also free you from the material realm you are sentenced to live in."

His ramblings made no sense.

"I can't do anything. Those men didn't even see me. I don't understand."

The man pursed his lips and shook his shaggy head. John's frustration grew as the man chuckled at him.

An uplifting sensation overcame him, and John realized, for the very first time, the overwhelming dread was gone. Relief washed over him. He could finally be a husband to Nora. Take Maggie to paint in the tree house. He stepped back, breathed in his new resolve, and screamed at the man.

"You're a liar. I'm not dead. What are you, some freakin' magician?"

The man's image blurred, and when John blinked his eyes, his torso disappeared. But his head. It hung directly in front of John, lips curled and eyes swirling, his laughter thundered like the sea.

"You can cut the third-rate magic act, buddy. I'm not buying it. My daughter needs me so I'm leaving." John wanted to laugh, cry, and scream all at once. Each new sensation was so strong, together, they pushed him backward into the sand.

John searched his pockets for the keys to his truck. He had to get out of this place. Away from this wacko. When he stood up, the weight of the man's hands gripped the back of his shoulders.

Dead man walking. The voice drifted in on the crest of the waves.

"Bullshit." John looked around, but no one was there.

Dead man walking. In his head this time.

A seagull squawked so loudly it pierced John's ears. He clenched his hands into fists and stood his ground. He heard a phone ring. A woman gasp.

No time to waste. He turned and floated across the first sand dune.

THREE

———

Large gray clouds crept across the sky, blocking the sun's warmth and chilling the morning air as it drifted past the open bedroom window.

Nora shifted in bed, her slumber disrupted by the drop in temperature and a distant ringing. She pulled the blankets up over her shoulders and covered her head with John's pillow.

She buried herself in his familiar scents. Cologne mingled with cherry pipe tobacco and a slight hint of walnut oil soothed her back to sleep.

The ringing started again. Louder this time, more persistent than the cold breeze forcing its way across the room.

Damn phone. Answering machine, pick up. The ringing stopped and started again.

Nora reached over and patted John's side of the bed. "Answer it, hon. It's probably Steve."

She moved her hand across the bare sheet and a flash of anxiety bolted her awake. She sat up and grabbed the receiver before the phone had a chance to ring again.

"Hello?"

"Nora. It's Steve." Her younger brother's voice sounded stiff and formal.

"What's going on? Is it John, Steve? Did something happen to him at the beach?"

"I'm right outside. Can you come down and let me in?"

"What? Here? Why are you at my house?"

"I knocked and rang the doorbell. I need to talk to you, Nora."

"Fine." She wasn't about to play his cop cat-and-mouse games. "I'll be right down."

Nora threw the cordless phone on the nightstand and tripped over John's slippers. Why the hell was Steve here? She grabbed a nightshirt and pulled it over her head as she headed out the bedroom.

She peered inside Maggie's room as she rushed by. Good. She was still sleeping.

When Nora opened the front door, Steve wrapped his arm around her shoulder. His firm grip sent a chill rippling down her spine.

"Steve? Why are you in uniform … and where's John?"

"We need to talk, Nora."

Steve led Nora into the kitchen and sat her down and then sat down next to her. His face was blank, and he seemed to struggle with what he wanted to say. Nora knew she couldn't listen and jumped up out of her chair.

"I'll make coffee." She pulled the carafe out from under the basket filled with yesterday's coffee grounds.

"Please. Nora. Just sit down."

Steve's voice was so hoarse he sounded like he did when he got his tonsils out when they were kids.

"Are you hungry? I'll cook breakfast. Blueberry pancakes?"

"It's Maggie, Nora. She's at Mercy General."

Nora's knees buckled, and Steve grabbed her before she slid to the ground.

"She's going to be fine. She's pretty shaken. The two men that found her said she almost drowned."

"That's ridiculous, Steve. I just saw her sleeping in her room." Nora jumped to her feet and ran upstairs before Steve could respond.

She almost laughed at the familiar bundle of blankets Maggie cuddled under each night. She hurried over to wake her, and as she leaned forward, she saw a pile of cushions under the comforter.

Oh, dear God, no. Her heart pounded so hard her eyes hurt as she raced back downstairs.

"But she's all right, isn't she, Steve?" Nora collapsed into the kitchen chair. "And John, he's with her, right? I mean how could she get there if he didn't take her? She could never get to North Beach alone … and why … why was she there?"

"Nothing's clear right now." Steve shifted in his seat and when he looked at her, Nora suddenly remembered—Steve was supposed to be with John.

"Where were *you*, Steve? Why weren't you with them?" Steve's astonished look scared Nora. "I mean, I'm sorry, but he told me—"

"Nora, the last time I talked to John, he was wrapped up in one of his painting frenzies, said he'd call me. That was almost two weeks ago."

"That doesn't make sense. He told me last night. You were going with him. To the beach … clamming …"

"I'm sorry, Nora. John didn't talk to me about going clamming." Steve took on a professional tone as he continued talking. "How was he feeling last night, Nora? Was he … in good spirits?"

The air in the kitchen felt cold. "Of course he was. Now please, please tell me what is going on. Where's John?" Nora crossed her arms over her chest and shivered.

"Let me get you a sweater."

"No. Just talk to me, Steve."

Steve stood up and leaned against the kitchen counter. "The only thing they found was Maggie's backpack. There were tire tracks moving away from the location. The deputy over at North Beach said they could've come from a pickup."

Nora's hand trembled, and she walked over to the counter and picked up her cigarettes. Steve took the pack away from her.

"Hey, come on, Nora. You quit smoking, remember? Besides, it's not even nine o'clock yet."

"Just give me the damn cigarettes, Steve."

He opened the pack and lit one, then handed it to her. Nora knew she shouldn't start smoking again, but he offered, so she took the cigarette and inhaled deeply.

"Where the hell is John?"

Nora twisted the filter between her fingers and regretted that first drag. She turned the kitchen faucet on and doused the cigarette out as she waited for his response. Steve didn't look at her when he answered.

"They don't know, Nora. I just … I mean, they're searching for him right now."

Oh God. She should've insisted John eat dinner. Pot roast was his favorite. He would have felt better if he'd eaten, even if all he had was a piece of apple pie …

"We have to leave right now, Steve. Go to the hospital. Make sure Maggie's all right. And then we're going to find John."

Nora ran back upstairs, tore off her nightgown, and dug frantically inside her armoire for something to wear. She dressed, stuffed her rosary inside her purse, then ran downstairs, and shoved the pack of cigarettes in her pocket.

Steve was waiting for her in the squad car. She jumped inside and with lights flashing, the vehicle careened out of the driveway.

* * *

Nora knocked over an orderly as she barreled toward the nurse at the admitting desk. Steve followed close behind, helping the man up and offering a quick apology as he rushed after his sister.

"My daughter, Maggie O'Brien. My brother, a policeman. She's here."

The woman looked at her computer screen to confirm. "Yes, Mrs. O'Brien. Maggie is on the sixth floor. Room 618. You'll need to fill out paperwork first."

"I'll take care of it." Steve spoke for Nora as he turned to the nurse. "I'm Maggie's uncle. I'll take them to Nora for signatures when I'm done."

Steve gave Nora a shove toward the elevator, and she veered over to the stairwell.

"No time to waste. I'll take the stairs."

Nora took the steps two at a time. She was out of breath when she arrived on the sixth floor and rushed into Maggie's room.

Just seeing her daughter alive and sleeping gave her hope. Nora walked over to the steel railing, gave the sign of the cross, then folded her hands, and prayed. "O Heavenly Father, I ask that you take my daughter under your care. Pour your grace into her heart, and strengthen and multiply in her the gifts of thy Holy Spirit that she will come out of this experience, well and whole. Amen."

Nora watched the rise and fall of Maggie's breathing and could smell saltwater in her long, blond hair. Several locks were matted against her forehead, and her cheeks were flushed. Nora leaned down and kissed Maggie, then picked a blanket off the back of the chair, and sat down. She wrapped it over her shoulders and focused on her daughter. She wasn't going to move until Maggie woke up.

* * *

A cold chill swept across the room as Maggie grabbed hold of the blanket and pulled it under her chin. It felt bristly, not soft like the blankets on her bed. She opened her eyes, and sterile white walls glared back at her.

What happened to her castle? She sat up and grasped the metal bar, releasing her grip as soon as her fingers connected with the cold metallic surface. She was just about to scream when she saw her mother sleeping in the chair across from her bed.

"Mom?"

"Maggie, you're awake." Nora rushed over and cradled Maggie in her arms. She kissed her forehead and then took Maggie's face into her hands.

"Young lady, why did you sneak out like that? You know better, Mary Margaret …"

The warmth in her mother's eyes turn to anger. She couldn't be angry, not now. Maggie had to make her understand. "Please don't be mad, Mom. I was afraid. Dad was acting, you know, strange. And I didn't want Uncle Steve to feel like he had to take care of him."

Nora pulled Maggie close to her, and Maggie felt the anger dissolve as she snuggled into the comfort of her mother's arms. But then flashes of memory from the beach began creeping into her consciousness. Maggie pulled away and looked up at her mother.

"I saw him in the water, Mom. I was so afraid. I didn't know what he was doing out there all alone so I went in after him." Anxiety took hold, and Maggie gagged and started choking.

"Maggie … I'm going to get the nurse."

Maggie grabbed Nora's arm and pulled her back near her. "No, please, I have to … tell you so … so … we … can find him."

"Okay, Maggie. Just take a deep breath. Take it nice and slow, okay, honey?"

"Oh … k-kay."

Nora handed Maggie a cup of water, and Maggie took several gulps and then tightened the grip on her mother's hand.

"Breathe, Maggie. Just breathe."

Nora's hand felt warm and safe, and Maggie sat for a moment and closed her eyes. She could do this. She had to. *Stay calm,* she told herself.

"I'm sorry I didn't tell you, Mom, but I didn't want you to be all upset and everything. I hid in the back of Dad's truck and fell asleep. When I woke up, he wasn't there. I got really scared."

Maggie took a sip of water, and Nora brushed the hair out of her eyes.

"I followed his footprints in the sand to the ocean. That's when I saw him. I almost missed him because of the waves. And then suddenly, he was gone." Maggie started to cry.

"It's okay, honey. You don't have to talk about it right now."

Maggie crumpled the edge of the sheet and wiped her eyes with it. "But I do, Mom. I have to tell you what happened."

"Okay Maggie. I'm right here, and we have all the time you need."

Maggie could feel the tension in her mother's hand. She knew that once Nora understood what had happened, they would leave the hospital and go find him.

"I ran. As fast as I could. I hit the water, and a huge wave knocked me over. When I stood up, the sand sucked me under again. I kicked and screamed 'Dad!' and then I saw another wave, and it crashed over me, and I couldn't breathe."

Maggie's hands were shaking, and she felt her stomach churn.

"Then there was nothing but bubbles everywhere. And that's when I saw Dad again." Her legs shook so hard the blanket slid off, and Nora quickly covered her again.

"It's okay, Maggie."

Maggie let go of her mother's hand and leaned over the side of the bed, spewing vomit on the floor. She grabbed the sheet and swabbed it over her mouth.

"No, it isn't, because … he … looked … so … so … peaceful, Mom."

Maggie gagged and almost threw up again. "A-a-a-nd … then his fingers touched mine, and he took me in his arms, and when I tried to thank him … everything went black."

Nora crawled in bed next to Maggie and started to cry. She wrapped her arms around Maggie, rocking back and forth and sobbing.

"He isn't dead, Mom." Maggie whispered. "He carried me out—Dad *saved* me. I remember how strong his arms felt. Then the next thing I knew, those two old guys were standing over me, and they said they found me on the beach all by myself. I just don't get it."

Nora sat up suddenly and stared at the wall. Maggie waited for her response. She didn't look sad anymore, and Maggie didn't know if she should be glad or scared.

The nurse opened the door and gave Nora a surprised look and then looked down on the floor. "I'm sure it's just all the saltwater you swallowed. Goodness, young lady, you gave everyone a scare."

"Her father …" Nora got out of bed and walked toward the nurse, her voice so low Maggie had to lean forward to hear what she was saying. "My husband, he's waiting for us at the beach."

"The beach is a wonderful place to be, Mrs. O'Brien. Now don't worry. Your daughter is going to be just fine." She patted Nora on the shoulder and walked over to Maggie. "It's time to check your vitals, honey." The nurse turned and faced Nora. "Can you sit over in the chair just for a moment, Mrs. O'Brien?"

Nora moved out of the nurse's way, and Maggie watched her mother's eyes glaze over as she sat down. The nurse inserted a plastic thermometer strip in Maggie's mouth and stuck a stethoscope on her chest. Maggie was sure the pounding inside her would make the stethoscope shake.

The nurse gave Nora a quick glance and then pulled the thermometer from Maggie's mouth and looked at the number. "Good, your temp is normal, darlin'. Lungs are clear." She took a light and shined it in Maggie's eyes. "Pupils aren't dilated. Looks as if you should be able to go home this afternoon." She turned her focus to Nora. "Dr. Roberts will be here at four for rounds. I'm sure he'll release her then."

The nurse made an abrupt exit. Nora hurried back to Maggie's side. Her eyes were as huge as the headlights on her dad's pickup as Nora tucked the blankets almost too tight around Maggie's legs.

Nora walked over to the window and stood for a moment before speaking again.

"Get some rest, Maggie. We'll leave just as soon as you're released. We're going to the beach. Find your father. Bring him home."

FOUR

———

Nora found Steve waiting in the lobby. He jumped up and greeted her with a hug. "How's Maggie?"

Nora's whole body ached as she sat down next to her brother. "Fine. Well, she's scared. She said John carried her out of the water. He must be somewhere at North Beach. Have you heard anything?"

"I talked to the captain about ten minutes ago. No sign of him yet."

"Can you drive back to the house and see if he's there?" Maybe he's gone home. And realized what a stupid thing he'd just done, Nora thought.

"Don't you need me here?"

Nora sighed. What she needed was this whole nightmare to end. "I'll be fine, Steve, really. And John—well, he'll need a friend when he gets back home."

"So he's done this before." Steve's eyes narrowed when he spoke.

"No. Yes, well … about four months ago …" Nora took a deep breath. "I knew he was slipping away, and I tried to help him. But I couldn't. Then I got angry. We had a huge fight, and I let him leave. I thought he'd come right back. And when he didn't return the next day, I panicked. So I went to North Beach and posted flyers—missing-person flyers—and a couple found him on the beach and called me. I took him straight to the hospital. He asked, no, he *begged* me to take him—he said he wanted help. But when he called me and told me they were going to give him shock treatments, I picked him up. Against the doctor's orders. But I know what those treatments did to his mom. I know why he was so scared of having them."

"I see." Steve tightened his lips into a thin line.

"But then Dr. Roberts told me they'd never planned on giving John shock treatments. That they thought the new meds would help. But they didn't. Well, who knows, maybe they could have … but he hasn't taken any of them."

"You know that for sure?"

"Yes. No. I mean, he just started acting as he always does when he goes off his meds."

Steve stood up, and when he looked at Nora, his expression was cool. She suddenly felt like one of those women the cops knew couldn't be helped.

"Look, Steve. It's not all bad. He just gets a little crazy sometimes. But he's never done anything horrible to anyone. He's a good guy. And, well, I love him. That's all."

"Well, you always did like the crazy ones."

Nora smacked Steve in the arm. "I know. I know. But I meant it when I said for better or for worse."

"Yeah, well. It looks like the worst just happened."

"Come on, Steve. You have to help me." Nora stood up and followed Steve to the elevator.

"Nora. I cannot expect the police force to continue on a wild goose chase for an unstable man with a history of disappearing acts. I'm a cop, for Christ's sake. You know that. It costs taxpayers millions of dollars every year to go on …"

"Fine. Leave then. Tell them whatever you need to tell them. I'll find John myself."

Steve dug into his pocket and produced a piece of paper. "Take this."

"Now what?" As if a slip of paper was going to help.

"It's the phone number of one of the guys who found Maggie. He gave it to the receptionist. Maybe you should call him."

Nora crumbled the note and shoved it into her pocket. "Fine."

"Nora, I promise. I'll do whatever I can to help."

The tone in Steve's voice was clear. He had her pegged as the victim who would take back the abuser and live with him until that final disastrous moment. Well, she'd found him before; she could do it again.

"Great. Thanks, Steve. You go now. I need to check on Maggie."

Steve gave Nora a stiff hug, and when the elevator door opened, he walked inside and stared down at the floor, as if she wasn't there.

Each number above the elevator door illuminated as her brother made his downward descent. Nora stood and watched until the light for the first floor went on and the elevator began its journey back up.

Maybe Steve would be in there when it stopped. She could apologize for making his job harder and promise there wouldn't be a next time. But when the elevator door opened, an orderly with a cart filled with lunch trays was the only occupant.

Nora sighed and walked back into Maggie's room. She had dozed off again. Nora tiptoed out and sprinted down the stairs to the chapel.

The walls in the small prayer room were the same dull beige that covered the hallways in the hospital. The altar candles were nothing more than puddles of wax. Any attempt to light a candle was useless.

She sat down in the first pew, reached for the shoulder strap on her purse, and realized she'd left it in Maggie's room. She would have to pray without her rosary. The thought of facing God without her ritual was terrifying.

She clasped her hands together as tight as she could and lowered her head in prayer. "O Heavenly Father, I ask that you …"

The words that flowed so freely during prayer seemed impossible to formulate in her mind. The light of God that dependably illuminated her heart as a sign of her true faith felt as nonexistent as the flames on the candles in front of her.

"Dear Jesus, help me keep my faith … lead me to John. He is the only thing that is important to me, God—I swear to you—I cannot live without him."

When Nora looked up, a crucifix of Jesus demanded her attention. A wreath of thorns dug into his head, and the look of pain on his face mocked her request. Her hands felt clammy, and she trembled as she pressed them against her hot cheeks. She stumbled to her feet and bolted out the side exit in the chapel.

Nora sat down on a cement bench next to an ashtray. It was ten minutes past one. She couldn't wait until four o'clock for Dr. Roberts to show up for his rounds. Her head ached, and her heart was beating so hard it sent an icy tingling over her fingers.

She knew she had to be strong. But damn it, she couldn't help feeling that if Maggie had stayed home in bed where she belonged, none of this would have happened.

She rummaged inside her pocket and pulled out the pack of Marlboros. She lit a cigarette and decided she wouldn't buy another pack when this one was empty. A cup of hot coffee would be good, or a glass of water to quench the dryness that made her cough every time she inhaled. Her hand was shaking when she pulled her cell phone from her pocket. She had called Dr. Roberts's private number so many times about John that she had him programmed into her phone.

He answered on the first ring.

"Dr. Roberts, you have to call the hospital right now and release Maggie." Nora took a drag off her cigarette and flicked the ash into the overflowing ashtray.

"Nora? Of course. I should be at the hospital no later than four o'clock. I've already received a preliminary report. Once I see Maggie and am sure her condition is stable, I'll release her. That won't be for several hours. Why don't you go lie down and get some rest. God knows you've been through enough, and you must be exhausted."

Nora bit her lip and tightened her grip on the phone. "We don't have time to wait. John carried Maggie out of the water. I have to go to North Beach and find him."

There was a long pause. "Nora, you do realize that a near-death experience can cloud a person's perception of reality. What she believed was her father carrying her out of the water could have been one of the men who found her."

"What are you saying? Maggie's fine. I was just in her room when the nurse was checking her. She's worried more than anything—about finding her father." Nora hesitated and took a deep breath. "I know she's telling the truth. Dr. Roberts, we have to find him."

"The police are at North Beach right now, Nora. And taking Maggie there could traumatize her." The way Dr. Roberts enunciated his words mimicked her father's scolding her as a child.

"Please get here as soon as you can, Dr. Roberts." Nora looked at the ashtray filled with butts, then dropped her cigarette on the ground, and crushed it. The palpitations started again, and the throbbing crept up her throat. "I'm just so worried about John …"

"Of course you are, Nora. I understand. I'll do my best to get there as soon as possible."

Dr. Roberts hung up before Nora could respond. She snapped her phone shut and leaned forward, staring at the cold, gray cement. The black marks from her cigarette looked like the angry scribbling of a child. She dug at the remains of her Marlboro with her tennis shoe, tearing the thin white paper to shreds and scattering the tobacco. She pulled a tissue out of her pocket and shoved the entire mess under the bench, then moistened a new one with spit and rubbed at the charcoaled squiggle until it blended with the pavement. She had an odd satisfied feeling and, when she leaned back, felt dizzy and almost too tired to stand.

Maggie's nurse walked up and sat down next to Nora. "I'm so sorry about your husband, Mrs. O'Brien. I wasn't aware of your circumstance until after you left."

The rueful look the woman gave Nora was genuine, but her apologetic words triggered an adrenalin rush. Nora sprung to her feet.

"What do you mean, circumstance? You have no idea what's going on, and neither does anyone else. My husband is at North Beach, Nurse whoever you are. And my daughter and I are leaving to get him."

Nora's glare challenged the woman. She was pleased when the nurse sank into the back of the cold cement bench.

"I didn't mean anything, Mrs. O'Brien …"

Nora moved so close to the woman that their noses almost touched. "Well, keep it that way, thank you."

Nora twirled around so fast she almost tripped over the ashtray. She stood erect and steadied herself, then headed for Maggie's room on the sixth floor.

Her anger played back in her head, and she was appalled at her own behavior. How could she act so crazy when sanity was the only thing that could keep her from crumbling?

She reached into her jacket and pulled out her cigarettes. She looked around for the nearest garbage can.

Shit. This was not the time to quit smoking again. She ran her hand through her hair, shoved the pack back inside her jacket, and opened Maggie's door.

Nora tiptoed over to the bed. She saw her daughter's soft expression cloud with fear. Maggie whimpered, her eyes flickered open and shut, and her mouth curled into a terrified frown.

Nora reached down and stroked Maggie's hair. Maggie whispered something so low Nora couldn't make out the meaning. But the fear etching Maggie's words sent shivers down Nora's back. She knew she couldn't make Maggie feel safe. And the only way Maggie could ever feel safe again was to find John. And bring him home.

FIVE

———

Mom, I thought we were supposed to go home." Maggie pressed her feet into the floorboard and gripped the edge of the car seat. "You're driving awfully fast, aren't you?"

"No and no." Nora gripped the steering wheel as she hit the gas.

"You're going to get a ticket …"

Lights flashed behind the car, followed by the high-pitched whine of a siren.

"Shit," Nora mumbled under her breath. She eased the car over to the side of the road. A police officer walked up to the driver-side door, and she opened the window.

"Afternoon, ma'am. License, please."

Nora searched inside her purse and pulled out her driver's license and insurance card. She was afraid to talk because she might burst into tears, so she kept silent as she handed the cards over to the patrolman.

Nora looked over at Maggie. Her daughter was staring down at the floor, her face white, hands folded in her lap. A flush of guilt washed over Nora, and she reached over and took Maggie's hand.

"Honey. This isn't the first time your father has disappeared."

"I don't understand, Mom. What are you talking about?"

"You remember right before he went to the hospital the last time? When I told you he was off visiting a friend of his in Oregon City? Well, I didn't tell you the truth. We got in a fight, and he left. And then he just disappeared." Nora choked back a sob. "And I shouldn't be telling you all this because you're just too young to understand and …"

"It's okay, Mom. I understand. I know how Dad's moods are, and I want to find him just as bad as you do."

"Oh, Maggie …"

"Mrs. O'Brien?" The policeman startled Nora.

"Yes, officer?"

The man gave her a reassuring smile. "I understand your need to drive fast. The police at North Beach are wrapping up their investigation, and the chief wants to talk to you."

"Oh my God, they found John?" Nora thought her heart would explode, and she grabbed Maggie's hand and squeezed it.

"Well, no, but I'm sure the chief can explain. I can escort you there right now. I may not drive as fast as you'd like, but I guarantee you and your daughter will arrive safely." The officer smiled as he handed Nora her ID.

"Thank you so much, sir. And yes, I'll follow you. Thank you …"

"No problem, Mrs. O'Brien."

The police officer jumped in his car and pulled on to the highway with his lights flashing.

"Buckle up, Maggie. This won't take long. I promise we'll go home after I talk with the police chief."

Nora buckled her seat belt, and just as she turned the ignition back on, Maggie let out a scream.

"Mom—he just passed us—Dad's truck!"

Nora slammed the gas pedal to the floor and flipped the steering wheel full circle.

A horn honked, and Maggie shrieked. There was a moment of flying, and then a jolt of metal on metal brought them to a grinding halt.

Nora wondered if maybe Maggie was mistaken. But Maggie knew her father's pickup. How could she make such a huge mistake? Yet she whimpered as if something bad had happened.

When Nora reached over to comfort her daughter, an unbearable pain sliced through her left shoulder. All she could do was scream.

John slouched into the front seat of his truck and hugged the passenger side door.

Whoa, buddy, slow down. John didn't like the way the kid ignored him. *I told you I don't mind you driving my truck. But hey ... I think you just caused an accident.*

John turned around and watched Nora's car spin around twice and then plow into an SUV.

Ah shit ... That's my wife ... You just made her crash, you stupid drunk punk!

Nora's scream filled the pickup. He could feel Maggie's heart beating inside his chest as he yelled at the kid.

You have to stop. Go back there. NOW.

The air inside the truck was so hot it burned John's skin. He tried to grab the steering wheel away from the kid, but an excruciating pain ripped his left shoulder, and he buckled over and closed his eyes.

When he opened them again, he was sitting between Nora and Maggie.

Someone banged on the driver side window. John turned and looked, but he couldn't tell who it was until the door opened.

"Mrs. O'Brien? Can you move?" The officer leaned his head inside the car.

"Yes, but my daughter. She's bleeding."

That's right. Help her, please ... John felt the air sweep inside the car, and when he looked over at Maggie, someone was carrying her out of the front seat. *What are you doing with my daughter? Oh my God, what have I done?*

"Please. My husband. He just passed us in his truck. You have to radio in ..."

Oh God. Nora. I'm right here. John lunged toward the driver side.

Nora screamed. The pain in her voice ricocheted through him so fast he couldn't breathe.

"My shoulder. Oh please."

When the officer touched Nora's shoulder, John trembled, and the intensity of Nora's pain made John feel as if he was going to pass out.

"Your collar bone. It may be broken. Bear with me. The paramedics are going to move you out of your vehicle, ma'am."

Can't you give her something for the pain?

When John looked up through the sunroof, the sky looked cloudy, and he thought it was going to rain.

"You're going to be fine."

What? But it still hurts. Please do something.

John's eyes burned as he looked over at the crumpled hood on a late model Jeep Cherokee.

Oh God, did someone die?

"The other car." Nora wheezed. "Did anyone die?"

"No, ma'am. Just shook them up. Let's get you out of the car. They're going to be fine."

Thank you. Please. I can't stand this. Do something please. John waited to feel the sting of a needle or cool water flushing the medication down. Yet the pain, her pain, riddled John, and each time he screamed out, Nora moved farther away.

The car door slammed shut. John started to fall and couldn't stop. Backward. Down through the seat. Past the floorboards. Into the darkness.

* * *

The light in the room was dim, and the sheets cold against Nora's aching body. She struggled to a sitting position, but the sling around her left arm and the sudden movement sent shooting pains across her shoulder blade. She fell back and tried to talk, but her mouth was so dry that all she could do was squeak.

Dr. Roberts sat on the bed next to her and took her hand. "Your left shoulder was dislocated in the accident. I've prescribed muscle relaxants and pain medication. It was a minor injury and shouldn't take long to heal. Maggie is fine; her forehead was cut from the shattered windshield. Superficial head wounds. They always look worse than they actually are."

Nora shivered, and Dr. Roberts tucked the blankets around her.

"Would you like me to get you a heated blanket?"

Nora shook her head no and started to cry. "We saw him, Dr. Roberts. At least Maggie did. He drove right past us in his pickup."

"I talked with Steve before I came in." Dr. Roberts studied Nora's face before speaking again. "He said some kid found the truck—keys still in the ignition. He'd been driving it drunk—up and down the beach, then decided since it was abandoned, he'd take it home."

"But that doesn't make sense. John would never leave his keys in the truck. That … stupid truck … it was his baby."

Dr. Roberts gave her two pills and a cup of water. She popped them in her mouth and then took a long drink, allowing the cold liquid to moisten her dry throat.

"The truck has been impounded, Nora. And the kid swears he never saw John."

Nora sank back into her pillows. "Then Maggie couldn't have seen John. And I could have killed her."

"You're very lucky, Nora. Your shoulder will heal. And Maggie, well, her injuries are more emotional right now than physical. You both need to go home and rest."

Nora wanted to tell Dr. Roberts she wasn't going back home and she wouldn't leave North Beach until she found John.

"Steve told me about the last time, Nora. Due to the circumstances, the police are treating this as a voluntary abandonment now, not a missing person."

Nora sank into the cold sheets. Once again, her brother was trying to take charge of her life.

"I want you and Maggie to stay overnight." The doctor's voice sent shivers down her arms, and she pulled the blanket up as far as she could with her right hand.

"Can I see her?" Exhaustion set in, and she wasn't going to argue.

"Yes, of course. But you have to promise me one thing."

The guilt overwhelmed Nora as she thought about her daughter lying in a hospital bed because of her recklessness.

"Of course." Nora was too tired and scared to try to find John by herself.

"You mean that?" Dr. Roberts stared at her in an uncommonly professional manner.

"Anything. Anything I can do to get this whole mess resolved."

Dr. Roberts waited so long before speaking that Nora was afraid she had ruined any chance of him trusting her again.

"Once I release the two of you, you must promise me you'll take Maggie home and let Steve find John."

Nora sighed and Dr. Roberts took hold of her hand again.

"Nora, I know this disease isn't easy to live with. But you have to trust that your brother will find him. I've given Steve instructions and a new sample prescription I want John to try. And once he's found, well, maybe a few weeks' stay in—"

"He won't go back, Dr. Roberts. He still insists they want to give him shock treatments. Maybe that's why he took off. I should never have agreed to his release."

Dr. Roberts gave Nora a reassuring nod. "Just let me talk to John once Steve finds him. Get some rest, Nora. I'll be in touch."

SIX

———

Shane stared at his aging reflection in the mirror.

"You're not even sixty yet," he muttered aloud, "but you look as if you're damn near seventy."

He rubbed his hand across his gray beard and thought about shaving, but doing so could end the cover he'd cultivated over the years. Unraveling the web of deceit and correcting all the lies was impossible. And he had to maintain anonymity. After all, a promise was a promise.

Shane splashed cold water over his face and brushed his teeth. He went to the kitchen, poured a cup of coffee, and then walked over to the window overlooking the weeping willow tree and the valley below.

The afternoon sun had already dried the moisture he'd provided his tomato plants that morning. It was going to be hot today. And not a single cloud in the sky. Another day for the records for sure.

He carried his cup outside and picked up the morning newspaper. He scanned the headlines as he walked back inside the house.

SOUR NEWS ON WINE GRAPES
MOTHER'S TRIAL SET ON PORN CHARGES

"When in hell did motherhood take such a disgusting *U*-turn?" he muttered.

Shane threw the paper on the coffee table and turned on the TV. He flipped the channels on the remote and had settled on a local newscast when the phone rang.

"Hello?"

"Shane, its Angie. Have you been watching the news?"

"I just turned the TV on. Why, what's up?"

"John's missing. And Maggie was found unconscious at North Beach early Saturday morning. I just called Mercy General. Maggie was released on Sunday."

"Oh, thank God. Then she's fine? Whom did you talk to? You didn't tell them why you were calling, did you?"

"My next door neighbor's daughter works in admitting. She told me Maggie was rattled but physically doing fine."

"What about John?"

"John was never admitted. The last I heard on the news, he's still missing."

Shane sank into the couch and shivered. John would never leave his only child alone on the beach to die.

"I'm going to North Beach, Angie."

"What? What if someone recognizes you?"

"They will think I'm there because of Genevieve."

"Ahh, yes ... dear Genevieve."

Shane hated the sarcasm in Angie's voice whenever she said Genevieve's name.

"Look Angie, I know how you feel. But I promised her—"

"Yeah, and Genevieve waited for you after you went MIA in Vietnam."

"She thought I was dead."

"Well, you weren't. And she had no right to get married to someone else when she was—"

"Angie, for the fifty-seven millionth time, I am not having this conversation with you."

Shane waited for Angie's response. The phone was silent on the other end for a change.

"Do I have your support, Ang?"

"You have my support, Shane."

"Thanks, sis. I'll call you once I get to North Beach."

"Love you, little brother."

"You too, sis."

Shane positioned the phone back on the charger and went upstairs to pack. He was glad he had decided against shaving. The cover up was more important now than ever.

* * *

The stress from the two-hour drive made it feel longer than usual. Shane smiled at the receptionist as he walked into the hotel lobby.

"Mr. O'Shanahan. So good to have you back with us again. You're a bit early this year, aren't you?"

"Thanks, Theresa. It's good to be here. I'll be back again end of November, just like always. Just had a longing, you know."

"I completely understand. Let me check and see if your usual room is vacant."

"Thanks. Sorry I didn't call first."

"No problem. And good news. Room 165 is available."

Shane thanked her and headed for his room. He stood at the entrance and ran his hand over the embossed numbers on the door before entering.

The curtains hugged the windows and gave the room a surreptitious glow. He plunked his bag on the bed and slid the sliding glass door open.

No matter how many times he'd stayed there since her death, he still expected to see Genevieve sitting on the deck overlooking the ocean. She would smile, and on a good day, the cool ocean breeze would echo her laughter back into the room. And on those other days, her somber request was always the same.

"When I die, I want my ashes scattered right out there—on our beach."

When Shane stepped outside, the warm breeze forced him to take in a deep breath. Today was not a day to be melancholy. He had to focus his energies on finding John.

Lighthouse Rock would be his starting point, then he would work his way down the beach, and then back up over the sand dunes lining the boardwalk.

But first, he would see if John was hiding out in any of the adjacent hotels. God forbid that he really did leave Maggie on the beach. Shane knew that just about anything was possible. He was all too familiar with the delusional side of a manic swing.

Shane started his search at the Seaview Hotel. When he entered the lobby, he was surprised to see a missing person's poster with John's photograph already hanging on the bulletin board.

"You know the guy?"

The voice—a woman's—startled him. He turned around. She was standing behind the desk, straight faced, her lips drawn into a tight thin line.

"No. Don't know him, just curious. Why?" Shane tried to remain calm.

"You have a spooked look on your face, that's all." The words came across like an interrogation. Shane knew she was a local and considered him guilty before proven innocent so he slipped into tourist mode to avoid a full cross-examination.

"I live down by LA. Things like this happen down there every day. But here? Damn it all. It just always upsets me when tragedy strikes in God's country. Were they staying here?"

"Look, I don't know what you mean by *they*. The Rock Squad, local police that is, already drilled me four months ago. That's when that particular flyer was posted. His wife was the one who came in with it. All I know is if there is a *they*, his wife didn't know about it. Now, did you want to check in?"

Damn. This wasn't the first time.

Shane forced a smile as he met the woman's steady glare.

"No, I'm staying at the Winds."

"Then what can I help you with?"

Her question turned accusation as she crossed her arms over her large chest. Shane knew if he didn't back pedal fast, she'd report him for no good reason. His neck felt hot, and he could feel his face flush as a whiff of fresh baked cookies filled the air. A buzzer went off, the woman glanced back into the office, and when she looked back at Shane, he smiled sheepishly at her.

"Okay, I'll be honest. I was lured in by the smell of cookies baking. I'm a sucker for homemade, and my wife … well, she's watching my weight." He reached down and patted his rounded belly. "When I walked in and nobody was at the counter, I just wandered around the lobby. When I saw the flyer, the guy reminded me of my son. He died recently. And it honestly, the picture, it spooked me."

The woman glanced at the wedding ring on Shane's hand. An empathetic look spread across her face when she looked at him.

"Oh my God, I'm so sorry for your loss."

"Thanks. That means a lot." Shane hoped his remark about someone dying wasn't a sixth-sense reaction.

"I have a fresh batch ready to come out of the oven. Wait right here."

She disappeared, and Shane wiped the sweat off the back of his neck. He chuckled. He never dreamt his paunch would come in handy one day.

The woman reappeared with a plate of warm cookies. "Have one. My mother's secret chocolate chip recipe—it's usually only available to our residents. But I'll make an exception just this once."

Shane took a cookie. When he bit into it, the warm dollops of chocolate made his dry mouth water. "Now that's a chocolate chip cookie."

The woman smiled and leaned over the counter. "A man went missing ten years ago and was found murdered about four miles down the beach from here. I always felt there was something I should have done to help the investigation. Like maybe the murderer had casually walked into the lobby here and I wasn't alert enough to notice."

"I understand completely. After 9/11, you just don't know who you can trust."

"Exactly. I'm sorry if I was—"

"No problem. But can you do me a favor? If my wife comes in here trying to check up on me, will you cover up my sugar addict tracks?"

"You bet." The woman laughed. "What's her name?"

"Genevieve. Genevieve O'Brien. I'm sorry, I meant O'Shanahan. She always went by her maiden name. Real women's libber, my wife."

"Well Mr. O'Shanahan, your secret is safe with me."

Shane smiled as she offered him another cookie.

"One more for the road?"

"Absolutely." Shane forced a laugh then walked out the lobby as if he was just another tourist looking for a sugar hit.

"Damn. This wasn't the first time." An eerie feeling of déjà vu swept through him as he quickened his pace.

Once he hit the beach, Shane threw his cookie in the sand and hurried down the coastal wetland as fast as he could.

* * *

Nora stared at the computer screen and studied the flyer she'd created just four months earlier. She decided to update John's picture. Not that he'd changed much, but she wanted to be sure that the image on the poster was identical to the man who had once again abandoned her.

She scrutinized the digital pictures on the computer and settled on one she'd taken several weeks ago of John painting in his art studio. It was more … like him, deep in his latest painting, unaware that she was anywhere near.

She reread the description and decided to be more honest this time, even if it sent John into a fit if he happened to see it. After carefully selecting her words, she read the description aloud:

> MISSING: 42-year-old man suffering from schizoaffective bipolar disorder and post-traumatic stress from the Gulf War.

She stopped. Was that too much? She deleted the text and started over, the next line in caps and bold font:

**LOVING FATHER. NOT CONSIDERED A DANGER
TO HIMSELF OR OTHERS.**

Now what should she say? That he was driven away by a bunch of voices arguing in his head? That, in his delusional state, he thought the doctors were going to give him shock treatments—just as they had done to his mother?

Nora highlighted the text and deleted it. Got to keep it simple. She typed up a new description and read it out loud.

MISSING: 42-year-old loving father and husband suffering from bipolar disorder. Not considered dangerous, but his condition requires medication. If you see this man, please call Nora O'Brien at 253-555-1729.

She printed off 25 copies and grabbed her purse. Maggie was spending the day with Becca, and if Nora hurried, she could be home in time to cook dinner.

* * *

The cold saltwater felt good on Nora's feet. She was glad she'd decided to hit every hotel and motel on North Beach from the shore rather than the highway.

The last time John disappeared, he bunked out in a sand dune. He hadn't slept in days, and the wild animal look in his eyes made the couple who discovered him shriek and run. John followed them—to apologize she supposed—and that's when they found a large piece of driftwood to use as a weapon. John got down on his knees and begged their forgiveness and then blurted out his home phone number. They called, and Nora came to his rescue. Mystery solved.

But this time. Nora had an eerie feeling, as if she was being watched. Or followed. She kept as close to the crowds as she could and constantly looked over her shoulder. She was relieved when she saw Steve walking toward her on the beach.

"What are you doing here, Nora? Where's Maggie?"

His voice was so professional it scared her. "I made up some flyers. I'm going to post them. Maggie's with Becca. What's going on? Did they find him, or some clue?"

Steve walked up and put his arm around Nora and steered her back in the opposite direction. "Nope, no new clues. I just think you should start posting the flyers in this direction."

"Well that doesn't make any sense. Are you sure you don't have something you want to tell me?" Nora tried to get Steve to look at her.

"No, no. No news is good news. I'll hand out flyers for you then swing by the house if I hear anything." Steve took some of the flyers out of her hand, waved, and headed down the opposite end of the beach.

"Well fine, little brother. I'll just retrace your footsteps and make sure you keep your word."

Nora walked across the sand and headed for the Seaview Hotel. She walked into the lobby and went straight to the bulletin board.

"You're the second person who's been looking at that flyer today."

The receptionist startled Nora. "What do you mean?"

"Older gentleman, said he lives in LA. Reddish gray hair and beard. Nice enough. Said the guy in the flyer looked like his deceased son."

"The man in the flyer is my husband."

"I'm sorry. I recognize you now. Nora, right? Well, you found him didn't you?"

"Well, yes. But, well, he's missing again. And he doesn't have his medication."

The receptionist stiffened behind the counter. "I see."

"He's not dangerous. He's really a gentle, loving man. It's just when he goes off his meds … and I'm worried. Do you mind, can I post this new flyer?"

"Of course, go right ahead. Is your phone number on there?"

"Yes, yes, it is." Nora let out a deep long breath. "He really is a nice person."

"I believe you, Nora. And I'll call you if I hear anything. Anything at all."

Nora thanked the woman under her breath and hurried out the lobby doors. She was shaking by the time she got back to the beach. And embarrassed. Maybe she should let the police handle the investigation and Steve post the flyers.

Her shoulder ached. She pulled a pain pill from her purse and swallowed it without water. She should have worn that stupid sling Dr. Roberts had given her, but she'd felt fine this morning.

Nora groaned as she looked at her watch. It was a quarter to five. Damn, too late to cook. She'd just grab a pizza and head back home.

SEVEN

Saturday evenings turned into weekly confessional sessions. Nora was certain that if Maggie recited the rescue to the priest, she would somehow uncover the missing piece that would bring John back home again.

And every Saturday night for an entire month, Maggie repeated the event verbatim, cementing the rescue so deep in her mind it became easier to field her mother's constant questions.

Maggie entered the small, stuffy confessional and began. "Bless me, Father, for I have sinned. It has been one week since my last confession."

"What is your sin, child?"

"Well. I guess you can say I've been lying. Well, not really lying, just maybe forgetting an important detail."

"About what, child?"

Maggie leaned against the confessional wall and let out a huge, frustrated sigh. "I don't really know, Father. I've tried to remember ever detail about what happened to Dad, just as it happened. But Mom. Well, she keeps saying I must be missing something, that if I keep coming here and confess to you, then maybe I'll remember what she thinks is missing."

She squirmed on the solid oak bench. "And, well—I wish I did leave something out, forgot a part …"

"Maggie, listen to me."

Maggie sat upright and gasped. "You know it's me, Father? But aren't these sessions supposed to be, you know, anonymous?"

"You're always the last one here, Maggie. And I'd really like to talk to you about this face to face. It might help if we just chatted in my office. Because to be honest, Maggie, I don't feel as if we're dealing with any kind of sin here."

Relief flushed through Maggie as she bounced out the confessional. Father Paul greeted her with a hug and led her to his office. Maggie sat down in the brown overstuffed chair directly in front of Father Paul's desk.

"All right, Maggie. We've recounted everything about the rescue. So many times now, I think I know it by heart." The priest smiled. "Now, tell me everything that happened after you woke up on the beach."

Maggie was happy to move on. "Well, the two old men were there. I remember the one guy's name is Henry. And the paramedics had a stretcher. They used that to carry me on to the ambulance. I'd never ridden in an ambulance before." She squinted her eyes and looked up at the ceiling.

"And I was crying. And begging them to search for my dad. I wanted them to go back into the ocean—get divers, search boats, anything. Because I knew if Dad stayed in there too long, well …" Maggie choked back her tears. "And then Henry said 'I know, honey; I saw him.'"

Father Paul leaned against his desk. "What did you just say, Maggie?"

Maggie jumped up out of her chair. "Oh my God, Father Paul, Henry saw my dad!"

She raced out the door, then flew back inside, and ran around the desk and hugged the priest. "Thank you so much, Father. This was way better than sitting in that tiny confessional."

He laughed. "You're welcome, Maggie. Now go. Your mother is waiting for you."

Maggie was out of breath when she reached Nora. "We found it, Mom. In Father Paul's office."

"Found what, Maggie?"

"Come on, you have to talk to Henry. He saw Dad standing next to me when I was lying in the sand. Henry *saw* Dad, Mom. You have to find him."

Nora scrambled to her feet and grabbed hold of Maggie's arm. "I'll drop you off at Becca's house."

Maggie stopped abruptly. "But how are you going to find Henry? We don't even know his last name."

"Henry gave Uncle Steve his phone number when we were at the hospital." Nora sat back down and dug frantically through the scraps of paper tucked inside her billfold. "It was on a green notepad, I'm sure I stuck it in here."

"Uncle Steve gave you Henry's number, and you never called him? Why? Why didn't you call him?"

"I don't know, Maggie. I figured he was just an old man, and well, I was going to wait and thank him after we found your father." Nora continued searching and, when she found it, held it up in the air as if it was the winning lottery ticket. "Here it is. Now let's get moving. I should be able to meet him before it gets dark."

✳ ✳ ✳

Large white clouds strolled like lazy sheep across the horizon. The ocean calmed, and the blue sky deepened to sapphire, signaling the end of the day.

John heard a newborn baby cry. Its tiny wails begged for its mother's breast. The infant's need to be fed, loved, and comforted overwhelmed him.

He staggered over to a bench on the nearly abandoned boardwalk and clamped his hands over his ears, but the sensations kept coming.

Young lovers hidden behind a sand dune, their hearts pounding so fast John thought his chest would burst. He could feel the tingling in his mouth as their lips met and their passion exploded inside him as they explored each other's bodies.

John jumped up and sprinted between the few remaining tourists and avoided physical contact with each person as he ran. He feared the slightest blending with one of these strangers would ignite their emotions inside him. He knew now that death provided no solace from feeling someone else's pleasure … or pain.

The sun continued its descent behind Lighthouse Rock. John ran down to the abandoned beach seeking refuge. The icy cold ocean waves beckoned, and the sand burned his feet.

He walked over the foam at the water's edge. He wondered why he had never questioned the footprints he once created and how death could take your body but not your emotions. They lived on. Stronger, more intense than when he was a living human being.

It baffled him how he could clasp his hands together and feel his fingers intertwine. His body was as real to him as it was when he was alive. Yet when a cool breeze washed across the beach, it blew through him as if he weren't there.

He longed to feel the softness of the wind against his skin. The air was so crisp with life he wanted to scream, to beg his way back into his body.

The waves thundered. John walked into the raging surf and prayed it would consume him. He heard a familiar voice and strained to decipher it.

He heard it again. It was Nora, her voice so sweet and warm. He struggled toward the source and lost his balance. He plunged into the water and was carried back on the shore. As he floated up toward the boardwalk, he heard her voice again.

Nora was sitting at a small table at Café Breeze. An older gentleman sat across from her. When John moved closer, he was certain the man made eye contact with him. His aged face turned red, and he stopped talking.

"Keep talking, Henry. I want you to give me every detail." Nora reached over and took hold of Henry's hand.

"That's all, ma'am."

The statement sounded abrupt. John thought Henry looked at him again.

"What do you mean, that's all? You just told me you saw John. Standing right next to Maggie. And he was screaming, 'Help me; help my daughter.'" Nora's voice rose above the crashing waves.

"I'm sorry, ma'am. Now that I think about it again, well, I'm sure it was just the ocean breeze. You hear some mighty strange things in the air that early in the morning." Henry stiffened in his chair. "And the mist on the beach, well, it can play tricks on even the sharpest eye."

So you did see me, didn't you, Henry? John moved over to the table and stood next to Henry's chair. *Why are you lying to my wife?*

"Listen, I don't understand. You just told me you saw him." Nora tightened her grip on Henry's hand.

John reached over and placed his hand on her shoulder. *Nora, I'm here. Nothing else matters.*

Nora jerked her head in John's direction and grabbed her shoulder as if she were in pain.

"Are you all right, ma'am?" Henry's voice was filled with concern.

"My shoulder. It's throbbing. I dislocated it in a car accident. It still acts up." Nora reached into her purse and pulled out a bottle of pills. She opened it, popped two into her mouth, and downed them with the rest of her wine.

"Listen, if that's all you have, I'm afraid I must leave." Nora stood and looked beyond John, searching the shoreline as if she expected to see someone waiting for her. "It's just so cold, I mean warm, here all of a sudden. And I'm not feeling well. But thank you, Henry. Thank you for taking care of my daughter."

"You're welcome, ma'am. And please, give Miss Maggie my best. If you want to talk again, please don't hesitate to call."

"If you think of anything else, here's my cell number." Nora scribbled her number on a napkin and then turned and walked away.

John's anger boiled over, and he lunged at Henry. *Why did you lie to my wife? I know damn good and well you saw me on the beach that day. And you see me now.* John tried to grab hold of Henry's shoulders, but his hands went right through them.

Henry picked up his beer and finished it off as if John wasn't there. He signaled the waiter for the check, dropped his money on the table, and started down the boardwalk.

The breeze picked up, and a thin mist covered the shore. John tried to follow Henry, but every time he moved his feet, the wind kept him trapped next to Nora's vacant chair.

John yelled, but the words dissolved before leaving his mouth, and he was so dizzy everything started spinning around him.

Except for Henry. He stopped suddenly, turned around, and walked back toward John. Henry opened his mouth to speak, and before John could decipher what Henry was saying, the mist thickened and everything went black.

* * *

The sun crept behind the horizon, and the evening air cooled as Maggie sat impatiently on the front porch waiting for her mother. Every time she heard a car drive by, she jumped to her feet and waited for headlights to appear in the driveway.

Where was she? Maggie paced the length of the front porch and looked at her watch. She'd been gone for two hours. It couldn't take that long for Henry to tell her what he saw and what direction Dad had headed down the beach that day.

Damn. Maggie bit her bottom lip and wished she'd been awake when Dad had carried her out of the water. Why did he leave? There she was, all by herself, and he just left her there? It didn't make sense.

No. That isn't what happened. He saved her life for God's sake—maybe the whole ordeal sent him into one of his tweak outs and he was afraid that she was …

No. Maggie sat down on the porch railing and examined her fingers for a cuticle in need of removal. Dad left to get help. And when he ran up on the boardwalk he tripped and hit his head on the cement and …

Headlights lit up the driveway. Maggie waited until she was sure it was her mom and then rushed off the porch to greet her.

Nora gave Maggie a weak smile as she turned off the ignition. Maggie backed away from the driver's door and stood, hands on hips, waiting. The door barely opened before Maggie began speaking.

"Where have you been? Did you meet Henry? What did he say? When are we going to leave to get Dad?"

Nora stared at Maggie. Her left shoulder drooped as she tried to balance several bags under her right arm.

"Mom, give the bags to me. I can carry them. Is your shoulder bothering you again?" She paused. "Did you talk to Henry?"

"Yes, take the bags. My shoulder hurts." Nora sighed and rubbed her forearm. "And yes. I talked to Henry."

Maggie took the front steps in one giant leap, turned, and faced her mother. "Well?"

"Maggie, I just want to go inside and sit down for a minute."

"Okay, you're right. I'm sorry, Mom." Maggie grappled with the bags and the front door and let Nora walk inside first. Maggie followed her into the kitchen and set the bags on the counter. One held groceries and the second a large bottle. She pulled it out and placed it on the counter.

"Bourbon. What's this for?" Maggie couldn't hide the disgust in her voice. Her mom's dad drank bourbon, and Maggie figured that was what killed him. He should have stuck to the lighter stuff—wine or maybe beer.

Nora took a glass out of the cupboard, filled it with ice, and then added water. "For your information, it's for me. My shoulder hurts, and a drink will help."

"But you aren't supposed to mix pain pills with alcohol, Mom."

"And you're not supposed to tell your mother what to do." Nora glared at Maggie as she took the cap off the half gallon and poured it into a glass.

"That stuff reeks."

Maggie put her hand over her nose as she emptied the bag of groceries and put them away. She plopped down on a chair at the kitchen table, crossed her arms over her chest, and stared at her mother.

Nora took a sip of her drink and pulled a pack of cigarettes from her purse.

"Ah, come on, Mom. You quit! What is wrong with you? What did Henry say to you, anyway? Was it really that awful?"

Nora lit her cigarette and blew the smoke over her shoulder. Maggie was glad she didn't send it across the table in her direction.

Great. Now the whole house is going to smell like a big fat ashtray again. She'd have to keep air fresheners in her room so her clothes didn't get contaminated, too. Oh well, when Dad got home, he'd put a stop to it.

"Dad hates it when you smoke."

"Your father isn't here right now."

"Well that's why you went to see Henry. Can you please tell me what he said?"

Nora rolled the cigarette between her fingers and took another drag. Maggie dug an old ashtray from a cabinet and set it down in front of her mother.

"Well?"

"Well, Henry said that when he thought about it again he wasn't certain if he saw anyone with you."

Nora sat her cigarette in the ashtray and rummaged inside her purse.

"That doesn't make sense, Mom. He told me he saw Dad and they would find him."

Nora popped the top off a bottle and poured a pill in her hand.

"Uh, Mom—you're not mixing pain pills with alcohol, are you?"

"Just leave me alone, Maggie! I need some time to think. To be alone."

Maggie wanted to scream at her mother and make her take her to see Henry. She needed to talk to him herself. But the vacant look on her mother's face made Maggie realize one thing.

No matter what she said, even if her mom wanted to listen, there was no way she could. Not right now anyway.

EIGHT

The blinds were pulled shut the day after Mom met with Henry. The two months since her father disappeared felt more like two hundred years. Even with the heat on, the house never felt warm. And sometimes, it was so cold Maggie thought she could see her breath.

Her mom didn't see the rotten apples on the ground. Or notice the chill in the air every morning when she went outside in her cotton bathrobe and bare feet to check the mailbox hours before the scheduled delivery.

Maggie hated the smell of bourbon and the pale liquid that remained in her mother's glass left sitting on the coffee table every morning. Every day was the same. She emptied the ashtray before Mom woke. Washed her drink glass and stashed it back in the cupboard as if it had never been removed.

The only time Maggie saw kindness on her mother's face was on Sunday morning when they sat together during mass. Somehow, the priest's words would soothe her. But as soon as they walked out the sanctuary doors, her despondency returned. The ride home was filled with a silence now painfully familiar.

Maggie retreated once again into the backyard. She was halfway across the lawn when she saw Becca peering down from their hiding spot in the apple tree.

Maggie was glad Becca didn't have to sit through the priest's boring chants or search her mother's face for a hint of reassurance. Becca's mom was into the mysteries of life. Maggie much preferred her softness of possibility to the black-and-whiteness of mass.

Becca swung down off the lowest branch. The grin on her face was so wide she looked like Kermit the Frog.

"I think I know what happened to your dad."

The triumph on Becca's face was more annoying than usual.

"Yeah, right. And the Pope isn't Catholic."

Becca crossed her arms over her chest and kicked a rotten apple in Maggie's direction.

"Fine. Don't listen to me then."

Maggie sighed. She surveyed the ground for a spot that wasn't swarming with hungry ants feeding on apples so pulverized they looked like store-bought applesauce.

She found a semi-clear spot and sat down. Becca hesitated and then sat next to Maggie. Her lips pursed so tight her mouth turned into a thin white line.

"You're going to punch holes in your lips if you squeeze them any tighter, Becca. You're such a dipshit."

Maggie picked up a rotten apple and shoved it in Becca's face. "Here, eat the poison apple; it will rid you of all your sins."

"They're only sins if you think they are," Becca mumbled as she pushed the apple out of Maggie's hand.

"Hah! I knew you couldn't keep your mouth shut for more than two seconds."

Maggie grabbed another apple and threw it against the fence. Becca stood up abruptly and stomped her foot.

"Fine. I'm going home. Just because your mom's such a bitch doesn't mean you have to be one too." Becca gave her head an indignant shake.

"Don't go stomping your foot and shaking your head at me. You're just rude, you know that, Becca?"

Maggie saw Becca's lips quiver as she turned to walk away. Maggie reached up and grabbed her hand. "Hey, wait. I'm sorry, Becca. You're right. I don't have to be all bitchy to you."

Becca sat back down next to Maggie. She picked up an apple covered with ants and threw it over the fence.

"Nice throw, girlfriend." Maggie slugged her in the arm. "Ok, I'm listening, Becca. Let's hear your latest theory."

Becca scooted deeper into the grass and began gesturing with her hands.

"The way I see it, your dad got sucked way out into the ocean. There was a man out there in a fishing boat. All by himself. And he didn't even see all the commotion—"

"Who didn't see?"

"The fisherman. So he was out there—the fisherman—and saw your dad floating in the water and thought he was dead. Then when he pulled him in the boat and found out he was alive because he coughed up some tadpoles or something and—"

"Doesn't work, Becca."

"Why not?"

"Because tadpoles don't live in saltwater."

"So maybe they were baby crabs …"

"Still doesn't work. There weren't any boats out there."

"Well, how would you know? I mean, you said you blacked out. You weren't looking for fishing boats, were you?"

"Dad carried me out, Becca. He was on the shore."

"But you didn't see him when you woke up, Maggie."

"Yeah, well …"

"And your mom said that Henry guy didn't see him either."

"Well, Henry lied to my mom. I don't know why, but he did."

"Well, maybe your dad has amnesia—and he's in California right now. Maybe working for a paint company."

"Yeah, maybe we should just quit talking about it." Maggie got up and stomped on an apple and then kicked it against the tree trunk.

"Well, Maggie, I'm just trying to help you figure it out. It keeps me awake at night too, you know."

Becca's chin crinkled into a pout. Maggie reached over and gave her friend an affectionate shove.

"Come on; I get enough pouty from my mom. And you know I appreciate your wanting to help. It's just, well …"

"I know Maggie. Hey, why don't we go hang out at the park?"

"I'd love to, but Mom has a ton of chores for me." Maggie sighed and Becca followed her across the back lawn and out the side gate.

* * *

Nora was already passed out when Kathy Harper called. She wanted to know if Maggie could come have dinner with Becca. Of course, Kathy told Maggie her mom was welcome to join them as well.

Maggie jumped at the chance to escape another evening worrying about her mother. She thanked Kathy for the invitation and then covered the receiver with her hand and pretended to ask her mom.

Maggie didn't feel one bit guilty when she told Kathy that her mom wasn't feeling well and was going to try to sleep. Mom had a migraine, Maggie explained, and she hadn't slept well the night before. Kathy said she'd call and check on Nora in the morning. Maggie thanked her and made sure her mom was covered with a blanket before she slipped outside.

A blast of cool September air rustled the trees and felt good against Maggie's flushed cheeks. She swooped up a handful of maple leaves that had fallen prematurely. She threw them in the air and watched them dance freely in the wind.

That's what Dad was—free. He didn't have to see Mom going to the mailbox every single day. Never mind that mail doesn't get delivered on Sundays. Mom checked it just the same. Or maybe she thought a mail fairy made special deliveries to their mailbox. Just to deliver a letter to Her Highness, Queen of Bourbon, to let her know that her husband was safe and sound and as far away from her sorry ass as he could get.

God, how she hated her mother sometimes. If she had just let Maggie talk to Henry. She could have gotten Henry to tell the truth. She could find the missing link. There had to be something. A simple explanation for why he hadn't come home.

Maggie even checked her mother's purse for the green note the number was written on, but all she found were several scraps. Which made her sure that her mom had torn it to pieces and thrown the rest away.

Maggie took slow deliberate strides and found herself searching every inch of the sidewalk. As if concrete could talk. Maybe the tiny green bugs living in the moss were going to jump up and say, "Hey

Maggie, we know where your dad is!" Then she could follow them and leave this hellhole and never have to see her mother again.

But then there was Becca. Her BFF who was quite frankly, not mature enough to live without her. They were all each other had since neither of them had brothers or sisters. And at this point, Maggie was just fine with being an only child. It just wouldn't be fair for another kid to live in her screwed-up mess.

Maggie stood on Becca's front porch and took several deep breaths before knocking on the front door. The light from the foyer formed a welcoming glow around Becca's dad as he opened the door.

"Maggie, honey, come right in. We're so sorry your mother is sick again. We'll send dinner home with you tonight. A nice meal might help her feel a little better."

"Thanks, thanks very much, Curt." Maggie warmed up as she walked inside the door. She hoped Curt didn't notice the guilt flush across her cheeks. Even a hot meal made by somebody else's nice parents couldn't sober Mom up tonight.

As Maggie took off her jacket, the coziness of just standing in the entry was overwhelming. Becca's house was similar to hers. The foyer had hardwood floors. The reddish oak banisters were identical. But the layout of the house was just the opposite. And so was what happened inside. Maggie cringed as she hung her jacket on the coat rack.

"Becca's in the kitchen helping Kathy with dinner. If the two of you want to play, I mean, hang out, in Becca's room, I can call when dinner is ready."

"Okay, actually, I don't mind helping. I'll just go into the kitchen and see what I can do." Maggie sighed when she walked past Curt. Playing? Seriously. They were almost fifteen.

Bacon crackled in a frying pan, and the aroma of caramelized onions filled the kitchen. Kathy placed a pan of potato wedges coated in melted butter in the oven as Maggie walked over to the table. Kathy closed the oven door and smiled at Maggie.

"How does home fries, green beans with bacon, and my famous crispy fried chicken sound, Maggie?"

"Like so amazing. All my favorites."

Becca made a weird squeal and gave Maggie the silliest grin. "Help me snap these beans. Last harvest from Mom's garden. And she saved them for you."

Maggie was surprised Becca hadn't called her cell and told her at least a hundred times what Kathy was making for dinner. At least Kathy remembered that Maggie was still alive. Mom hadn't cooked a single meal or gone grocery shopping since forever. Well, at least since she had stopped looking for Dad.

"Maggie, did you hear what I just said?"

"Yeah, Mom isn't here because she has the flu. Puking too much to leave the house."

"I didn't ask you about your mom, dumb ass," Becca whispered.

"Whatever." Maggie snapped a bean in two, and Becca leaned closer to her and spoke even softer.

"What's really going on, Maggie? Is it a headache, the flu or a hangover? Or is she just passed out again?"

"Shut up, Becca—not now." The words whistled passed Maggie's tightly gripped teeth and tickled her lips. "We'll talk about it later." Maggie hated it when Becca brought up her mom's issues when one of Becca's parents was in the room.

Kathy walked behind Maggie and squeezed her shoulder. "Everything all right, Maggie? Should I call your mom and make sure she's all right?"

"She's fine. Everything's fine. Thanks for asking, Kathy." Maggie grabbed several beans at once and glared in Becca's direction as she ripped them in two.

"Becca, if you do two at a time, it goes faster." Maggie forced a laugh and mouthed *shithead* at Becca.

Curt wandered into the kitchen. Maggie watched him hug Kathy's shoulder and brush a kiss across her cheek.

"Geez, do you have to? How embarrassing." Becca rolled her eyes and acted disgusted.

Maggie didn't see anything disgusting about it. The soft way Curt held Kathy close to him. The nice way he kissed her.

He sat down, and Kathy brought him a cup of coffee without even asking if he wanted one. She sat it in front of him, and he held her hand

and then added two scoops of sugar and a dash of cream. He stirred it three times and took a slow, satisfied drink.

"Looks as if you two are done with the green beans." Curt winked at Maggie as he sat his cup on the table.

"Yep, almost." Maggie looked down at the table; her pile of green beans was gone. She didn't even remember snapping the last one.

Kathy started humming as she dumped the fresh beans in a large kettle. Maggie couldn't believe that Kathy was actually humming. Becca's parents seemed happy just to be in the same room together.

That's how Maggie wanted it when she got married. No demands. No yelling. Nobody making you feel like you were nothing but a burden. Of course, Dad never thought that. But he was gone now.

"Okay, we're done already, Maggie. Let's go upstairs and listen to some tunes."

Maggie followed Becca upstairs and sat down on the bed.

"Sorry my parents are such perverts." Becca stuck her finger down her throat like she was going to puke.

"You're lucky. You know that, retard?" Maggie tried hard to swallow the lump in her throat.

"What do you mean?" Becca fiddled with her CD player before she sat down next to Maggie.

"You have a family. That's all."

The familiar lyrics of "Boulevard of Broken Dreams" drifted out the speakers, and Becca turned the volume up just loud enough to mute their voices. She wrapped her arm around Maggie's shoulder, and Maggie leaned against her.

"This is my dad's favorite song." Maggie's voice was so soft the music quickly absorbed her words.

"I know, Maggie. I thought if you heard it, you might feel better."

Tears clouded Maggie's eyes as she listened to the lyrics. She had bought the single for Dad on his last birthday. She'd walked into his studio, it was playing on the radio, and he just stood there—in front of his latest attempt at the willow—and sort of stared out the window like he was hypnotized or something. Maggie had to ask him twice what he was doing. When he didn't answer the first time, she knew he'd tripped back into that world of his, and she wasn't even sure if she should try to talk to him at all.

"I never understood what your dad sees in that song, Maggie. I mean, empty streets and broken dreams and being all alone. What's up with that?"

"You'd have to understand my dad to understand the song. I just think he related to it. He's bipolar, and the song talks about walking down a line that divides the mind. He knows he's bipolar but can't change that. And I just think that it's the first time he'd heard anything except doctor babble that made sense to him."

"Well yeah, but that's kind of weird, don't you think?"

"No, I don't."

Kathy yelled from downstairs saying dinner was ready. Maggie wiped the tears out of her eyes. At least tonight, she could eat dinner with people who loved each other and forget about the nightmare that was her real life.

NINE

There was nothing but miles and miles of beach. People came and went as John drifted in and out, connecting and disconnecting with the sights and sounds around him. At times, the beach goers seemed to swarm through him. The feel of their bodies and surging emotions would push him back into the dim world he lived in.

The weeks blended into months, and the only way John could measure how much time had passed was how quickly the sun set each day.

On those days when the sun was the brightest and the beach fullest, the aloneness would wrap around him like a thousand octopus tendrils, each one reaching inward, pinching his soul and racking him with guilt for what he'd done.

John moved away from the crowds and walked toward Lighthouse Rock. The tide and waves were too high for the beach goers to navigate, and he decided to take refuge inside the rock's largest cavern. He floated inside a tunnel time had carved into the stone and sat down on a bed of barnacles. The water inside his hiding place was much calmer than the waves lapping outside. The barnacles had no effect on his weary body, and he lay down and closed his eyes.

It felt like minutes, but John knew hours had passed because the light inside the cavern was gone. He shifted to a sitting position and heard shouting and screaming, and then a horrible stench drifted up from outside the cave entrance. He bolted forward; the shrillness of the sounds and the putrid odor rendered each step weightless and heavy at the same time.

When he emerged from the cavern, the tide was lower than he'd ever seen it. He crawled over a large rock and stumbled upon a bloated body.

A flock of seagulls swarmed over the corpse, and he flailed his arms over his head, trying to ward off the attack. Each bird glared at him before taking its turn diving down on the pile of decomposed flesh and then flew off to feast on the tiny morsel it had picked off after making its landing.

John recognized the red plaid shirt that clung to the dead man's left arm. He staggered over to the nearest rock and sealed his mouth and nose with his hand as someone screamed.

"Oh my God, it's a body! The smell is coming from that body. Nobody get too close." The man staggered backward, reeled to the left, and vomited several feet from the corpse.

"Oh God, poor soul," said another man, his voice overflowing with emotion as he collapsed on a piece of driftwood next to a clump of kelp. "Must have family, someone who is looking for him right now."

Yes, that's right, my daughter and my wife. I love them, please …

John sat next to the stranger, praying he would feel his fingers as he pressed them on the man's shoulder. John's hand ruffled the man's shirt, and the man rubbed his shoulder and stood abruptly.

"Did you see that? Something touched me, right here on my shoulder."

Yes, I'm here … right here. Just look at me!

The first man wiped the residue from his mouth. "It's just the breeze, buddy. Come on, we have to get help."

The men disappeared, and John crouched next to his human remains. A tiny crab circled inside the hollowed eye socket, and he tried to remove it. The creature continued its feeding frenzy as if John weren't there.

Stop it, right now! His words dissolved without making a sound, and he floated aimlessly toward the clouds. A free-falling sensation took over, and just as suddenly as it started, it stopped, and he crashed down inside the rotting flesh. The fall connected him to his human remains. As he struggled to move out of the void, he integrated with his decomposed arm. John felt the wedding ring attached to his finger and the memories engulfed him.

He soared upward, the vast blue sky blending with the sparkling sapphire and whitecapped waves.

A vision of Nora floated across the sand below him. The edges of her white gown glistened and flickered like a million tiny diamonds as she moved across the beach and in to the raging surf.

No, you can't take her. John reached down to stop her and tumbled through the air.

He crashed back down inside his body, and when John clenched his fingers around the ring, it burned his palm. It happened so fast he tightened his grip. The stronghold sent blisters bubbling up his arm, and the fiery collision between his life and his death thrust him onto the rocks.

The sun dimmed, and the sound of the violent waves moved from the ocean inside his head.

Please, Nora, forgive me for what I have done.

A wave crashed against the rocks, reverberating and propelling him back to the corpse.

John grabbed at the ring again and again, but each time he did, his fingers whispered through it leaving the ring dangling on the exposed bone. The sound of a man's voice reeled him away from the body and onto the beach.

"It's way out there, wedged between those two big rocks."

It sounded like the person was standing right next to him, but when John stood up, he realized it came from a group of people several hundred feet away.

"Everyone, clear out. We have everything under control."

"Any idea who it is?" A woman's voice, softened with sadness, thick with impending grief.

"Not yet. Now go. We'll notify next of kin as soon as we know who it is."

Two men with rubber boots, gloves, and white facemasks walked toward him.

John rushed toward the first man. *I'm right here. It's my body. Please help.*

The insanity was more than John could bear, and he couldn't organize his thoughts as they cascaded into silent jumbled sentences.

Excuse me. I'm John O'Brien. Ignore the body, please. I don't need it, you see, but I need to—I have to—help my daughter … and my wife …

The first man walked right through John and began talking.

"Clothing fits the description. Body's too bloated to make out any physical features."

Yes, that's right … John turned to follow him, and when he read the bold black CORONOR printed on the back of his shirt, he stiffened and couldn't make his feet take another step.

"Poor son of a bitch. It's got to be him, same red plaid shirt he had on when they reported him missing. His daughter was right; he did go back into the ocean but never made it out alive."

The other man nodded. "Yep, must a drowned right after he saved her. Still don't understand why he went back in. I guess an experience like that would confuse anyone. Poor little girl, that Maggie. And her mother. All they're left with are broken hearts."

The man reached down and moved the corpse's left arm. When he did, the wedding ring slipped off onto a rock.

"Now that's nothing short of a miracle. All the flesh gone on his finger, and the wedding ring still hung on."

Yes, Nora gave me that ring. Please give it to her … The reality was becoming too much, and John could feel himself fade.

Something flashed around the corpse's neck. One of the men pulled back the collar, and a gold heart dangled in the bloated flesh. He reached down and took the necklace off and rinsed it in a small pool of water. He opened it, revealing two pictures inside.

"I'll be damned. There isn't a drop of water on these pictures. Sure enough, that's her, the little girl found on the beach two months ago. This should be enough to identify the man as John O'Brien." He closed it, and then gently tucked it inside a Ziploc bag. "Ain't that something? The guy's body is rancid, and the pictures in this here heart are as fresh as the day he went missing."

The man nodded in agreement. "Sure hope this jewelry will comfort his family."

"Not enough here for a casket. Way too much decomposition. Looks like a cremation on this one for sure."

Fire and damnation. John closed his eyes and welcomed the darkness.

TEN

———

The noise sounded like a wounded animal. Loud, growling, almost sobbing. Maggie stumbled out of bed and tried to pull herself together. What was making that noise?

She raced out of her room, slid down the banister, flew over the landing, and collided with the front door. Maggie shivered as she stood up and looked outside.

Rain gushed from the skies and pounded across the front porch. The thick heavy clouds made the living room dark, and Maggie hesitated as she peered around the corner.

Nora sat next to Dr. Roberts, eyes rimmed in red. She looked startled when Maggie walked into the room.

Dr. Roberts wasn't wearing his customary suit, and he looked odd sitting there in jeans and an old sweatshirt. Maybe he came over to help Mom mow the lawn. After all, the backyard looked like an abandoned lot, and Maggie didn't know how to use Dad's new power mower.

"Dr. Roberts, you can't mow the lawn in the rain," Maggie whispered so low she didn't think he heard her. She took several steps closer to the couch.

Nora reached out to Maggie. When her sobs began again, Maggie recognized the sound that had woken her.

"What's the matter, Mom?"

Dr. Roberts wrapped his arm around her mother's shoulder, and Maggie wondered why he didn't just go out and mow the lawn. Maybe that would make Mom stop crying.

Nora pulled away from Dr. Roberts's embrace, grabbed hold of Maggie, and tried to pull her closer. Maggie scrambled out of reach and backed away.

"Please, just tell me. What's the matter with you, Mom?" Maggie took several steps backward and looked toward the kitchen.

"It's your father, Maggie ..." Dr. Roberts's words echoed inside Maggie's head but his mouth wasn't even moving.

Everything in Maggie's heart fell inside out and swarmed around her lungs so fast she almost lost her breath. Her head wobbled back and forth on her neck. A burning sensation filled her chest, and she knew it was going to cave in, and her mouth just sprang open and closed like a puppet on a string, and all she could say was, "No, no, no!"

"They found his body," Dr. Roberts said.

Mom sat there. Blubbering.

Sadness and panic consumed the room, and Maggie watched her mother's face deflate like a red balloon someone had beaten with a bat.

"Maggie, come sit down ..." Dr. Roberts spoke again.

Maggie tried to cover her ears.

"I'm sorry, honey. I know how upset you must be." Dr. Roberts's voice was gentle as he moved off the couch.

Nora attempted to stand but fell backward. "Please, honey, Maggie come here. I need you."

Mom's face contorted, and her words came from a million miles away. She just sat there, whimpering on the couch.

"No ... I don't believe you! I hate you! Nooooo ..." Maggie's stomach churned, and a long wail tumbled from her mouth.

The words followed Maggie as she ran down the hall. Her feet skimmed the kitchen tile, and she flew off the back porch without touching the steps.

The howling echoed inside Maggie's body as she staggered across the rain-soaked backyard. She stumbled and then collapsed onto the soggy grass.

Maggie lay down flat and allowed the September rain to beat against her skin. She kept her eyes wide open and didn't blink when raindrops landed inside.

They were lying. Dad wasn't dead. He carried her out of the ocean and rescued her from drowning. Besides, adults only believed what they want to believe. Maggie wasn't going to allow them to distort her memory. She felt her father's arms as they sailed out of the ocean. Just because they didn't see what happened doesn't mean it wasn't real.

Maggie heard water splashing in the puddles leading from the house. She closed her eyes and clenched her fists. Her mother shouldn't be outside in her condition.

Maggie sealed her lips together as tight as a zipper. She opened one eye just wide enough to look in the direction of the footsteps slogging across the lawn.

Dr. Roberts's legs were soaked up to his ankles. The rain slid down his shiny bald head. He sat down in the grass next to Maggie and stared out at the pouring rain.

Maggie was glad he didn't try to talk nonsense to her. She loosened her fists and opened both eyes.

"Why doesn't anyone believe me?"

She wanted so badly for someone, anyone to tell her she was telling the truth and Dad was resting comfortably at Mercy General in the exact same bed she had slept in the day he had disappeared.

Maggie watched Dr. Roberts hesitate before he looked down at her.

"I believe you, Maggie."

She heard the sincerity in his voice, but Maggie knew he was just trying to make her feel better. And right now, she didn't want to hear anything else he might want to say.

"Thank you," she whispered, then stood up and raced across the lawn.

Water sprayed her ankles, and the cold rain felt good as it splashed against her burning cheeks. She knew if she didn't make it to her bedroom as fast as she could, Dr. Roberts would start talking his medicine language. And that was more than she could handle.

Maggie flew inside the back door and slid down the hall.

"Maggie, is that you?"

Nora's voice pierced the silence, and Maggie scrambled up the stairs so fast she tripped three times. She didn't look back until after she had slammed her bedroom door shut and had braced a chair underneath the doorknob.

* * *

John wavered against the ceiling of a room painfully familiar. He spun through the air and collided with bits of sand and earth. Suddenly the whirling sensation stopped, and he dropped to the floor. He kept his arms tucked under until his head stopped spinning, afraid to open his eyes.

He recognized the fluorescent stars spattered across the ceiling and the castle painted on the walls. The coat rack he had hand carved still held the multicolored shawls created from fabric remnants, but their vibrant colors produced an ominous tone. The shiny tiara John surprised Maggie with when she was eight lay tarnished on the floor. The carpet Maggie once thought was magic was rolled up under the bed, and John shivered from the room's desperate glow.

Maggie's easel stood where the mirror had been, holding a half-painted canvas, splashed with colors so dark John understood the anguish he had created in her world.

The wind swept the room. It pulled John to the window seat where Maggie was sleeping. Her cheeks burned red from crying, and faint whimpers escaped her lips as he watched.

Despair flooded the room and splashed over the walls. John inhaled as deeply as he could, a hopeless attempt to draw the grief inside him. The sorrow surged around him like a swarm of vengeful bees. It stung his heart and then swept back out and consumed everything in the room.

What in God's name have I done?

When John reached over to touch Maggie, the sound of glass shattering inundated his senses. Shards of anger pierced his skin. He turned away from his daughter and drifted down the flight of steps.

Nora was sitting on the coffee table holding a bottle of bourbon. The glass she had been drinking from was shattered at the base of the stairs. Her long blond hair was pulled back in a ponytail and matted with hairspray. It looked as if she had tried to apply lipstick but, instead, had caked pink into the creases around her mouth. Mascara spread down her cheeks, her eyes wild with fear. Her clothes were so crumpled it looked as if she hadn't changed them in days. John let out an involuntary moan as Nora placed the bottle to her lips and took a huge drink.

"You weren't ever supposed to leave me." Nora stared as if John wasn't there. She took another huge swallow and choked it down.

Nora, I'm so sorry. John walked down the last three stairs and into the living room. Nora's focus remained on the staircase.

John sat on the couch in front of her. The circles beneath her eyes appeared even deeper up close, and the gray color accented the pallor covering her skin. Her pain was audible in every ounce of his being and paralyzed him against the cushions.

Nora sat the bottle down and fumbled with her cigarette pack. She wrestled with the matches until her cigarette was lit. She took a deep drag in, and her shoulders slumped as she exhaled.

"If Maggie hadn't gone in the water, you'd still be here. You saved your daughter and left me."

Nora's words pummeled John. He tried to grab hold of Nora's hand, but his fingers glided right through it.

"She was always between us, John. And I'm so angry at her I can barely look at her." Nora crushed out her cigarette and fumbled for another one. "Why, John, why did you leave me?"

The words sent torrents of resentment around the room and hammered John deep into the back of the couch.

The air grew cold and so calm John couldn't breathe. A sudden warmth filled the room, and Maggie's voice followed. He clawed at the darkness as bits and pieces of conversation floated past him, each word scratching his remorse deeper inside.

Your fault

Never would have happened

I hate you, Mother

The last words cut right through him. He tried to scream out to his daughter.

Maggie, you don't mean that. Please listen …

Before he could finish his sentence, the darkness washed over him, and he floated away.

ELEVEN

Maggie gripped Uncle Steve's hand as she walked inside the funeral home. A piano played "Amazing Grace," and the melody etched sadness into all the familiar faces.

She saw her best friend standing next to an old lady dressed in a faded mint-green pantsuit. Becca's hair looked fire-engine red against her china-doll, ivory skin. When she saw Maggie, she rushed forward.

Maggie let go of her uncle's hand, and he bent down and kissed her forehead.

"Will you be all right, Maggie?"

"Yeah, yes I will Uncle Steve, thanks. I just need to be with Becca right now."

"No problem, princess, I understand. If you need me, I'll be right here."

Uncle Steve hugged her shoulder and disappeared into the crowd.

Becca and Maggie greeted each other with a dry-eyed hug.

"I can't cry anymore," Becca whispered into Maggie's ear.

"I know. If I cry one more tear, I really am going to drown." Maggie clung to Becca and didn't want to let go. She didn't want to acknowledge the ocean of sad faces, the hands trying to touch, to hug her. She wanted them all to go away.

"You okay?" Becca's voice comforted Maggie as they moved to a quiet corner.

"I suppose, but nobody believes me, and I'm afraid I'll forget what really happened." Maggie could feel her bottom lip quiver as she talked.

"How's your mom doing?" Becca frowned at Maggie as she spoke.

"Sure, change the subject. Mom's just great. Dr. Roberts gave her a new med. Not that she needs another bottle of pills. And last night, well, she got wasted and blamed me for everything. And right now, I just hate her."

"I'm sorry, Maggie. Your mom's just sad right now. She didn't really mean that. Once this is all over, she'll be back to her old self."

"Yeah, right. Like that will ever happen." Maggie looked down at the red-and-cream swirled carpet. She traced the pattern with her foot and fought the urge to dig her heels in as deep as she could.

"Do you want to go in and sit down now, Maggie?"

"Not yet. Just give me a sec. I just need to be by myself before I go in there and have to look into all of those sad, creepy faces."

Maggie walked into a private room next to the entrance of the sanctuary. The lights were out, and it had a one-way window that overlooked the people sitting inside the chapel. There were cushioned chairs and a speaker that she decided was used to hear the service without disturbing those sitting on the other side.

She sat down in a chair tucked in the far left corner and covered her face with her hands. She exhaled slowly, and when she inhaled, a hint of cherry tobacco jolted her senses.

Maggie took her hands away from her eyes and looked around the dimly lit room. There was only one person she knew that used cherry tobacco. Could it be?

"Dad?" When Maggie stood up, she saw movement, then a shadow behind the door. She rushed over and swung the door wide enough to reveal a man who looked so familiar it startled her.

"Dad? Is that you, Daddy?" The words barely escaped, and Maggie stepped back and rubbed her eyes.

An unfamiliar voice answered. "I'm sorry, Maggie. I didn't mean to scare you."

Maggie couldn't stop shaking. She heard the shock in the stranger's voice and watched him struggle to maintain his composure as he walked over and turned on the lights.

"Who are you?" Maggie demanded.

"We met once, a long time ago, Maggie. My name is Shane. I'm a friend of … your … your father's."

"You're too old to be one of his friends." Maggie folded her arms across her chest, narrowing her eyes as she glared at him.

Shane tilted his head to one side and smiled. Maggie wanted to smile back, but his smile touched the sadness she tried so desperately to avoid.

"Well, your father and I, we had our differences. But I cared deeply about him. I'm so sorry this happened, Maggie. Your father loved you so much." Shane's words intensified the scent of cherry tobacco.

"Can't you smell it?" Maggie moved closer to Shane.

"What?"

"Cherry tobacco. It's all around you. Do you smoke a pipe?"

"Well, no, Maggie, I don't."

The scent dissipated, and Maggie suddenly realized who he was.

"You know my mother, don't you?"

"Yes, I do. But it's complicated."

"Yeah, well, everything's complicated right now. Where do you live?" Maggie waited to see if Shane had lied to her.

"I live in Angel's Corner …," Shane began.

"That's where Grandma Genevieve lived. Did you know her?" Maggie watched Shane's face flush. "Well, did you?"

"Yes, I knew your grandmother. I just wish I had time to explain."

Maggie was captivated with the warm gold speckles in Shane's hazel eyes. They were just like …

"Well, it doesn't matter where you live or what anyone says. He isn't dead."

"What?" Shane sounded surprised.

"Dad. He isn't dead. I know he's still alive."

"Well, Maggie, are you sure?"

"Of course, I'm sure. I was with him. He carried me out of the water."

Two old ladies moved into the room. One of them wedged herself between Maggie and Shane. She talked in a soft, sad voice and pressed Maggie into the fleshy folds in her chest. The puffiness of the old woman's arms threatened to strangle Maggie. She wiggled out from beneath them and pushed the old lady away. The woman yelped indignantly, and when Maggie could finally focus on the other people who'd drifted into the room, it was too late.

Shane was gone.

* * *

John paced back and forth inside the private room at the funeral chapel. He watched the church volunteers pick up the programs and tissues left in the pews after his memorial service. For once, he was grateful he couldn't be seen; there was so much for him to process now.

Like Shane. Hiding behind the door. John tried his best to shield Maggie by standing directly in front of Shane. He had hoped the resentment he felt toward the intruding old man would create a barricade and keep Shane trapped behind the door.

But when Maggie walked over and stood in front of John, all he could feel was his undying love for his only child.

And Maggie. She knew I was here.

That's when it happened. Maggie whispered, "Dad, is that you, Daddy?" The pain in her voice drove John back into the darkness. Before he could console her. Tell her he was really right there. That he wasn't really gone.

How dare Shane attend my funeral, he thought. Shane had already taken everything he had treasured in his life. Why was he here, wreaking havoc on an afterlife he had no control over?

Shane knew how much John resented him, how much John blamed him for his mother's rapid demise.

John heard a phone ring. The ringing grew so loud he covered his ears and fell to his knees.

"I'm so sorry, John." The words Shane spoke on that dreaded morning flooded the room.

"Oh my God, it's Mother, isn't it? What have they done to her?" John felt those old emotions boiling inside him as he remembered the day his mother died.

A dead silence filled the room, and then Shane spoke again.

"John, I'm so sorry."

And then John knew. The shock treatments had killed his mother.

She was too fragile. Why didn't Shane do something to stop them?

John raised his fist in anger and slammed it into the wall. He flinched, and when he looked at his knuckles, they were red from the contact.

He hit the wall again and reeled backward from the pain. His knuckles were skinned and bleeding this time, and he rushed over to the door.

He's not going to destroy Maggie's life. Anger shot through John as he grabbed the door knob. *I'm going to stop you this time, Shane.*

John's hand drifted through the doorknob. He staggered backward and placed his hands over his face.

"Love heals all wounds."

The voice came from behind John, and when he whirled around, there was no one there.

He looked for the thick mist that had preceded the wacked out man he had met on the beach. Maybe he really was some sort of archangel. And John had finally passed his test and he was going to help him.

John waited. And waited. Then he heard the voice repeat the same words again. He struggled to place the voice and tried to determine if it was male or female. It boomed so loudly and then was gone so fast.

If it was female, could it be his mother? Maybe she entered the realm he lived in just long enough to deliver the message. And the last time he'd heard her voice … Shane was there.

Anger bubbled up and threatened him again. *I will not feel anger. I'll only feel love. Love for my mother.*

John clenched his fists and tried to concentrate on Genevieve. But every time he saw his mother, Shane was there.

The memories surged again. He'd never forgive Shane for taking his childhood home. And the tree house in the willow … the only place he had ever felt safe.

"Shane is a wonderful man, John. If only you'd give him a chance."

John searched the room for his mother and remembered the whisper of sadness that had filled her eyes when she asked John to forgive her—and Shane.

The image disappeared in a blur of wet sand. John found himself standing on the cold, deserted beach.

That man. My mother.

John turned back to the sea and shook his fist. *I don't understand your motives just yet, Shane, but believe me, I will not stop until I do.*

He stomped away from the rain-soaked shoreline toward the first sand dune. When he turned around and looked down behind him, he was sure he saw his footprints imbedded in the sand.

TWELVE

Silent mourners crammed their way into every inch of Becca's house. Their jaws moved up and down as they shook their heads and dabbed at their eyes.

The scene was more than Maggie could bear. She ran out of the house, her feet barely touching the freshly mowed lawn in Becca's backyard. She took the fence in one huge leap, raced over the jungle of overgrown grass, and ran straight inside the back door.

She rushed into the kitchen and sat down to catch her breath. Her heart was pounding so hard her ears hurt, and she didn't think she could ever breathe normally again.

Maybe Mom locked Dad up in the psych ward so he could get his strength back. God knows he must have been just as scared as Maggie was after he carried her out of the ocean. And, well, something like that would make him sit and stare at the walls in his studio. He wouldn't even pick up his paintbrush for at least a month.

The last time he stayed at the hospital, Maggie found the paperwork in the file cabinet in her parent's room when Mom was having coffee with Kathy Harper. Maybe there was new paperwork in the cabinet now.

The only way she was going to know for sure was to find proof. She walked into the foyer just as Uncle Steve walked through the front door.

"Hey, Maggie. Are you okay? Your mom asked me to check on you."

Uncle Steve walked up and gave Maggie a quick hug.

"Want to talk about it?"

Maggie avoided eye contact as she moved out of her uncle's embrace.

"No. I'm just tired of old ladies I barely know trying to suffocate me with their big boobs."

Uncle Steve knelt down next to Maggie and rubbed his chin.

"Ah, yes. There's a criminal term for that, Maggie."

"Of course there is." Maggie was more than happy to engage in a distraction. "And what is it exactly?"

"Armed assault, which is technically known as suffiboobafication."

Maggie laughed and gave Uncle Steve a triumphant smack on the shoulder. "See … I knew it was a crime when it happened!"

Uncle Steve kept a straight face as he talked. "The woman can get 5-15 in the big house for it. Want me to issue a warrant for her arrest?"

"Nah. We can let it go this time. She probably didn't know she was carrying double assault weapons when she left the house."

"How right you are, Maggie." Uncle Steve ruffled her hair. "So how about I stay and try to take that spit yo-yo crown away from you?"

"Absolutely not. Besides, you already broke the first cardinal rule."

"Are you accusing an officer of the law of premeditated cheating?"

"No, I'm just saying your beer breath is a dead giveaway." Maggie giggled. "Rule number one—alcoholic beverages produce an unfair amount of spit; therefore, they cannot be drunk prior to a challenge."

"You've been drinking, Maggie?"

"No, yo-yo head, YOU have, therefore YOU cannot challenge ME for a shot at the crown."

"Fine then. I'll just give you a big fat beer breath kiss instead!"

Maggie covered her face with her hands and ran half way up the stairs before turning around.

"Now go, Uncle Steve. Before I have you arrested for being drunk in public."

"I am not drunk. And I'm not planning on going public. So I'll just hang around downstairs. Let me know if you need anything, okay, kid?"

Maggie panicked as she raced back down to her uncle's side. She didn't want him to stay in the house while she searched through the file cabinet before Mom came home.

"You don't have to stay. I'm fine, really. Besides, Mom needs you right now. I just, well, hate talking to all those sad people. It creeps me out."

Uncle Steve pinched Maggie's nose and stared directly into her eyes. "Are you sure you don't want me to stay?"

"Positive. I'll call your cell if I need anything."

Uncle Steve cupped Maggie's chin in his hands.

"I love you, Maggie. And I will always be here for you."

"I know, Uncle Steve. I love you, too." Maggie tried not to cry as she hugged her uncle and then turned and walked up the stairs.

She stood in the hallway until she heard the front door close. She tiptoed back downstairs and did a quick search to make sure she was alone, locking all the doors as she went.

Once back upstairs, Maggie raced into her parents' room. She was stunned when she saw Dad's sweaters piled neatly on top of the bed. And the second dresser drawer, Dad's drawer, was open.

Maggie walked over and looked inside.

What was Mom thinking? Dad's clothes belonged in his drawer, not strung out on the bed like there was going to be a freaking garage sale. She grabbed one of the pullovers and pressed it against her nose. It smelled clean, like fabric softener and frustrated her so much she stuffed the remaining sweaters inside the drawer. She slammed it as hard as she could.

Dad's favorite sweater was crumpled over the end of the bed. When Maggie picked it up, she pressed it against her face. She searched for a hint of her father captured inside the tightly spun yarn. But it smelled as fresh as the others did. She threw it across the room.

Maggie moved away from the bed and opened the closet door. A huge pile of Dad's painting shirts cluttered the floor. Maggie sat down next to them. The familiar smell of cherry tobacco tickled her nose. She fell forward, breathed in deeply, and buried herself in the pile.

She lay still, closed her eyes, and tried to imagine her father standing in his studio next to his easel. But all she could see was Shane standing next to her at the funeral … and then he was gone.

Maggie dug frantically through the pile of clothing, pulling out every teeshirt speckled with paint and imbued with the heavy scent of cherry tobacco. She gathered them into her arms, and when she stood to leave, she saw Dad's ball cap, the one he always let her wear when he felt good enough to go outside. She plopped it on top of the teeshirts and then went into her bedroom and hid them under her bed.

It was getting dark. Maggie knew if she turned on her parent's bedroom light, it could be seen from Becca's dining room window.

She hurried back to the closet. She had to be quick when she looked inside the file cabinet. If there wasn't time to read right now, she'd have to hide the paperwork under her bed. The thought of doing that and getting caught made her palms sweat.

Maggie closed the closet door and flipped the light switch. She looked away from the burst of light, and when she looked back, she saw it.

A box, no bigger than the ones for microwave popcorn, sat open on the lowest shelf. Her dad's wallet, bubbled and tortured by the sea, rested next to the lid.

Maggie thought about turning the light off and leaving the room as fast as she could. But the box was open. She knew if she didn't look now, she might never get a second chance.

She peered inside. Shredded pieces of Dad's red plaid shirt lined the bottom of the box and cradled a clear plastic Ziploc bag filled with neatly folded pieces of red tissue paper.

Maggie couldn't tell what was wrapped between the sheets. If she unwrapped them, her mother would for sure know because who else would lay the plaid fabric bits so neatly in the bottom. And, she'd know exactly how that bag was sitting inside the box and well …

Crap. Shit. Damn.

Maggie needed to get hold of herself. If there was any way to make her heart stop ticking like a bomb, she needed to figure it out now.

Deep breathe in. Exhale. Just like her PE teacher taught when she introduced yoga as a way of relieving stress.

After several deep breaths and a couple of Hail Marys, Maggie was as ready as she'd ever be.

She examined the way the bag sat inside the box and memorized its position. She made sure none of the fabric was disturbed as she pulled the bag out. She unzipped it, and as she removed the tissue, something dropped on to the floor. She scooped it up and held it in the palm of her hand.

Tiny sprays of engraved gold roses wrapped themselves around the top of a heart-shaped jewel. It was Dad's locket. The one that was identical to hers. The one that he swore he would die before he took off.

Maggie's hands were shaking. All she could do was gasp as she backed out of the closet.

She stumbled over a pair of Mom's shoes and fell. The locket flew out of her hands. She almost screamed when it hit the ground outside her parents' bedroom door.

The front door opened and slammed shut. The sound of familiar voices in the foyer sent her scrambling to her feet.

The voices faded down the hall. Maggie grabbed the locket and turned off the closet light. Her hand was still shaking as she shoved the shoes back inside. Her heart skipped several beats because she knew Mom would notice they'd been moved.

Maggie tiptoed into the hall and clutched the locket so tightly her fingernails dug into her palm. She braced herself against the wall, crept back into her bedroom, and sat on the edge of the bed.

Maggie heard Mom talking to Uncle Steve. She knew if she lay down and leaned out over the top stair of the landing, she could see the kitchen table. She clung tight to the locket and positioned herself on the top stair.

"I was glad to see Shane. I didn't recognize him at first. I was surprised he came all the way from Angel's Corner for the funeral."

Her mother's voice drifted up. Maggie leaned forward and peered over the banister. She could see the kitchen at the end of the hall. The door was wide open. Uncle Steve was pacing in front of the kitchen sink.

Mom disappeared for a minute and then sat back down and placed a bottle on the table.

"And I love Shane's house. And the willow tree. John always wanted to take Maggie there."

So Mom *likes* Shane. Why didn't Maggie know this before today? Once again, Mom was keeping things from her like she'd done her entire life.

Ice jingled in a glass. She watched her mom take a long drink as Uncle Steve crossed his arms over his chest. He started talking so loud Maggie wondered what was making him so angry.

"Yeah, well, that's Genevieve and Rex's house, remember? Just because Shane married Genevieve after Rex died, it didn't give Shane the right to take that house from John. And when Genevieve passed, Shane should have moved out of there."

Uncle Steve's voice was so loud Maggie scooted up one stair.

"Would you please keep your voice down? You'll wake Maggie and get her upset again."

"Fine. But I can't believe he showed up, especially after I told him to get out of North Beach and never—"

Maggie heard her mother gasp.

"You saw him at North Beach? Why didn't you tell me?"

"I saw him that day you were posting flyers. You said yourself you didn't recognize him. I almost didn't either—which makes me wonder what the hell he's trying to hide. I didn't say anything because I knew how upset you'd get. Look, I get that you feel some sort of weird bond with Shane, but I'm telling you, my instincts say—"

"That as a cop, you've forgotten how to feel?"

"Fine. I'm going to ignore that remark. You're upset. And if you like Shane, so be it."

"Yes, I've always liked him. Did you even bother to ask him why he was there? Maybe he was just trying to help. And I'll tell you one thing for sure. I don't buy your bullshit theory about Genevieve. And you can't change how I feel."

Maggie leaned forward and watched Uncle Steve plant a kiss on Mom's forehead.

"I didn't mean to upset you, Nora. Listen, I'm going to go check on Maggie before I leave. Are you going to be okay here by yourself?"

"Yes sir, officer."

Maggie watched her mother place a pill bottle on the table.

"Come on, Nora, you can't mix—"

"My shoulder is throbbing, and you're making it feel worse."

Maggie watched Uncle Steve sigh and shake his head. "Nora, please."

"Just leave, Steve. I need to be alone now. I'm fine. We'll be fine. I'll figure it all out in the morning."

Uncle Steve threw his arms in the air and headed down the hall. Maggie scrambled off the stairs and rushed into her bedroom.

It felt like forever had passed before she heard his footsteps coming up the stairs.

"Maggie?" asked Uncle Steve.

She pretended she was asleep and hoped the twitch in her right eye wasn't visible. She felt a blanket fall across her body. She could feel the warmth of her uncle as he tucked the blanket around her.

"Sleep, Maggie. You'll feel better in the morning."

Maggie listened to Uncle Steve's footsteps disappear down the stairs. She loosened her grip on the locket in her hand and then rested it on the pillow next to her. She took off her necklace and strung her father's locket next to hers.

She knew for a fact that her father must have spiraled farther than ever. And she couldn't remember if he had his necklace on when he pulled her out of the water. It didn't matter. She'd keep it close to hers because she knew that is what he'd want. Besides, she couldn't think about that right now. Now that she'd met Shane.

So Grandma Genevieve was married to Shane? Why didn't they tell me I had a stepgrandfather? Maggie tiptoed over and shut her bedroom door.

Maggie had to find out why Shane was at North Beach. He had to know something—otherwise, why would he go there? And maybe he wasn't such a bad guy after all. He acted concerned at the funeral home.

Maybe he wanted to tell her where he thought her dad had gone— and maybe he could help her find Dad and bring him home where he belonged.

THIRTEEN

—————

Maggie tossed and turned all night and finally gave up sleeping. She tiptoed into her parents' room. It was weird seeing her mother lying in that king-size bed all by herself.

Her mom had Dad's pillow scrunched around her head. She even had Dad's teeshirt on, which was completely weird because she preferred to sleep naked. (This had, of course, grossed Maggie out the first time she'd seen it.)

Maggie understood wanting something of Dad's snuggled around her. And she was actually afraid that maybe his smell would just go away, and then she'd forget how he looked when he smiled and …

Stop it. Right now.

She hurried back to her bedroom and checked the time. Six o'clock. Becca would surely answer her cell right now, even if she was half asleep.

Maggie grabbed her phone and shut her bedroom door. The phone rang five times and went to voice mail.

Damn. How could her BFF not know she was desperate to talk to her? The phone rang in her hand, and Maggie started talking immediately.

"I know you were asleep, Becca, and if it wasn't so important, I wouldn't have woken you this early."

"This better be good, Mag. I'm exhausted. Half the people stayed and drank until four this morning, and your Uncle Steve, well …" Becca took a deep breath. "Hey, I'm sorry. That was a horrible thing to complain about. If it makes you feel any better, your uncle crashed on the couch."

"Yeah, that's great. But wait until I tell you what I heard him and Mom talking about."

Becca yawned, and Maggie almost felt guilty about waking her. She talked so fast she could barely understand herself. "Mom bought double-stuffed Oreos yesterday, and I thought maybe you could meet me outside. I think we even have grape juice."

"Grape juice with Oreos? That's like offering me a Quarter Pounder with a Double Whopper with cheese."

"Yeah, you're right. I'm sure we have milk. Can you come over right now?" Maggie didn't want to forget a single detail, and if Becca didn't hurry up, she was sure she'd miss something as she had when Mom kept hammering for details the day Dad had disappeared.

"Fine. But if my mom wakes up, what am I supposed to tell her?"

"That I woke up all tweaky and called you."

"Oh yeah. Then I'll just leave her a note on the kitchen table."

"You can't. If Uncle Steve wakes up and sees it, he'll come over, and then we'll never get any privacy." Geez, why did Becca have to make everything so darn hard?

"Fine. Whatever. I'll be over in five."

Maggie went to the kitchen, grabbed milk and cookies, and headed out the back door. A huge spider had taken residence across the back steps over night. The sun was out, and the dew on the web looked like tiny crystals. She marveled at its complex pattern. She decided to tell Becca she couldn't take the stairs. She'd just have to crawl up the banister or something. The spider must have been up all night. Destroying something so insanely beautiful was out of the question.

The air had that crispy-fall chill, and Maggie worried that Dad wouldn't be home before the first frost. What exactly was he doing for money wherever he was? Maybe he was hiding somewhere near Angel's Corner so he could commandeer Grandma Genevieve's house. Maybe that was what he'd planned all along. Go back to the willow. Take back the house—his house, as a matter of fact.

"God, Maggie, you know I hate spiders!" Becca stood with her sweatshirt wrapped around her and the hood planted firmly on her head.

"I am not eating on the back porch with a huge spider watching my every move. Can you believe how ginormous he is?"

Becca's stupid fear was making everything even more complicated. "We can't eat in the kitchen. Mom will wake up, and we'll never be able to talk."

"Fine. But we're not eating on the back porch."

"Geez. Just meet me around front." Maggie gathered the milk and cookies and hurried out the front door. Becca was already there, inspecting the railing and deck. She seemed satisfied that no multi-legged creature was waiting to join them.

Maggie sat the food on a table and started talking as soon as she sat down. "I was too freaked out to tell you what happened when I was in that room totally by myself."

Becca ripped open the bag of cookies and poured herself a glass of milk. "When I went back to that room, there were a couple of old ladies in there with you. So you couldn't have been sitting there by yourself for long."

"That's the whole point, Becca. I was never really alone in there. Not for one single second." Maggie moved closer to Becca and lowered her voice. "This old man—Shane—he was in there talking all morbid ..."

"What do you mean, morbid?"

"You know, the I'm-so-sorry-this-happened stuff. But the point is, right before I actually saw Shane, I smelled Dad's cherry tobacco, and of course I thought he was my dad. Until I got a closer look, and he only resembled him in an old sort of way."

Becca interrupted. "That doesn't make sense."

"Nothing makes sense right now. But when I looked around for Dad and didn't see him anywhere, that's when I asked this man who he was."

Becca dipped two cookies into her milk at once. "Asked who? Who's him? I'm totally confused. And these cookies aren't cutting it for breakfast."

Maggie shoved the bag at Becca and continued talking. "Who *him* is? Shane. The guy my dad never liked. And to top it off, when I looked closer at him, it just completely freaked me out. And then I heard Mom and Uncle Steve talking, and Mom said she liked Shane, and I could tell by the way Uncle Steve was saying Shane ripped off Grandma Genevieve's house that he doesn't like him one bit."

Maggie stopped for a moment and downed her glass of milk. "And get this. Uncle Steve saw Shane at North Beach."

"And that means something? Why?"

Becca's reply startled Maggie. The wheels were turning so fast in her mind it was giving her a headache. "Because he was at the beach right after Dad went missing. Don't you get it, Becca? Maybe Shane knows something. He lives in the house with the willow tree. Why else would he go to the beach after Dad went missing and then come to that funeral thing yesterday?"

"Huh? That is just insane, Maggie." Becca finished off her milk and took hold of Maggie's hand. "Listen, I know you still want to believe your dad carried you out of the water. But my mom said they found his body, and it was cremated. And my mom wouldn't lie to me about something like that."

"So what? You're saying I'm a liar? That I'm crazy just as everyone says my dad is—behind my back of course. Because, oh, we wouldn't want to mentally disturb Mary Margaret now would we? Because she's crazy …" The words escaped between sobs. Maggie stood up and knocked the glasses off the table. They shattered against the house.

"Maggie, I'm so sorry. That's not what I'm saying. Nobody believes that about you. You're nothing like—"

"My father? Well, for your information, I am just like him, Becca. And if you think he's crazy, then you think I'm crazy, too!"

Maggie shoved the table over, and the front door flew open.

"Maggie, what in God's name …" Nora stood in John's teeshirt, her eyes wide and her whole body shaking as if she'd seen a ghost.

Maggie glared at Becca. Her lips formed a thin line as she spoke. "Leave. Now."

"Maggie, I'm so sorry …" Becca wiped the tears from her eyes, and before Maggie could say anything else, she turned and raced down the front steps.

Maggie watched Becca run home. Her gut felt like everyone she'd ever loved had abandoned her.

"Maggie, honey, what's going on?" Nora moved closer to Maggie. But Maggie backed away.

"Leave me alone, Mom. Don't touch me."

Maggie shoved the overturned table between them. If her mother came one inch closer to her, she would scream. And she knew if that happened, she'd never be able to stop.

Tears welled up in her mother's eyes. All Maggie could do was glare at her. She tightened her hands into fists and slowly moved toward the front door.

FOURTEEN

Tiny streams of sunlight filtered through the attic window. The light found its way inside the room as daybreak approached. Each object in the long-forgotten crawl space took on a life of its own.

A rack of handmade maternity dresses, impeccably sewn, hung neatly, though the blues and reds of the fabric had faded with time. A rocking chair held baby blankets, hand crocheted and still intact, ready for the next arrival. A fire truck sat at the foot of a bentwood rocker, its ladder upright, while an army of soldier figurines surrounded it, positioned for battle.

John recognized a dump truck sitting next to an easel but was drawn to one of his earliest paintings resting on the stand. The colors were still bright. He still remembered when he completed it.

It was his fifth birthday. Genevieve had bought art supplies for him. John smiled as he recalled the reams of paper he splattered with pictures before receiving the first tools of his trade.

"I want big pictures, Mommy," he'd told her, and his mother rewarded his work with the easel and oil paints.

"Just like your father," she whispered and looked as if she was a million miles away. Yet when he asked his father to guide his work, Rex held the paintbrush like a shovel in his attempt to apply paint to paper.

"No, like this, Daddy." John tried to show his father how easy it was to make green out of yellow and blue. But Rex's turned more aqua than green. When John had said something to him, his father replied,

"I never was much good at this." John knew than it would be more of a chore to teach him than to do the work by himself.

The attic warmed, and he could feel the softness of his mother's touch. He smelled the baby powder she used after her morning bath.

John drifted over to a trunk and sat down on a stack of magazines. He ran his hand over the top of the chest, chasing the dust into the thin streams of light. His heart pounded as he took hold of the latch. It felt firm and powerful in his hand, and sweat ran down his forehead as he lifted the cover.

His apprehension surged as he opened the lid, and the scent of baby powder filled the room.

"Mother?"

John waited in silence for her response and then whispered again. "Are you here, Mom?"

The dust disappeared, and the air cleared as he waited. And listened. Then somberly looked inside the trunk.

A small stack of letters tied with a faded blue ribbon rested on top. He touched the first one lightly, and his hand connected to the paper. He grabbed hold of the ribbon. It stayed in his grip. He pulled the bundle out and onto the floor in front of him.

John untied the ribbon and scanned the date stamped on each one. Four of them were mailed in early 1967, and one envelope was blank. He examined the one on top.

It was addressed to his mother and bore her maiden name. The return address on all of them was the same: APO San Francisco from Jonathan O'Shanahan, Marine Private First Class. He shuddered when he saw the name and knew the letters were from Shane.

The first letter was dated seven months before John's birth. Odd. Why would this man be sending his mother letters when she was married to someone else? The confusion pushed him to open the envelope. He held it with both hands and read the contents:

January 4, 1967

Dearest Genevieve,
I am thrilled about the baby. This war won't last forever, and as soon as my leave is approved, we will be married.

The letter didn't make any sense. His mother was already married.

The postmark on the second was a month later. He scanned the contents that spoke about delays. The next letter was written three weeks later and gave an official leave date of April 12, 1967.

The front of the next envelope was blank, and when John opened it, each scribbled word on the page was smeared.

February 7, 1967

Shane,

I cannot wait another two months for you to come home. I'll be big as a house by then, and people will talk. Not that I care so much about the chatter, but I can't end up an unwed mother. My father would have confirmation that I am the whore he always said I was. God, how I hate that man.

I have decided to marry Rex O'Brien. He has promised to take care of me and my baby.

The words burned John's eyes, and he shook so hard the letter fell to the floor. He ripped the piece of paper out of the final envelope, hoping its contents would erase the nonsense his mother had written.

March 5, 1967

Dearest Genevieve,

I have to make this short. I've missed your letters. Please write. I love you and our baby, and nothing in this world means more to me. My leave was cancelled. There's nothing I can do.

I love you.

Shane

John dropped Shane's letter on the floor and picked up his mother's handwritten message. The edges of the paper were sharp and fluid in his hands. He tried to get a firm grip, but the letter floated back to the floor.

The air in the room thickened, and tiny dust clouds swirled in the blinding sunlight and tumbled across the attic. He leaned forward and reread his mother's message.

The words were so clear and the meaning so real that a rage of deceit surged through him. He looked back inside the trunk and saw a marriage certificate below the spot where the bundle of letters had rested.

Genevieve Mae Anderson
Rex Allen O'Brien
Married March 12, 1967

Memories thrashed him in ugly swarms. The tree house in the willow his father had built. He couldn't even hold a hammer. A paintbrush was like a shovel in his hands.

All of it. Lies. John kicked at his mother's letter and it drifted toward the rocker. The window in the attic clouded over, and the sunlight disappeared. He heard a noise at the base of the stairs and fought the darkness as the sound of footsteps moved closer.

"Who's there?"

The voice sounded urgent and familiar, but when John opened his mouth to answer, the ocean flooded in, and he disappeared into the angry waves.

* * *

Shane hesitated before turning on the light. He hadn't been in the attic since Genevieve's death. Whenever he ventured toward the upper staircase, heaviness filled his heart, and his legs turned to lead pipes. Each time he walked away.

A sense of urgency had enveloped him since he had woken up this morning. The scent of baby powder filled his bedroom. It was as if Genevieve was there, trying to tell him something. He called out to her, but when he sat up in bed, the scent was gone. The only thing left was a hollowness he just couldn't shake.

The unanswered questions. Genevieve never told him why she didn't wait for him. Yet he was relieved to know she'd been taken care of during the six years he spent in the POW camp in Vietnam. Rex had been his best friend. And Rex did the honorable thing. But what nagged at Shane was how fast Genevieve married Rex. She didn't even know Shane had been captured before she and Rex tied the knot.

And when Rex died, Genevieve called Shane. The only thing she asked was that he never reveal that he was John's father. He'd been reluctant at first, but the sound of her voice gave him hope that all the years they'd spent apart would be over and he could finally be with her again.

Besides, John was a grown man with a family of his own. Disclosing the secret would make his only son feel as if his entire life had been a lie. So he settled. Peace for his son and a few good years with the woman he loved.

Shane sighed as he flipped the light switch on and climbed the last set of stairs. The air in the attic smelled of cherry tobacco, and Shane scanned the room for its source. He walked further into the upper floor, drawn by the smell and the need to find something familiar.

The attic was filled with memories of a past he didn't experience. A lopsided shade sat on a Tiffany lamp, placed carelessly on a broken end table. Shane checked the damaged table and saw how easy it would be to repair.

He pulled the single drawer out and discovered a stack of old photographs. He took the first one out and dusted it off. Genevieve stood smiling in front of the stack of lumber Shane used to build the tree house.

The rest of the photos were a series of Shane trying to take their picture together. He remembered propping the camera on a tripod and then running back to her side. He flipped through them, and each photo evolved into an animated sequence with only his hand visible at first and Genevieve laughing, progressing like a miniature film finalizing with him grabbing hold of her and them dissolving into a passionate kiss.

The images stirred the love he felt for her. He ran his hand over the top photo, then placed the stack on the table, and looked around the room.

A rack of clothes demanded his attention. When he went closer, he saw a trunk, lid open, and envelopes and stationary scattered across the floor in front of it.

He picked up a letter and recognized his own handwriting. His heart stopped as he read it.

He held the letter close to his heart and heaved a sigh.

"If only ...," he said to the empty space. Shane reached down for another letter and noticed a folded piece of stationary resting on the ladder of a fire truck next to the bentwood rocker. He leaned over, picked it up, and then opened it slowly.

Scribbled handwriting sprawled across the stained and streaked paper. Shane had to read it several times to understand.

He turned back to the trunk and peered inside, looking for additional clues. When he saw the marriage license that took Genevieve away from him, he tore it to shreds. He waited for a feeling of satisfaction to come, but it eluded him. He pulled the remainder of papers out of the trunk and scattered them in front of him.

A large manila envelope stood out. When he picked it up, he recognized Genevieve's handwriting. It was addressed to John.

He waited for a moment, unsure if retrieving the contents was the right thing to do. The envelope seemed to move in his hand. When he opened it, everything inside tumbled to the floor.

The first thing he saw was two photographs, one of himself and another of John painting in the tree house in the willow. Shane was amazed at their identical poses and the way the photos showed similar drawings in progress. Two artists, photos taken years apart, each creating eerily comparable works of art.

The similarity in style and composition was so profound that Shane leaned back against the trunk to catch his breath. He leafed through the contents of the envelope and found a piece of stationary identical to Genevieve's handwritten note. Unfolding the letter, he read Genevieve's words.

July 17, 1996

John,

If you receive this letter, it is because I am gone. This is my final wish for you. I hope that when you read this, you will not feel I made your entire life a lie.

I loved your father, Rex, and will always be grateful for the loving parent he was to you, my only child. I cannot tell you how much he loved you or how he longed to participate in the natural talent so inherent to your being, yet so foreign to him.

Your artist abilities are a gift, and the source of your talent is your biological father. His name is Jonathan O'Shanahan. But you have only known him by his nickname, Shane.

I pray that someday you will forgive Shane and give him a chance. He can provide the missing link you have searched for your entire life.

Your artist ability rivals his, but the most important gift he can give you is his unconditional love. God speed.

I love you,
Mom

Shane held Genevieve's letter of confession in one hand and her letter to John over his heart. He had to decide what to do with this newfound information. He scratched the beard on his face as he placed the letter back in the envelope and leaned it against the trunk.

He hurried down the stairs and walked into the bathroom.

Shane peered at the bearded image in front of him and then reached inside the medicine cabinet and pulled out his razor. It was time for him to shave.

* * *

John's lungs filled with dust, and he struggled against the downward spiral that tangled and twisted his body.

A rocking chair flew past him. An army of soldier figurines shot tiny bullets into his heart, and just as he closed his eyes and tried to scream, everything came to a screeching halt.

John floated inside a dusty haze. He felt his body unravel as he settled against a hard surface.

The haze lifted, and John recognized the cedar chest sitting in front of him.

No!

The intense anger that always threw him back into darkness took over, and he welcomed returning to the abyss.

But it didn't happen.

A manila envelope perched against the chest screamed his name. John held firm to his spot and tried to look away, but his body moved closer. His hands reached down and picked up the envelope that bore his mother's handwriting.

His fingers tingled, and his hands shook so hard he dropped it.

The single word—his first name—jumped off the paper and floated between him and the floor.

John covered his eyes, and when he moved his hands away, two photos were lying next to his feet.

He leaned down and looked at the two prints. One in color. The other faded black and white.

He recognized the color shot. It was taken when he was a young boy. He stood in the tree house with paintbrush in one hand, head tilted to one side as he smiled at the camera.

The other photo was taken inside the tree house in the exact same spot. And the man in the picture looked just like John did when he was around nineteen. Yet he never painted in the tree house when he was a young man. By the time John turned nineteen, his father was dead. And the second photo—black and white, the edges so yellowed with age—it couldn't possibly be him.

Yet the poses in both pictures were identical—from the way each held his paintbrush to the paintings themselves.

John dug through the manila envelope searching for another clue. He pulled out a letter written on his mother's stationary.

He paused, holding the neatly folded document in his hand. He was hesitant to read.

The photos on the floor came alive, and the image of the young boy begged him to take a closer look. When John leaned down, the photos blended into one, and the man that stared back at John from the photo wasn't himself.

It was Shane.

John kicked the photos under the rocker and then unfolded the stationary. He scrutinized the shape and size of each letter that formed the message his mother had left him.

He read it and then read it again. He glared at the paper, hoping his anger would burn holes in it and make it sizzle, burst into flames … and disappear.

But the words refused his challenge. They swirled off the paper and danced in the dusty streaks of light filtering in from the attic window. The air was so dry and hot the words exploded and sparked and then turned to ashes on the floor.

Yet the original message, etched carefully by his mother's hand, held fast to the stationary, challenging John to believe.

FIFTEEN

Fifteen wasn't such a big deal. Not like becoming a teenager, which Dad had made this huge production.

"Becoming a teenager," Dad had told her on her thirteenth birthday, "is a rite of passage. But when you turn sixteen, the sweetness of your youth will turn you into a young woman."

"Is that why they call it sweet sixteen?" Maggie remembered trying to humor him and hoping she would finally get a cell phone for her birthday.

"Sweet sixteen refers to a young woman who has never been kissed." The look on her father's face was half pleased, half sad.

"Seriously? How lame is that is that?" Maggie was sure her cheeks were bright red.

"Oh no, Magpie. It is a celebration of the beauty and innocence of the girl. She has shed her youth, and as she accepts the virtue of who she is, she can also accept the responsibility of being a wife and mother."

"Whaaaat? Are you for real, Dad?"

Her father laughed then. And it had been such a long time since she'd heard him laugh it surprised her. "Sorry, Magpie—that is a very old interpretation. And I'm getting way ahead. Today, we must celebrate your becoming a teenager. Your sixteenth is three whole years away."

Her father always looked at the world through poetic eyes. Maggie was glad that he was missing this one. There was nothing poetic or even magical about turning fifteen. It was just another birthday.

Maggie walked into the kitchen, and Nora was sitting at the table. Maggie touched the top of the stove and then sniffed the air, but all she smelled was stale cigarettes and freshly brewed coffee.

"No scones, Mom?" Maggie tried to act nonchalant.

"Why would I ..." Nora stared at Maggie as if she was crazy, and then her mouth dropped open. "Oh, Maggie, it's your birthday. I ..."

"That's okay, Mom. No big deal. I'm meeting Becca right now, and I wouldn't have time to eat one anyway."

"Honey, I'll have a cake this afternoon. I don't have to work today, so I promise."

A cake was better than nothing because she knew for sure Mom couldn't afford to buy her a gift, the way she was going over the bills yesterday.

"That'd be great, Mom. Can Becca come over and have dinner with us?"

"Of course. I'll pick up some pizzas. We can have a party."

"Awesome. Thanks." Maggie hesitated and decided to sit down.

"What is it Maggie? I'm sorry I upset you. It's just—"

"That you have a lot to deal with right now." Maggie reached over and took Nora's hand. She thought her mother was going to cry. "But, Mom, well I have to talk to you about something ... someone."

Maggie took a deep breath.

"What?" Nora sounded scared at first and then smiled. "Is it boys, Maggie? Do you have a boyfriend you've been hiding from me?"

"No, of course not. All the boys I know are lame. Except for maybe Johnny Peterson." Maggie blushed, and Nora squeezed her hand.

"Your father actually likes, liked Johnny." Nora's voice faded, and Maggie was afraid she might lose her chance to talk to her about Shane.

"You never told me that, Mom. And you never told me why Dad and Uncle Steve hate Shane."

Nora sat up in her chair and pulled her hands into her lap. "How do you know about Shane?"

"I met him at the chapel."

"What chapel?"

"The one where Dad's, that service—"

"You mean your father's memorial? Maggie, honey, when are you going to come to terms with your father's death?" Nora choked back a sob. "He isn't coming home again."

Maggie stood abruptly and clasped her hand around the heart-shaped locket hanging around her neck. "Dad carried me out of the water, Mom. And Henry saw him, and I don't know why he lied to you. And even Shane knew Dad was missing because he went looking for him at North Beach."

"Who told you that?"

"I heard you and Uncle Steve talking when you got back from Becca's."

"I thought you were asleep."

"Well, I wasn't. And I need to know about Shane."

Nora sighed and patted the chair next to her. "Sit down, Maggie. I'll try to answer your questions."

The relief made Maggie's knees weak, and she practically collapsed in the chair.

"Uncle Steve said Shane was married to Grandma Genevieve. And Shane said that he and Dad had their differences. I need to know what that means."

Nora took a sip of her coffee.

"When Grandpa Rex passed away, Shane moved into the house three weeks later. And your father was angry because he felt it was disrespectful to Rex, your grandfather. You never met your Grandpa Rex—he died before you were born."

"I remember driving all the way to Angel's Corner to see Grandma. Dad drove up the driveway, and some man came out of the house, and he and Dad got into a really big fight and ..." Maggie thought for a moment. "And that man was Shane, wasn't it?"

Nora sighed. "Yes, it was Shane. Your dad went there because he decided he was going to kick him off the property. I was against it, and we argued for months about it. But your father, well, when he set his mind on something, nothing I could say would change it. And that's when Shane told him—he and Grandma were married."

"I saw Grandma in the upstairs bedroom window. And when I waved to her, she sort of hid behind the curtains. And then Dad got in the car, and we drove away."

"Yes, we did."

Maggie watched her mother run her fingers around the rim of her coffee cup.

"And your father refused to go back there again."

"But I don't understand." Maggie knew how obsessed her father was with the willow tree. "He told me he would go back. He was going to take me there. After he got rid of Shane."

"He was always threatening to do that, Maggie. He never really meant it. He just couldn't bring himself to go back there." Nora poured a fresh cup of coffee. "Maybe there were just too many memories, honey. And, well, after your father stormed away that day, your grandmother quit calling him."

"Seriously? Just like that? Do you think Shane had anything to do with it?"

Nora turned and faced Maggie. "No, I don't. Shane is an honest and sincere man. He understood that your grandmother was ... delicate. He was good for her."

"Did Dad ever see Grandma again?"

Nora stared into her coffee cup. "She called and said she wanted to see him. Your dad went to Angel's Corner by himself and met with Grandma Genevieve."

"And?" Maggie looked at her mother. She had the "it's complicated" look on her face.

"And ...," Nora took a drink, "your father came home and never said a word."

"You didn't even ask him what they talked about?" Maggie couldn't believe her father would drive that entire distance and then come home and say absolutely nothing.

"Honey, you know your father was moody." Nora walked to the kitchen counter and looked outside the kitchen window.

"Yeah, I know Mom." Maggie realized her mother could only give her so much information. But Shane. That was an entirely different story.

"Why do you think Shane was looking for Dad?" Maggie watched her mother sit down at the table. Her expression turned somber.

"Because. Your grandmother used to disappear."

"And Shane always managed to find her?" Maggie sat on the edge of her chair.

"Yes, Maggie. As far as I know, he did."

Wow. This was huge. Shane must know a lot more about Dad than Maggie could imagine. And he knows all about the disappearing acts. That's why he was at North Beach. To help. To find Dad.

"Then why did Uncle Steve get all bent out of shape at Shane? I mean, Shane knows the drill. He could have actually helped us."

"Maggie ... your Uncle Steve ... well, it's complicated."

"I know, Mom. Thanks." Maggie kissed Nora's forehead, and Nora reached up and gave her a loose hug.

Well, it certainly wasn't all that complicated. As far as Maggie was concerned, the complication had just worked itself out. Shane was the only person she knew that had dealt with this type of disappearing act. And it was time for Maggie to talk to Shane.

SIXTEEN

The willow branches crackled as hail pounded against the tree house roof. The sound comforted John as he accustomed himself to the dismal fall evening.

Genevieve's mood swings drove John to the willow when he was a child. He sought refuge in the tree house back then and used those stolen moments to strengthen himself—or rather, create a façade of strength, for his mother. He knew that, if he couldn't hold the weight of her erratic emotions, she would die. Rex never wavered even when his mother rambled on incoherently for days on end. The man John had thought was his father stayed as close to his mother's side as she would allow. Maybe Rex's love for Genevieve is what caused his heart to fail. God knew Rex would have loved his mother if she had allowed him close enough to demonstrate it.

At least now, John knew his mother's coolness to Rex was because her heart belonged to another man.

The hail subsided and turned to huge drops of rain. John walked over to the window and sat down on the bench below it. He longed to cover himself with the thick wool afghan his mother had knitted for evenings like this one—when you were sure winter had arrived before fall had one last chance to show its glory.

John stretched his legs across the bench and looked outside. The clouds that had brought the sudden downpour disbanded. A sliver of moon peeked out between them, and the stars twinkled as bright as they did on Maggie's bedroom walls.

John looked over at the blank canvas resting on the easel and longed for the feel of a paintbrush in his hand. If only he had brought Maggie here, given Maggie the opportunity to experience the wind as it whispered an image into her mind. Then when she closed her eyes, just as he'd done, she could have allowed the wind's melody to orchestrate her creation.

If only he'd kept his promise.

John sighed and thought of his mother. She had always insisted John's talents emerged from the tree house—that his gift was born on the wind and the willow held the mystery of their lives. Once, she said John's destiny would unravel those mysteries, and then, and only then, would his life be right.

But he never let that happen.

John lay down and covered his face with his hands. Why was his life cursed with confusion and his death haunted with clarity?

A flash of light emblazoned the floor, and shadows danced across the room. John bolted upright and watched the light move across the floorboards and shine under the trap door in the floor.

He heard the ladder hit the ground with a thump, and the light bounced upward and then stopped. Metal scraped against metal, the trap door flipped up onto the floor, and light filled the room.

John watched Shane poke his head up and survey the perimeter of the tree house before climbing inside.

Shane seemed agitated. When John walked up next to him and waved his hand through Shane's shoulder, Shane didn't flinch. It was clear his preoccupation was keeping him from sensing John's presence. Relieved, John went back to the bench under the window and sat down.

Shane stood in front of the easel and closed his eyes. John watched Shane's breathing slow with each deep breath he took. A sense of calm filled the tree house.

He is my exact opposite, John whispered to himself.

Shane opened his eyes and loosened his fingers before picking up a tube of white paint and placing a generous dollop on his palette. He mixed a hint of black with it, stroked it onto the canvas, and quickly outlined a child's face.

A sense of tranquility overtook the room as the childlike image on the canvas turned into a portrait of Maggie.

The exactness Shane displayed when he added the sparkle to Maggie's eyes was the same technique John always used—one he thought belonged solely to him.

Each brushstroke Shane made was as if John had made it himself. The calmness Shane radiated was an emotion John longed for but never achieved.

John watched Maggie's face light up the canvas, and when Shane finished the portrait, he fell to his knees.

"Dear God," Shane whispered, "watch over my granddaughter, Maggie. I want so much to be with her. Give me a sign, Lord. Please help me to know what I should do."

SEVENTEEN

Maggie pushed her head into her pillow and screamed. The surf crashed over her head, and just when everything went black, Dad grabbed her.

The water calmed as she wrapped her arms around his neck, and they floated the sea like two feathers in the wind. She didn't care when she took a breath of water because she was safe again in her father's arms.

They glided past a school of fish and taunted a shark on their way to the top of the ocean. They walked down the crashing waves, and Maggie breathed in the lightness that took over her body. They hit the sand, and Dad howled, and then she couldn't feel him anymore. When she tried to open her eyes, her lids hung like steel shades, and Dad's howl turned into a scream. She felt the wet sand hard against her back. When she tried to find him and pull him next to her, she felt him walk back into the water.

"No, Dad, no!"

Maggie sat up in bed, her pillow drenched with sweat. Darkness blanketed her room, and she couldn't stop shaking.

She was so afraid her father would never come home and her mother would never be happy, and all of it was her fault. She should have held on tighter. She should have told him she was in the back of the pickup. She should have insisted he keep his promise.

Maggie reached under her bed, pulled out one of John's paint shirts, and slipped it over her head, wrapping herself inside.

She pulled her pillow down on the floor. The feel of her father's shirt against her skin reassured her as she drifted back to sleep.

* * *

The cool October breeze dampened the early morning sunshine as Nora walked into the studio. She had avoided this room since John's death. But doubt still consumed her mind and convinced her to search his hideaway.

The easel held a painting so dark the images scared her. The area was immaculate, paintbrushes clean and palette tightly covered with Saran Wrap as though he planned to return.

Nora's throat tightened. She went over to the desk and sat in John's chair.

She repressed her grief as best she could and turned her attention to the contents of the desk. She wasn't sure what she was looking for and felt guilty rummaging through John's papers. Still, she needed a clue, something that would help her understand what had happened.

She found a large manila envelope in the bottom drawer and pulled it out. It contained a stack of half-finished poems. When she saw John had dated each piece, she arranged them in sequential order.

The first was written several years back and uttered his profound love for her. She traced each word with her finger and then placed the sheet up to her nose and inhaled a hint of his cherry tobacco. She held back a sob as she placed it on the desk.

The second was written just two months before he died. The words were scrawled on the paper, some so small she could barely read them. The others, loud and profound, recorded his frenzied state. Nora recalled that familiar confusion and crumpled the paper into a tight wad and threw it in the trash.

The remainder of the poems exposed his raw descent into hopelessness. But the final sheet of paper held a single line that distressed her more than any of the others she'd read.

Life is merely existence when Death is the only reality.

Nora ripped the paper into tiny pieces. The bits scattered across the floor as she angrily plunged the remaining words into the garbage can.

She sat back in the chair. A rage she had not known existed welled up in the pit of her stomach. How could he write of death and profound love and keep her at such a distance, locked outside but always near enough to make her love him?

And death. That was absurd. His life was full, wasn't it?

Nora bit her lip.

The manic episodes damaged John long before he did his time in the Gulf War. His mother's illness started the spiral.

And somehow, John blamed Shane. If Shane hadn't married her and taken over her life, if Shane hadn't convinced Genevieve to have the shock treatments, his mother wouldn't have died. John repeated it so often it burned a permanent mantra in Nora's mind.

After he shipped out to Kuwait, Nora spent the days that followed waiting anxiously for John's letters. Each letter she received was filled with gruesome details of murderous rampages and inhumane bombings.

When he returned from the gulf, he wasn't the patriotic man who had left to fight for his country.

He woke up in cold sweats. And when he did sleep, he thrashed and churned so violently Nora was forced to sleep on the couch.

Then came the first round of medication. Followed by a blessed reprieve. And the birth of their only child.

Maggie brought John back to Nora. They were joyous and happy— a normal couple. For a while.

Then came months of hospitalization and the eventual diagnosis.

Schizoaffective bipolar disorder. Post-traumatic stress. Delusional.

They'd squeaked by on Nora's job and John's Veterans disability. Sure, there wasn't enough money for luxury items. But they had each other. They were a family. She thought it was enough. Until he spiraled out of control once again.

Yet his art always brought him back to her. Not solely to her, but it allowed her to be on the side line while he taught his protégé, Maggie, the fine art of losing one's self into the colors on a canvas.

Nora shoved the remaining papers back into the bottom drawer and kicked it shut. She rubbed her hand over the desktop and whisked the last bits of torn paper on to the floor. She scanned the book titles on the shelf searching for more evidence. When she found nothing, she opened the top drawer.

A picture of John and Nora on their wedding day rested on top. The memories surrounded her. She felt the cool ocean breeze as she picked up the portrait and the warmth of John's kiss as she pulled the picture close to her heart. She closed her eyes and imagined the two of them, dancing on the beach until the sun went down.

She opened her eyes and looked back inside the drawer. Nora dropped the picture in disbelief when she saw what had been sitting under the portrait. A letter. Addressed to her. The sight of John's familiar scribble scared her.

She sat down. Then stood up and began talking aloud. "Why in God's name would he write me a letter?"

She covered her mouth and the tightness in her throat made her cough.

"Probably a poem. And there's no date on it. Nothing to worry about." Her words echoed across the studio walls.

"Or pictures. John loved to take pictures. Yes, that must be it."

She sat back down and ran her hand over the top of the envelope. The bold black ink and the desperate scrawl of John's handwriting forced her to pick it up.

"Doesn't feel like pictures."

Nora held it with two fingers. The letter was so light it twisted and turned in her hand. She almost dropped it before she stuffed it back inside the drawer.

"Maggie will be up any minute. I have to make her breakfast."

Nora looked at the clock. It was a quarter pass seven. And it was Saturday. Maggie wouldn't be up for hours.

"All right then."

She reached back inside the drawer and pulled the envelope out, planting it firmly on the desk. Her hands were shaking so hard she anchored them on her knees.

"All right then," she repeated, hoping the sound of her own voice would provide some sort of distraction.

She studied the single word, letter by letter, searching for a reason to open the envelope. She noticed John had placed a period at the end of her name. A period. Nobody ended a name on an envelope with a period.

Unless …

She grabbed the envelope and tore the sheet out so fast the envelope fell to the floor. She sat for a moment, paper still folded, and tried to put her mind at rest.

When she exhaled, the ends of the paper fluttered back at her. It startled her so badly that she grabbed hold of the edge and plastered it to the top of the desk, scanning the contents.

The shock treatments will turn me into nothing more than a mindless body. I will lose my ability to paint.

You won't know who I am, Nora, and I won't know myself either.

The ocean is my refuge. That is why I chose to go there. My death is not an end for you; it's the beginning of a consistent direction for your life.

Be there for Maggie. You are all she has.

She read the letter and tried to comprehend the meaning. How could he know he was going to die?

Nora sprang to her feet and paced back and forth across the studio floor. She ran out to the living room and grabbed her rosary.

"Hail Mary, full of grace …" Her voice was so low she could barely hear herself. Her heart felt as if it was going to explode.

She squeezed the rosary beads so hard in her hand she thought she would crush them. She dashed back into the studio and read the letter again. This time, the meaning cemented in her mind.

"Holy Mary, Mother of God. He committed suicide."

Nora's anger consumed her as she slammed her rosary against the desk. The chain broke and scattered the beads across the floor. They spun in every direction—like a mob of lost and betrayed souls.

She scrambled to her feet and ran to the kitchen. She opened the dishwasher and searched the silverware basket, pulled out a steak knife and serving fork, and then reached under the sink and grabbed a large garbage bag. She turned to run, but the cigarette lighter caught her eye, and she plucked it off the counter and dashed back to the studio.

A blast of cold air hit Nora when she walked back inside the door. The desk was screaming, *Get rid of the evidence,* and the knife trembled in her hand.

"She can never know. Maggie can never know." Nora repeated the words under her breath, and the colors of John's paintings were so bright they hurt her eyes.

She ran over and gouged them, one by one with the steak knife. The frenzy used to create his works of art took hold, and she stomped on each one, shattering the wood-framed canvases into splinters that wedged in her feet. She swooped up the remains and stuffed them in the garbage bag and then looked wildly around the room for the next battle location.

The suicide note came alive on the desk. She sobbed as she thrust it inside the bag. All Nora could see was the devastated look on Maggie's face if she knew the truth.

Nora's feet were bleeding, and the splinters crept deeper into her skin. She wanted to scream, but the sudden sound of Maggie's voice stopped her.

"Mom, are you okay?"

Nora whirled around. Maggie stood wide-eyed in the doorway, dressed in one of John's painting shirts.

"Oh God. What are you doing here?"

Maggie was so white Nora didn't recognize her at first. Her daughter's eyes were dark with fear, and her blond hair, damp with perspiration, matted to one side of her face. Her entire body shook under the protection of her father's old shirt. The smell of cherry tobacco and hopelessness filled the air.

"You're bleeding, Mom."

Her child's voice was so broken by death and frightened by life that Nora struggled to compose herself.

Pain inched up Nora's calves. When she looked down at her bloody feet, a throbbing sensation grabbed hold of her, and it felt good.

"I have splinters. Splinters from the frames." Nora wiped at her eyes and sat down on the desk chair.

"Can you get me the tweezers, Maggie?"

Maggie gawked at her, and Nora grabbed the bag lying loosely at her side and sealed it shut. She looked up at Maggie and forced a smile.

"We're going to burn some trash today, honey. Now hurry, these splinters have to come out before I can walk outside."

EIGHTEEN

The evening sun crested behind Lighthouse Rock. A cascade of light illuminated the waves as the glittering whitecaps met the seashore.

Henry rarely missed a sunset on the beach, and as he watched, the light reflected off a hazy object near the oceanfront. Each time a fading sunbeam bounced from heaven to earth, he thought he could see the shadow of a man lingering on the shore.

Damn glasses. He took them off and cleaned them on the edge of his shirt. When he shoved them on again, the shadow moved toward him.

This presence was much stronger than any he'd seen before. And when it continued its ghostly stagger, Henry recognized the red plaid shirt and hollow look of pain on John O'Brien's face.

He grabbed a sand dollar and brushed off the seaweed clinging to the shell. He acted as if he were interested in the garbage that littered the beach. But Nora's desperate questions and Maggie's sorrow convinced him he could no longer ignore a spirit seeking his assistance. Especially this one.

"Damn humans. A sacred place like this should remain clean, not littered."

He sent his comment in John's direction, and John stopped suddenly.

Henry bent down and picked up a McDonald's drink cup. "It all started happening when those fast-food chains popped up everywhere." He picked up a beer bottle and an empty cigarette pack. "Most likely a bunch of punks down here drinking after dark."

Henry walked past John and nodded and then headed back up the sand dune. He could feel John follow him. As John neared a large piece of driftwood, the air swirled, and John stumbled forward onto the weathered log.

Henry wasn't sure what to do next. In all the years he'd been seeing apparitions, they vanished when he didn't respond. He had never actually communicated with one. But it was different this time. He had witnessed this man's final moments and had felt Maggie's pain.

Henry picked up a super-size French fries carton, crumpled and stuffed it inside the drink cup along with the cigarette pack, and set them on the ground.

"Look, I've never really tried to talk to a ghost before."

Henry looked around to make sure no one was close enough to hear his crazy one-sided conversation. He walked over to the log and stood in front of John.

"You're going to have to work with me, John."

John reached forward and clamped his hands on Henry's shoulders. The lightness of John's touch and the determination on his face begged Henry to remain calm.

"I can feel you, John. What do you want me to do?"

The form in front of Henry rippled like the waves of the sea. John's emotions ricocheted so fast through his fluid form that they burst into sparkling beads of light.

"Hey, buddy, calm down. You're going to explode before I find out what you want."

John patted the log next to him and motioned for Henry to sit down.

"That's right, buddy, I'll sit down. Now you breathe ... or do whatever it is in the spirit world you do. Well, you know, just center yourself or something."

Henry bit his lip and winced. He hated the whole New Age thing and getting-to-your-center bull. His method of two beers before bed worked like a charm. He wiped the perspiration off the back of his neck. Tonight it was going to take a six pack.

"Thank you." John whispered as Henry sat down next to him.

John's voice drifted in on the ocean breeze, and Henry felt it ruffle across his face instead of actually hearing his words.

"Okay, John. Good. Now, well, let's get started."

Henry kicked at a patch of grass. Trying to figure out how to start the conversation was awkward. Especially since Henry's consent to help had now turned into full-blown curiosity. He was actually sitting next to a dead person and having a conversation. Nobody would ever believe him. No matter how many beers they had.

Henry tingled with apprehension as he talked. "That little girl of yours was heartbroken. I didn't tell anyone—except Lefty, and well, he didn't see you so he said I was seeing things again. What happened, John? Why did you take your daughter out so far? Or were you going in after her?"

John solidified next to Henry and then turned into vapor. Colors rose inside John like swells on the ocean, and Henry knew John's grief was beyond his control.

"Hey, I didn't mean anything by that, really. I know it wasn't your fault."

"Please listen." John's voice floated past him.

John took shape again, not solid, but sort of like a transparent film. Henry knew if he reached over and tried to touch him, his hand would slide right through John, as if he wasn't there.

"Okay, buddy. I'm listening."

John looked at the ocean as he talked.

"She wasn't … supposed to be with me."

"Then how did she get in the water?"

"She must have hid. In my truck. Decided to follow me."

"Well that doesn't make sense. Why would Maggie hide in the truck?"

"I was sick then. I didn't know. I was supposed to be, I planned … to be alone."

The driftwood Henry sat on felt like a huge piece of ice, and he jumped up and faced John.

"Planned what?"

"Suicide."

John's body was fluid again. It filled with white foam and the sound of the waves crashing filled the air.

"Oh Jesus, I'm sorry, man. But why in front of your daughter?"

"I said ... she wasn't supposed to be there."

The anger in John's voice dissolved into white foam, and he faded into a steaming hot vapor. Henry backed away and covered his face with his hands.

"Control yourself; you're going to blister the skin right off me."

"I'm trying ..."

John stood up and sucked in the heat from the steam until it cooled into a warm mist.

"That's better, buddy." Henry walked back over to the driftwood and sat down.

"I'd never harm Maggie. I love my little girl so much. She ... kept me sane."

"I see."

Henry tried to imagine being so distraught that taking your own life would be the only way out.

"It wasn't right ... I can't change that now."

"No, you certainly can't."

"Maggie has to know. I cared for her. Find the package. Buried in the sand. Take it to her."

"But where in the sand?"

"Right here Right here Right here ..." John's voice floated out toward the ocean, and he faded into the waves.

Henry looked around the sand dune. The only thing that made sense was to begin digging in the spot John had been sitting. Why else would a ghost sit in that exact spot on that exact piece of driftwood?

NINETEEN

Maggie could never forget the last fall storm and the turbulent winds it brought. But today was different. The air was filled with electricity. The blue sky was spattered with bulging white clouds, edged in black, begging to burst.

It was the kind of day when Maggie retreated to her room with her paints. She'd throw the window open and then listen and wait for the exact melody the wind played before beginning her next creation. She shivered with excitement as she leaned out her bedroom window and watched the cool wind ruffle across the overgrown grass.

The feather boas whispered with the wind and danced on the hand-carved coat rack. She grabbed the red one and threw it around her neck. The wind filled her room, and she danced back and forth before stopping in front of the mirror.

How silly. She was fifteen years old. And playing make-believe was not something she should be doing. But the wind kicked up again, and Maggie felt the feather boa tickle her bare arm, and she giggled with anticipation.

She draped the boa over the dragonhead rack and opened her dresser drawer.

She picked up a pair of shorts and then shoved them back inside. It was almost Halloween. Too cold for anything but jeans. She dressed with one of her dad's painting shirts and a thick sweatshirt to hide it under and then hurried downstairs.

Nora was sitting at the kitchen table with a cup of coffee, dressed neatly in her navy blue suit and ruffled white blouse. Her clothes couldn't mask her unhealthy pallor. Maggie thought the pathetic way her chin tilted downward deepened the puffy, dark circles underneath her eyes.

The previous evening hadn't been kind to her. She had reeked of bourbon when Maggie had kissed her cheek.

Nora jerked her head around and had a startled look on her face. "Why are you up so early? You're not going anywhere today, young lady. And since there's no school today, you can clean the house."

The energy in the air muffled the edge in Nora's voice. Maggie looked at her mother and felt sorry for the cold way she stroked the handle on her steaming coffee cup.

"But, Mom, can't I just have this Friday off?"

"Did you hear me, Maggie? I have things for you to do today."

"Yes, Mother, I heard you. They will all be done by the time you get home."

"Well, that won't be until late. We have inventory today. I probably won't be home until almost midnight."

"Want me to cook dinner?"

"I can grab a bite in the cafeteria."

"Mom, what's going on? Are you all right?"

Nora stood abruptly. She looked at Maggie and started to say something, then pursed her lips together, shook her head, and walked out of the kitchen.

The front door slammed, and the hopelessness seemed to lift. Maggie welcomed the reprieve. The gray clouds had broken apart, allowing the pale blue autumn sky to reach above the apple tree. She unlatched the kitchen window and slid it open.

A gust of wind rattled the screen, tickled the curtain, and then tenderly brushed across her face. And the smell. So crisp and fresh and ... well, brand new. Maggie inhaled the invigorating breeze before closing the window.

Nora's list sat neatly in the center of the table. Maggie scanned the contents: vacuum, dust, wash the windows if she had time.

"Is she for real?" Maggie flipped the list over. "Like she's ever washed the windows. What am I, the new Cinderella?"

Maggie stomped halfway up the stairs and then turned around. The urge to paint was overwhelming. And not in her room ... in Dad's studio.

She hadn't been inside since her mother's rampage. When she opened the door, her father's easel still held his last picture—the only one to escape her mother's tirade. It made her shudder, and she quickly removed it.

Maggie looked out the picture window and imagined a willow in the exact spot where the apple tree stood. Dad had wanted her to paint in that tree. Now that she was sure Shane wasn't the bad guy, well, she knew he would let her. She just had to figure out how to get there.

Maggie pulled off her sweatshirt and untucked her father's paint shirt from her jeans. She found a fresh canvas and placed it on the easel. She stripped the clear plastic wrap off his paints, then grabbed a pencil, and sketched out the image in her mind.

Maggie layered each shade of green paint with gold. She lost herself in her creation as the long spindly branches on the willow tree came to life on the canvas in front of her.

She stood back and examined her work. She wondered how close to the real willow she'd come. The branches fluttered in the wind, and the tree house peeked out from the highest branches, just as she had always imagined.

Maggie glanced up at the clock. It was almost three thirty, and she hadn't even started the list her mother had left for her.

She cleaned the brushes with walnut oil and gave the painting one last critical look before she left the studio. As she walked back to the kitchen, she heard the doorbell ring.

Maggie peered through the sheer curtains on the side window. A man, wearing wire-rimmed glasses, his gray hair short on the sides of his balding head, stood on the front porch. He was holding a small bag in his hands and looked extremely familiar. She opened the door just wide enough to get a better look.

"Hi, can I help you with something?" When she looked closely at the man, she tried to place his face.

"Hi, yes you can. Maggie, I don't know if you remember me or not ..."

She studied him for a moment, and when she didn't reply, the man continued talking.

"That day at North Beach ... I'm Henry. Lefty and I ... we found you and called the ambulance and ... well, I found something buried in the sand last night. You can imagine how surprised I was when I discovered it belongs to you."

Maggie recognized Henry's kind eyes. "Yes, of course. I remember you. How are you, Henry? I mean, I'm not sure what you could possibly have that's mine. Is it in that bag?"

Henry reached inside the bag and removed a package wrapped with brown paper and covered with clear packing tape.

"See, right here. It's addressed to you."

Maggie opened the door. She took the package and brushed at bits of sand stuck in the folds of the packing tape.

It didn't register at first. The handwriting. She ran her fingers over the letters that spelled her name twice before she could finally speak.

"I don't understand. Where did you get this? My father. He wrote my name ... and my address ... and where exactly did you find it?"

Maggie felt her voice rise, and her hand shook as she tried to pull the tape away from the wrapper.

"Damn it. It's stuck. I need something to cut the tape."

The familiar handwriting scared her. She leaned against the door.

"I'm so sorry, Maggie. I hoped this wouldn't upset you. I have a pocket knife. I can cut the tape. But please, let me help you sit down."

"I didn't mean to yell at you like that. Yes, help me ... no, I mean, yes, please come inside."

Henry held Maggie's arm and steadied her as he closed the door. Every time Maggie looked at the package, she felt faint. She was grateful when they made it to the couch and she was able to sink into the comfort of its cushions.

Henry took the package, carefully cut the tape, and unsealed the brown paper. Sand drifted out the open ends as he handed it back to Maggie.

She held it in her hand for a moment before sliding the contents out on her lap.

The hand-carved wood case. The one her grandfather had handed down to Dad. The one Dad had always promised would be hers.

Maggie leaned into the arm of the couch and took a deep breath. "This belonged to my grandfather. My father was going to give it to me. I looked for it after he disappeared. I don't understand. Can you please tell me where you found this?"

"It was buried in the sand. Not far from where Lefty and I found you on the beach that day." Henry hesitated. "I didn't open it."

Maggie ran her fingers over the top of the box. She had loved this wonderful, ornate container. Before she learned to paint, she filled it with seashells from her collection while she watched her father orchestrate a scene on canvas.

"I didn't open it." Henry repeated.

"What?"

"Your package. It was addressed to you. That's why I delivered it."

"Thank you. Very much." Maggie bit her lip and avoided eye contact.

Henry shuffled his feet and took a huge breath then continued. "I just want to tell you that I remember everything that happened that day, Maggie."

She looked at Henry, stunned at first. "What do you mean, everything?"

"I know I shouldn't be saying this. Lefty gets so darn mad at me because he tells me I act like a crazy fool sometimes."

Maggie watched Henry as he paused for a moment. "But I saw someone carry you out of the water, Maggie. I turned and yelled at Lefty, and when I looked back, the man was gone."

Maggie wiped the moisture from the corner of her eyes and then glared at Henry.

"Why didn't you tell my mom the truth? Or at least call the police?" Maggie's anger startled her, but she kept yelling. "Good God, Henry, you could have stopped him. And my mom, she needs to know that I wasn't imagining things. She needs to know that Dad is still alive!"

"Maggie, no. It's not that simple. It's … well, I believe I saw someone, but he disappeared so fast, maybe I was seeing things or something. I can't always be sure."

"That's the story you laid on my mom. I'm not buying it. I remember what you told me that day." Maggie tightened her lips into a thin line and strengthened her hold on the wooden box.

"I know it sounds confusing, Maggie. And I don't have any real explanation for what happened or what I saw. Then I found this. And anyway, well, I hope it helps you."

Maggie ran her hand over the top of the container. Holding the wooden case in her lap calmed her and gave her a new resolve. All she wished for right now was an answer to her one crucial question. She prayed the keepsake would provide an answer.

"I should go now, Maggie."

Henry stood up and walked to the front door, and Maggie followed him.

"Listen, Henry. I just want you to know, well … this means so much." The lump in her throat came on so suddenly she had to swallow hard to keep from crying. "Anyway, thanks. Thanks so much."

Henry trembled when he took hold of Maggie's hand. He looked much older than when she'd first met him. She was afraid he might actually cry.

"Oh, you're welcome, Maggie. I'm sorry I upset you." He squeezed Maggie's hand and, before she could say another word, turned and walked out the door.

Maggie closed the door and braced herself against it. Her knees felt weak, and her heart and head were so dizzy she was afraid to move.

The sun flashed across the foyer. She leaned over and looked out the side window.

Clouds rolled in and the air crackled. She took a deep breath and stood up. She'd have to wear her waterproof jacket. She'd need it. It was going to rain.

Maggie stuffed the box inside her jacket and then ran down the hall and out of the kitchen as fast as she could. She bolted out the back door and raced up the trunk of the apple tree. The wind danced through her hair, and she shivered. Large raindrops began soaking the earth's surface, and the sudden cool felt good against her hot cheeks.

Once safely up inside the trees branches, Maggie collapsed against a large limb. She carefully opened the clasp on the worn container.

She recognized the old paintbrushes resting inside the case. She pulled out the largest one and examined the fluorescent paint on the wood handle. It was one they had used to paint the stars on the ceiling and across her bedroom walls.

It wasn't until she removed all the brushes that she found the neatly folded piece of paper. Her hands trembled as she carefully unfolded the sheet and read the words her father had written her.

July 22, 2006

Maggie,

This letter allows me to tell you the things my chaotic mind wouldn't let me say. I trust that this will somehow get to you at the right time in your life so you will understand why I had to leave.

Live your life to its fullest. Take your loving, open spirit and share it with as many people as you can. It is that spirit that I admire most in you. The wonderful way you look at life. The way you take things into your own hands and process them until you understand.

Embrace the good in people. Look through to the inside; ignore the crutches they use, the emotions that seem to cover them. You have the gift of seeing into the depths of their character.

Never stop painting. Take these paintbrushes and use them to create and color your world. And if paints aren't enough, grasp a sheet of paper and pour your words onto it and let them be expressions of your soul.

Never forget that I will always be with you. Climb the willow tree and listen to the song the wind has to sing, for it is my song to you. Always remember, Magpie, that up there, you will find my love and it will fill your heart.

I love you,
Dad

TWENTY

I t was dark when Maggie tiptoed in the kitchen door and down the
hall to the landing. She was glad Mom wouldn't be home yet. She
didn't want to explain her rain-soaked clothing or swollen eyes.

The possibility of her father's death always brought an overwhelming
feeling of despair that only sleep could relieve. Now, the second line of
her father's letter reinforced what she already believed.

Dad isn't dead. He just went away.

She couldn't wait any longer. The letter was a sign. She had to go.
Find Shane's house and climb the willow tree. That is where Dad would
look for her, she was certain now.

Maggie walked up the stairs and was about to open her bedroom
door when she heard her mother.

"Maggie, is that you?"

The sound of her mother's voice shot up from the living room and
startled her. Shit, she's going to ask a hundred million questions.

"Yes, Mom. It's me. I'll be right there. I need to change my clothes.
Becca and I went for a walk in the rain, and I'm soaking wet."

"Well hurry. I need to talk to you."

Great. Another sermon. Maggie wasn't sure she could handle listening
to how she didn't finish the chores and how she didn't appreciate all her
mother did for her.

Her room was dark, and when she turned on the light, she was surprised at how faded the castle walls had become. She had never noticed
it before, but the dark gray outline around the towers had taken on
a washed-out tone, and the blue in the sky had paled.

She hurried over to her dresser and pulled out a sweatshirt and sweatpants. She changed, then stuffed the wood case under her pillow, and carefully folded the letter inside her pocket. Maggie towel-dried her hair and hurried back downstairs.

Nora was sitting in the living room without a single light on. Maggie turned on the old lamp next to the couch and sat down next to her mother. There was no telltale evidence of her usual nightly bourbon. The only odor that lingered in the air was the stale smell of cigarettes.

When Maggie sat down, Nora didn't look up. She sat, with her hands clasped in her lap, staring down at the coffee table.

"Did Henry come to see you?"

"How did you know that?" Maggie moved away from Nora and folded her arms across her chest.

"He called my cell." Nora's voice was flat.

"You never told me Henry had your cell number, Mother." Maggie winced at her own accusing tone, but Nora ignored it and continued talking.

"Henry was worried about you. Thought you might have been really upset."

"About what?" Oh God. Did Henry tell Mom why he came?

"The package, Maggie."

Nora looked up, and Maggie stiffened in her chair. Her clothes felt wet again, and the pain in Nora's voice sent chills down her spine.

"Did your father tell you, Maggie?"

The fear etched between each of Nora's words didn't make any sense.

"Well, yes, Dad said in his letter he had to go away."

Nora stood up and went to the bar in the corner of the living room. Her hands shook as she filled a glass half-full of bourbon and then added ice and a splash of water. She took a drink, then turned, and faced Maggie.

Maggie couldn't tell if Nora was going to laugh or cry.

"He isn't coming back, Maggie. You have to believe me."

Maggie wasn't sure if it was Nora's words or the look on her mother's face that made Maggie hate her. She wanted to throw something at her, make her pay for the bitterness that always gushed out of her mouth.

"You drunk old bitch. You're a liar," she whispered, knowing if she talked any louder, all the rage boiling in the pit of her stomach would burst out and spew across the room.

"Don't you talk to me like that, Mary Margaret O'Brien. And I'm not a liar."

A surge of hate filled the room, and Nora teetered against the bar. She finished her drink and then stared at Maggie as she poured straight bourbon into her glass.

"You really don't understand, do you?" Nora sat her drink on the edge of the bar and then shuffled over to her purse. She fumbled with the contents and then pulled her cigarettes and lighter out.

"Understand what, that Dad hated you so much he never wanted to come home again?" Maggie choked the words out. Hate suddenly felt like love, and she wondered if a hug could actually kill.

Nora sat on the edge of the coffee table. "No, Maggie. What you don't understand is—when you went into the water after him—why he was there. Why he died."

Maggie repeated the second line in her father's letter over and over in her head. *I trust that this will somehow get to you at the right time in your life so you will understand why I had to leave.* He went away. He didn't die.

Nora pressed her hands over her mouth, and her eyes were so huge she looked as if she'd just awakened from a nightmare.

"Oh God, Maggie. He really did drown, and it isn't your fault. I'll make it all up to you. I want to take you to the willow tree. We can go there together."

Maggie clutched her chest and felt like her heart was going to explode. Nora stood up and extended her shaking hand. Maggie walked backward toward the living room entrance.

"Shane still lives in that house. Maybe we can go see him. I think you'd like him …"

"No, Mother, I don't want to go anywhere with you. Don't touch me. Just leave me alone."

Maggie felt the bite of her own words. The sadness on her mother's face numbed out her anger, and all that was left was an empty void between them.

Nora walked back over to the bar, and her shoulders drooped lower with each fumbled step. Her cries, loud at first, were softened by the tinkling of ice as it hit the bottom of her glass and scattered across the bar as she tried to mix another drink.

The ice on the bar chilled any warmth remaining between mother and daughter. The empty house was nothing more than the place where life ended as soon as Maggie walked inside the front door.

Maggie felt an odd sense of comfort as she stared at her mother's back. If she walked away this very second and never came back, Mom wouldn't even notice. She knew she couldn't have picked a better time to leave for good. She would go to Shane's house. It was the right thing to do.

Nora's second drink appeared to go down faster than the first, and her hands seemed steady enough to keep the ice from falling outside her glass. Maggie watched her mother garnish her drink with several lemon slices and sit down on a barstool. Nora lit a cigarette, and when she inhaled, Maggie realized it was the only time she saw a hint of pleasure on her mother's face.

When Nora glanced around the room, she stared past Maggie as if she weren't even there.

Maggie took the opportunity and rushed into the den. She turned the computer on. She was sure now. If she went to Shane, he could help her.

She navigated to the Greyhound bus station's home page and then to the local page for Rockaway Beach. She searched the schedule and found a bus departing Rockaway Beach for Angel's Corner on Saturday morning at eleven thirty.

She wrote the time and bus number on a sticky note, shoved it in her pocket, and shut the computer down.

Maggie left the den and didn't even look in the living room before she bolted upstairs. She pulled her books out of her backpack and shoved them under her bed. She searched inside the dresser drawers and pulled out several changes of clothing, clean underwear, and a pair of warm wool socks, and stuffed all inside. She placed the wooden box containing the paintbrushes on top and the picture of her and Dad went below it.

It was only a two-hour bus ride. Once she was at Shane's house and they found her father, she would come back to the house and get the rest of her things. And maybe, Dad was in the willow tree right now, waiting for her.

Maggie made sure her door was shut before she picked up her phone. She touched Becca's number. She answered on the second ring.

"Becca, it's me."

"Hey, Maggie. What's up?"

"Everything."

Maggie knew she couldn't say what she wanted to say on the phone, and she hoped Becca would follow along without asking a bunch of stupid questions.

"And that means?"

"Can you meet me outside?"

"It's dark outside, Maggie. And creepy. You know I don't like the dark."

"Becca, this is important. It will only take a minute."

"What am I supposed to tell my parents, Maggie?"

"What are they doing right now?"

"They're in the den, watching a movie."

"Well, fine then. Sneak out, and I'll meet you by your garage."

"What if I get caught?"

"Tell them you thought a bird hit your window. Just think of something, Becca. This is urgent."

Maggie threw the phone on her bed, pulled her sleeping bag from the closet, and walked downstairs. She didn't worry about her mother firing off any more questions as she rushed out the front door; the blank look on Nora's face assured her she was invisible now.

Becca was standing by the garage door in her Sponge Bob slippers. The quizzical expression on her floppy footwear matched the look on her face.

"What are you doing, Maggie? Why do you have your sleeping bag with you?"

"I'm leaving."

"What? I don't understand. Why?"

"I can't live here anymore, Becca. I have to leave before I end up a basket case like my mother. And I know for sure now I need to talk to Shane."

"All your mom has to do is quit drinking, Maggie. She could go into rehab, like my Aunt Cindy did."

The desperation in Becca's voice saddened Maggie. Becca was the best friend she ever had, and it would be hard living so far away from her.

"She's not going to quit, Becca. Besides, I don't think she could, even if she tried."

"Then we should do an intervention. You know, like they do on TV."

Maggie wished it were that simple.

"I don't have time for that shit, Becca. Please, just listen, okay?" Maggie took hold of her hand. "Henry came to the house today, Becca."

"Henry who?" Becca sighed and looked down at the ground.

"One of the men that found me on the beach when Dad disappeared."

"Oh, that Henry."

Becca looked at Maggie, rolled her eyes, and then crossed her arms tight against her chest as she looked down at the driveway again.

"Well, that Henry gave me something today." Maggie placed her hands on Becca's shoulders. "Becca, look at me. This is important."

Becca looked up at Maggie, her lips drawn in a tight line.

"It's a letter, Becca. Henry brought me a freaking letter. And it's from my dad!"

Maggie didn't know if she should laugh or cry, so she threw her arms around Becca's shoulders and hugged her instead.

Becca squirmed out of Maggie's embrace, and when she looked at her, Maggie burst into laughter.

Becca kicked the planter and threw her arms in the air. "Oh fine, this is a big fat joke. Well, it's not funny Maggie O'Brien."

"No, Becca. I'm not joking. I just, well, sometimes I just laugh when I should really cry and, well anyway ..." Maggie reached into the deep pocket of her sweat pants and produced the neatly folded letter from her father.

"This is from my dad. Henry gave it to me today."

"What? Are you kidding me?"

Becca's eyes were as big as streetlights, and she clamped her hand over her mouth in disbelief.

"No, I'm not kidding you. Take it, Becca, please. I want you to read it."

Maggie watched Becca unfold her arms. When her hand was loose, Maggie handed the letter to her.

Maggie jiggled back and forth and then hopped from one foot to the other as Becca read. When Becca was done, all she said was one single word.

"WOW."

"I know, WOW," Maggie repeated. "Do you understand what this means? It confirms everything! He went away, Becca. And I'm supposed to climb the willow tree. Well, we don't have a willow tree for God's sake. We have an apple tree so you know what that means, don't you? Duh! Shane is the one with the willow tree—I'm supposed to go to Shane's house!"

"Your dad's weird, Maggie. Leave it to him to make you unravel riddles just to find him."

"He's not weird, Becca. He's an artist." Maggie wasn't even annoyed by Becca's remark. It didn't matter. He was alive, and she was finally going to see him again.

Becca folded the letter up and gave it back to Maggie.

"So you believe me now, right, Becca? I mean, it all makes perfect sense, doesn't it?"

Maggie shoved the letter back in her pocket and giggled.

"I mean, Dad and I always made everything an adventure. Like painting the castle on my bedroom walls and pretending like that Persian rug was a magic carpet and the feather boas and the princess crown and—"

"But what if it's just a good-bye letter, Maggie? I mean, he did say his mind was chaotic, and well, it's sort of like telling you to live your life after he's gone. And look at the date. It's the day before he died."

"Of course, it's the day before he LEFT—not died, dim wad." Maggie winced and stomped her foot. "Well for your information Miss Know-it-all, I knew my father better than anyone, and I know exactly what he's trying to say in the letter."

Becca crossed her arms over her chest and shivered.

"He's telling me exactly what I need to do. Don't you get it? I'm supposed to go to Shane's house."

Becca's shoulders drooped, and Maggie reached over and hugged her and then grabbed hold of her best friend's chin.

"Becca, it's not like I won't ever see you again. Shane lives less than two hours from here. We can stay together over long weekends during school and a whole week in the summer. And I'll have my own bedroom with plenty of room for both of us."

"Yeah, but it won't be the same."

"I know, Becca. But my life, well, it's never going to be the same here. Ever again."

Becca looked up at Maggie. "I know, Mag, I know."

Maggie fought the urge to cry and squeezed Becca's hand.

"Then you'll help me?"

"You're my best friend, Maggie. Of course I'll help you."

The relief made Maggie light-headed. She leaned against the garage door for a moment before she let go of Becca's hand.

"Here's the plan. I'm going to hide my sleeping bag at the park tonight. I'll tell Mom I'm spending the night with you tomorrow. I already checked online for the bus times. The bus leaves Rockaway Beach tomorrow morning at eleven thirty. I'll go over to your house at nine thirty. We'll pretend we're going for a bike ride. You go back home by yourself. I'll pick up my sleeping bag and ride my bike to the bus station. You make sure you go through the alley. Not in front of my house. Mom can't see that you're by yourself. Got that?"

"Why are you taking your sleeping bag?"

"Well, because, Becca," Maggie tried to sound calm in her response, "just in case my bedroom isn't ready. I can sleep on the living room floor."

Maggie watched Becca think over the plan.

"How far is the bus station from here?" Becca asked.

"Just a mile or so. Not that far."

"Where are you going to get the money, Maggie?" Becca looked as though she'd just discovered the reason Maggie couldn't go.

"I have at least sixty dollars. That should be plenty."

Becca started pouting. "What if your mom calls my mom?"

"She won't, Becca. After the fight we had tonight, she'll be drunk until Sunday night. Which will give me plenty of time to get to Shane's before she even knows I'm missing."

Becca's body started shaking, and Maggie took hold of her shoulders.

"Becca, please, you can't cry."

"I don't think I can tell you good-bye tomorrow, Maggie."

"But you have to go with me." Maggie's chest tightened, and she was sure her heart skipped a beat. "Please, Becca."

"I'll go as far as the park. That's it. And when we get there, I'm not going to stop or say anything at all to you, Maggie. I'm just going to ride away as fast as I can."

"Okay, okay. I understand. And I promise I'll call you just as soon as I can."

"Yeah, well, you'd better take your cell phone with you."

"Of course I will." Maggie hesitated. "I'll call you as soon as I'm at Shane's house."

Becca looked down at the ground and didn't say a word. Maggie was glad Becca didn't talk because Maggie knew if she had to say good-bye to her best friend she might not be able to leave.

"Go back inside, Becca. I'll meet you out front tomorrow morning."

Becca turned and hurried away. Maggie leaned against the garage door until Becca disappeared around the corner.

When she heard the front door close, Maggie threw her sleeping bag over her shoulders and raced to the garage. The side door squeaked when she opened it, but Maggie didn't care. She maneuvered her bike outside and raced through the sudden downpour of rain. She rode into the playground, jumped off her bike, shoved her sleeping bag under the bench inside the baseball dugout, and then pedaled full speed all the way home.

It was just after midnight when Maggie crept back down into the living room. Nora was lying on the couch, and a half bottle of bourbon sat on the coffee table next to an ashtray filled with butts.

Nora's breathing was so shallow Maggie thought she might not take another breath. She bent down and placed her ear against Nora's chest and listened for the steady beat of her heart and then placed her cheek near Nora's nose until she felt a light exhale.

Maggie sat down on her knees and took hold of Nora's hand. Sadness etched her mother's eyes and wrinkled the corners of her lips. When she exhaled again, her lips quivered, and she let out a small, hurt-filled cry.

"Someday, I hope when I do finally have to see you again," Maggie whispered, "you won't still be blaming me for everything that happened."

Maggie covered Nora with the afghan. And just like any other night, she removed all traces of her mother's binge from the coffee table and, without question, went upstairs and crawled into bed.

TWENTY-ONE

Nora pulled the afghan tight over her shoulders. Her head throbbed every time she opened her eyes. The living room was so quiet she heard ringing in her ears. She took short, shallow breaths hoping they would stop the waves of nausea.

Knowing John didn't want to live made Nora want to die. Each remembrance she had treasured as a sign of his life was now a glimpse of his suicide.

And she felt like such a fool. She had forced herself to believe the lapses between his delusional episodes were always temporary. Once he made it past them, she swore he was coming back to her for good.

But instead, he left for good. And she had nothing left of their marriage except a stack of unpaid bills and a daughter who refused to hear the truth. All Nora could hope for now was that Maggie would eventually believe her father was dead. She knew once the truth finally settled in, it would hurt her deeply. But she was still young; time would heal her pain.

If the bathroom weren't so far away, Nora could get up and take a handful of ibuprofen and a couple of pain pills. But even the thought of standing made her head hurt more.

"Mom?"

Maggie's voice cut the silence and pounded inside Nora's head. Nora opened one eye and peered at her daughter.

"Please, Maggie, don't talk. Just bring me the ibuprofen. And the prescription sitting next to it in the medicine cabinet. And water."

"Are you all right, Mom?"

"Just get it for me, Maggie. Don't talk."

Nora closed her eyes and tried not to move. Maybe a piece of toast would help the nausea. No, she reasoned, that would require sitting up and chewing.

"Here, Mom."

"Just shake out four ibuprofen and a couple of the prescription pills and give them to me."

"But the prescription says to take one every—"

"Just hand me the pills and the water, Maggie."

The sound of pills rattling out of bottles made Nora grit her teeth.

"Can you sit up?"

"No."

"Well, you have to …"

Nora swung her feet off the cushions and grabbed the water from Maggie.

"Stop yelling, Maggie. Just give me the damn pills."

Nora reached forward and opened her hand, and Maggie dropped the pills onto her palm. Nora threw them into her mouth and chased them down with as little water as possible.

"I'm leaving now, Mom."

"Where?"

"To Becca's. I'm spending the night, remember?"

"Yes, fine. I remember. I'll see you tomorrow."

"But I won't be home until late Sunday. We're going over to Becca's grandma's house for Sunday dinner."

Maggie stood next to the couch, and Nora could feel her staring at her.

"What now, Maggie?"

"Nothing. I just wanted to tell you good-bye, that's all."

"Fine. Good-bye." Nora pulled the afghan back over her shoulders and shivered as she lay back down on the couch.

"Maggie?" Nora squinted in Maggie's direction. Good. She caught her before she walked out the door.

"Yes, Mom."

Maggie was biting her lower lip, and for a minute, Nora thought she was going to cry.

"What's the matter with you? Quit biting your lip and turn the heat up before you leave."

"Yes, Mom."

"Now go."

Nora turned her back to Maggie. She buried her head in the pillow and prayed she would fall asleep before she puked all over the sofa.

* * *

Maggie stomped off the front porch and into the garage.

"If I never see her drunk bitch face again, that will be too soon."

She didn't bother lowering her voice and didn't care if old man Murphy was out on his side of the yard nosing into the whole neighborhood's business. Right now, all she could think about was how great it was going to be to wake up in the morning and not smell bourbon or see an ashtray filled with nasty cigarette butts sitting on the coffee table.

"Good morning, Maggie."

Maggie shrieked as she grasped her chest and steadied herself against the garage door.

"Mr. Murphy. I didn't see you." But I should have known you'd be standing over there with your big fat nose hanging over my fence.

"You going somewhere today, Maggie? You have your backpack on."

That's really none of your business you old goat. "I'm spending the night with Becca."

"Leaving awfully early, aren't you?" Mr. Murphy peered over the top of the fence.

Not soon enough, Mr. Nosey Nose. "We're going on a bike ride right now."

"How's your mom?"

Drunk and hung over as usual. "She's not feeling so well this morning."

"She have the flu?"

Yeah, the bourbon flu. "Something like that."

"Well, have a nice bike ride."

"Thanks."

Maggie stuffed her backpack in the front basket, swung her leg over the bike, and pedaled down the driveway. The rain clouds were gone, and she welcomed the clean autumn air.

Becca was waiting for Maggie in front of her house. As soon as Maggie pulled out from her driveway, Becca jumped on her bike and pedaled down the road so fast Maggie couldn't keep up with her.

"Hey, Becca, wait up."

Maggie raced after Becca, but she didn't slow down until they arrived at the park.

"What's the deal, Becca?" Maggie asked as she brought her bike to a halt. "Why did you take off like that?"

Becca jumped off her bike and threw it to the ground. She turned around, stood with her hands on her hips, and glared at Maggie.

"For your information, Maggie, I'm going along with this only because you're my best friend. I still think it's crazy that you still think your dad is alive, and if your mom wasn't drunk all the time, well, I would tell her what you're going to do."

Becca's lip trembled, and she stomped over to the merry-go-round and plopped down. Two younger boys came over and tried to get on, but Becca jumped up and yelled at them.

"Girls only. Now get out of here."

"That's not fair," the older boy yelled back.

"I don't care what's fair, and I'm older than you, so just leave."

Maggie rolled her bike into the bike rack and then sat down on the merry-go-round next to Becca.

"I'm sorry, Becca. But it's not like we won't ever see each other again."

Becca started sobbing, and Maggie wrapped her arm around her shoulder.

"I'll call you, Becca, as soon as I get to Shane's. And I'll give you his phone number, and you can call me any time you want."

"But it won't be the same, Maggie."

Becca turned her back on Maggie, and when Maggie walked in front of her, Becca kept her arms folded and refused to look her in the eye. Maggie glanced at her watch. It was almost ten thirty, and she knew if she didn't leave soon, she might miss the bus.

"Listen." Maggie took hold of Becca's hands and pulled them away from her chest. "I promise, Becca, I will call you as soon as I get there. You have to believe me."

Becca squeezed Maggie's hands and then let go.

"But I'm not going to say good-bye." Becca raised her head just high enough to look up at Maggie.

"There is no good-bye, Becca. I'll call you when I get to Shane's house tonight."

"Whatever." Becca walked over to her bike and picked it up off the ground, then turned, and looked at Maggie. "You promise you'll call me the minute you walk into Shane's house, Maggie?"

"I promise, Becca. The absolute minute."

Becca scowled and, without saying a single word, jumped on her bike and pedaled as fast as she could out of the park.

TWENTY-TWO

The Greyhound station hummed with anticipation. A woman cuddling a baby wrapped in a blue receiving blanket made Maggie long for a brother, but she decided one runaway in the family was enough. Besides, there was no way she could have taken a brother with her, and she would never have left him with her mother. So maybe being an only child her whole life had turned out to be a good thing after all.

Maggie checked her watch. It was ten thirty-five. She tried to act casual as she walked inside the crowded bus terminal and into the restroom.

She pulled out the makeup she'd taken from Mom's gift with purchase stash and loaded on black eye liner, brown eye shadow, and voluminous mascara. She outlined her lips in hot pink and filled them in with a deep burgundy.

Maggie waited until the bathroom was empty, then went into the handicapped stall and pulled out a pair of scissors. If she was going to run away, she had to make sure no one would recognize her once she left the bus station.

Maggie hung her backpack on the hook behind her and sat the sleeping bag on the floor. She snipped each long strand of hair, measuring it against the last cut the way Mom's stylist always did when she cut Mom's hair short.

She flushed the hair down the toilet, grabbed a tube of gel out of her bag, and lathered it through her hair, and then spiked it up on top and sprayed the ends with black hair spray.

When she walked out of the stall, she gasped at her reflection in the floor-length mirror. "Wow," she whispered as she walked toward the restroom door.

"Bus Forty-seven, bound for Multnomah Falls, will begin loading at Gate Three in ten minutes."

Maggie looked at her watch. It was eleven o'clock. She threw the can of black hair spray in the trash and rushed out the restroom and over to the ticket counter.

The man standing in front of Maggie kept flipping his wallet against his hand and muttering under his breath until it was his turn at the ticket counter.

"Do you think you could just move a little bit slower?"

Maggie wasn't sure she heard him right until she looked at the embarrassment on the ticket seller's face.

"Good afternoon, sir. Where are you traveling to today?"

The girl selling tickets had a snake tattooed on her neck, and it looked like it was trying to nibble on her ear. She had an obvious third earring hole in her nose. Maggie was certain she wasn't allowed to wear an earring in it to work.

"You can't even figure out if it's morning or afternoon." The man turned around to see if anyone heard him and then laughed out loud.

"I'm sorry, sir. We're extremely busy today. If you'd provide me with your destination, I can have your ticket ready without delay."

The man behind Maggie walked up and grabbed the rude man's shoulder. "Leave the girl alone, just buy your ticket, bud. We're all in a hurry this morning." He turned to the ticket seller. "Miss, do you want me to call security?"

"Yeah, well ..." The rude man shoved the other guy away from him. He looked down at Maggie and then back at the woman. "One way to Portland and make it fast, Ink Tramp. I don't have all MORNING."

Maggie pretended she didn't hear the conversation or notice how shaken the young woman was when she walked up to the counter.

"Good morning," Maggie said in her most adult voice. "I'd like one ticket to Angel's Corner on the eleven thirty, please."

"One way?"

"Yes, please."

"In order to ride unaccompanied, you must be fifteen years old." The woman's voice sounded accusing.

"Oh, I'm fifteen. I'm just very short for my age. You see, I got my height from—"

"Ma'am, can you hurry please?"

The man moved up to the counter. "My bus leaves at eleven fifteen, and I can't miss it—my husband, he's in the hospital, and I have to get there, be with him."

"I'm so sorry, ma'am. This will take only a minute." The ticket seller looked flustered as she looked back at Maggie.

"All right, young lady, that will be forty-eight dollars. And I'll need to see your ID."

Maggie fished through her purse and pulled out two twenties and a ten and the picture ID her father had insisted she carry.

"Miss, please. I'm going to miss my bus."

"I'm sorry. We're almost done here." The woman behind the counter handed Maggie her change and ID card—without even looking at her picture.

Maggie breathed a huge sigh of relief and grabbed the items as fast as she could. She hurried over to the line forming for Bus Forty-seven.

The bus driver's eyes looked tired, and his movements were so slow Maggie wondered why he wasn't retired. Yet, when he looked each traveler up and down, it was as if he could size up the person's entire life before taking the ticket. The bus driver's psychic ability made Maggie nervous.

A man with a dark complexion and a turban over his hair was first in line. He clutched his overnight bag like it held some deep, dark secret. The driver looked him over and then suggested he store his bag in the storage compartment outside. The man fidgeted and then mumbled something about medication, and when the driver asked to see inside his bag, Maggie saw the man look out into the crowd. Like he was trying to alert an accomplice.

When she saw his face, it sent her on a mental search trying to match his mug with the terrorists she'd seen on TV.

The bus driver checked the contents and handed the foreigner his bag before Maggie could make a match.

The next to board were three old ladies. They told the bus driver they were vacationing nuns from the Sisters of Sorrow convent. Maggie hoped the name of their order wouldn't bring her bad luck. Nonetheless, she felt safer with them on board. If the man really was a terrorist (after all, the driver didn't inspect his shoes), she would have a straight shot to heaven with the nuns on board.

Maggie rehearsed all possible answers to any prying question the bus driver could ask her. She was third from the last at the end of the line, and once the terrorist and nuns boarded, the rest of the passengers moved ahead quickly.

When it was her turn, she decided to make eye contact immediately to avoid any suspicion on the bus driver's part.

"Just your backpack and sleeping bag today, young lady?"

"Yes, sir. Just staying until Monday when my mother picks me up."

"So you're traveling alone?"

"Yes, sir. I'm fifteen, you know."

"Awful short for your age."

Maggie hoped he didn't notice the flush creeping up her neck.

"Yeah, my grandmother's fault. At least that's what my dad told me. She was only five foot when she died."

"You're not much more than that yourself." The bus driver chuckled and handed her ticket back.

"And what does your dad think of that hairdo?"

"Oh, he's an artist. He likes me to express myself in any way I want."

"I'll buy that. Have a good visit with …"

"Cousin … Brie … short for … Sabrina."

"Okay, young lady. You have a nice time."

Maggie smiled and hurried up the stairs. The terrorist was sitting two seats behind the bus driver, and that made her nervous. She took the window seat one row behind the vacationing nuns. If there was any place to be safe on the bus, it was near them. She stuck her backpack on top of her sleeping bag in the middle seat, leaned back, and breathed a sigh of relief.

The driver boarded and gave safety instructions (Maggie was relieved to know the windows popped out in the event of an emergency).

He revved up the engine and was just about to leave the station when a policeman planted himself directly in front of the bus.

The driver shut off the engine and walked outside. Two men approached him and one of them boarded the bus while the other interrogated the driver.

"I'll need to see everyone's ticket and identification, please."

Maggie panicked as she clutched her ticket. She watched the policeman mull over the terrorist's ticket and then the woman sitting behind him. He was looking straight at Maggie when the other cop boarded the bus. They whispered back and forth, and when the first cop talked, she knew he was speaking directly to her.

"Thanks, everyone. Just sit and be patient. A new driver will be here shortly."

Maggie watched the man leave the bus and walk over to the other policeman. The bus driver was in handcuffs, and the cop was reading him his rights.

Maggie was relieved they arrested the bus driver and not her. But she still couldn't believe they did absolutely nothing to the terrorist sitting in the front of the bus.

A new driver boarded without saying a word, sat down, and started the engine. The bus made a swooshing sound as it moved forward, out of the bus station, and into the crisp autumn air.

TWENTY-THREE

Nora opened one eye and watched the dust swarm in the light coming in the front window. When was the last time anyone vacuumed? Didn't she tell Maggie to get that done before she went to Becca's?

Damn her.

Nora scooped the afghan off the floor and threw it over her shoulders as the grandfather clock chimed twelve times. She winced at the familiar throbbing between her eyes. Another pain pill and a double shot of caffeine would dissolve the headache. She couldn't let it get the best of her. She wanted to take advantage of her solo time.

She staggered into the bathroom and took one pill for her headache and then headed to the kitchen. She dumped in enough coffee for a triple shot and stared outside the kitchen window.

The autumn wind ruffled the long clumps of grass and she almost didn't recognize her own backyard.

The flowerbeds were overgrown. A layer of thick green moss covered the resin cherubs that once were Maggie's imaginary friends. On hot summer afternoons, when the heat was unbearable, Nora would sit with Maggie under the shade of the apple tree and wait for the cooling relief of nightfall. Maggie would take the cherubs one by one and christen them with angel dust made from the warm, soft earth.

Nora would weave lacy ferns with pink bachelor buttons and daisies into crowns, and Maggie would pretend she was a fairy princess and Nora was her queen.

Nora ran her hands over the sides of her hair and listened to the coffee spew the last drops into her mug.

Her hand shook as she poured the steamed milk into the coffee. She waited before taking a drink and kept her focus on the hot vapor drifting up from the cup.

Emptiness settled in her stomach. She reached up and pulled the kitchen curtains shut.

Maybe coffee wasn't what she needed. It couldn't possibly extinguish the vivid memories that dared to haunt her. It was different now. John was dead. Damn him. How dare he? Rage pulsed her veins. When would Maggie accept the truth and come to terms with it?

Nora bent down and opened the bottom cupboard door. She moved the boxes of scone mix, canned soup, and spices to get the gallon of bourbon hidden in back. She poured it into her mug, and it splashed up and onto the counter as it blended with the steaming coffee. She leaned forward and drank the overflowing mixture until it was safe to pick it up without spilling.

She downed her first cup and then brewed four more shots. She dumped the shots in her mug with a shot of bourbon and half-steamed milk and then walked over to the bar in the living room and lit a cigarette.

* * *

John stood in the center of Maggie's bedroom. As he surveyed his current surroundings, doubt sent waves rippling through him.

Maggie's bed was so perfectly made it looked like a picture of someone else's room. Each item on Maggie's dresser looked one-dimensional. Her easel was empty, as if it had never been used. John had an overwhelming feeling that everything froze once Maggie walked out her bedroom door.

Panic set in as John looked for vital signs of his daughter. When he saw the blank spot on the nightstand—the spot where Maggie kept the picture of the two of them—he knew Maggie was gone. And that something went terribly wrong.

Did Maggie understand what he said in his letter? Or did it come as a crushing blow and send her running?

John backed up toward the door, afraid that if he stood in Maggie's room any longer, something hideous would consume him, and he would never see his daughter again.

He had to do something. Find Maggie. Warn Nora. Tell Steve. Go back to North Beach. The ocean. The waves. His grave.

John whirled in circles as his thoughts pummeled him. He covered his ears and leaned against the bedroom door.

The solid surface turned to liquid, and John fell backward onto the hall carpet. The floor softened beneath him, and he floated through the floorboards. His body connected to the joists, each nail hammered the urgency deeper, and each electrical wire he passed singed the dread inside his heart.

John could feel someone just below him, and sadness pelted him as he fell.

Nora's hands were tightened into fists, and she was glaring up at the ceiling when John made his descent into the room. He waited until he felt the firmness of the hardwood beneath his feet before he sat down on the coffee table in front of her.

Nora, Maggie. Where is she?

John saw a flicker of recognition on Nora's face before her eyes glazed over. He looked at the grandfather clock. It was only one thirty, and Nora looked as if she'd already started drinking.

"Damn you, John."

Nora, no. Please, Maggie needs you. Where is she? I think she's in danger, Nora. Please, you have to hear me.

Nora grabbed her bourbon-laced mug off the coffee table, took a huge swallow, and slammed it back down.

"Why, God, why have you betrayed me?"

She sat up straight and covered her mouth with both hands, eyes so wide John thought she was going to laugh.

"You're not real," she whispered. "There is no God, is there?"

Yes, there is! John screamed. *Nora, please, I never meant to take your faith away!*

His words echoed inside the room, bounced off the couch, and dissolved before reaching Nora's ears. John watched Nora's arms drop to her sides and her whole body sway back and forth like a lifeless rag doll.

He leaned forward and cupped his hands under her chin. He could feel the quiver with his fingertips, and when he looked into her eyes, she screamed.

"No, don't do this to me!" Nora flailed her arms in his direction, and John recoiled with each blow.

Please, Nora. You must listen. Maggie needs you—help her. Help Maggie.

She screamed again and stumbled over the coffee table and into John's recliner.

"Leave me alone. Get away."

Nora sobbed and twisted in the chair. She jumped to her feet, grabbed a magazine off the end table, and threw it in John's direction.

John tried to stand, to go to her, but the love he never expressed to his wife paralyzed him.

"You never loved me, you crazy bastard."

I did. I do. His mouth disappeared from his face as the words screamed inside his head.

Nora grabbed a newspaper and tore it to shreds. She threw the tattered fragments at him. She screamed so loud she howled, and John's eardrums splintered with each hysterical wail.

Nora's fear was stronger than John's after-death confession. He covered his ears and tried to block out the sound of her sorrow. The tighter he held his hands, the louder Nora's sobs became, and her helplessness swallowed him. The room grew dim, and John struggled with the shadows.

Nora watched the confetti float through the air and fall to the floor. It fell so slowly she could make out bits and pieces of the headlines as the paper hit the floor. When she tried to piece the words together in her head all she could decipher was *Help Maggie,* and her confusion intensified.

Maybe mixing the bourbon and pain meds wasn't the right thing to do. And maybe it wasn't a pain pill. Maybe she grabbed the wrong bottle, and it was the sleep aid. And what if the sleeping pill pushed her into a delusional sleep state, and that's why she thought she saw John's face?

She should check the bottles. Count the pills. See if the count matched with the prescription date. But what if she'd taken so many there was no way to tell?

For God's sake, now she was acting just as crazy as Maggie.

John was—IS—dead.

Nora reached around her neck and produced the chain holding John's wedding band. She shoved the ring on her finger. It was way too big. She looked at the ring on her right hand and compared them.

They were still identical except for the size. She still knew John would never remove the ring from his finger voluntarily. The only way it could have been removed is if he were dead.

He's dead. Nora pressed deeper into John's recliner and curled up as tight as she could.

She desperately wanted a cigarette. And the afghan lying on the floor below the couch.

But she was too afraid to walk across the room. Afraid if she walked anywhere near the coffee table, John would touch her or try to talk to her again.

John looked down at the scraps of newsprint and then turned his focus on Nora. She sat wide-eyed, legs curled up to her chest and her arms clutched tightly around her knees. Her breathing had slowed, and the hysteria in the air began to dissipate.

He would wait right on the edge of the coffee table until she fell asleep.

The furnace kicked in. Nora jumped and tightened her grip on her legs, sinking her head into the small space between her knees. She leaned against the recliner's arm and clenched her eyes shut.

John felt the warmth from the heater fill the room. He rubbed his bare foot against the comforter on the floor and connected to the loosely knit pattern. He wanted to cover Nora and make sure she felt warm. But he knew if she saw the afghan float across the room it would send her over the edge.

The grandfather clock chimed twice. John hoped Nora wouldn't sleep long and would realize their daughter was missing.

TWENTY-FOUR

The Greyhound rolled to a stop at the Angel's Corner station at exactly 2:07 p.m. Maggie followed the three nuns off the bus. One of them said she was famished, and Maggie silently agreed. She tailed them to a McDonald's several blocks away.

A homeless man sat leaning against a fence. He called out to the sisters as they passed, asking them for spare change.

"God bless you, my son." One of the sisters told him. "And may you have the good fortune to find a job."

The nun stopped and slipped several coins into his cup. Maggie moved past the women and hurried inside the front door of the Golden Arches.

She ordered a super-size Big Mac meal and sat down near the front window. The bum was counting his change and seemed happy as he staggered to a standing position.

Naïve nun, Maggie thought. He's just going to go buy a couple of cans of beer.

Maggie watched the sisters drift in and order and then disappear behind a plastic arrangement of fern and ivy. She devoured her hamburger, and when she finished her fries, she looked out at the desolate people milling around on the street. Her stomach felt queasy, and she didn't know what to do next.

She scanned the road outside and noticed a phone booth on the other side of the street. She opened her backpack and pulled out her purse. Shane's number was still tucked away in the side zipper. She didn't want to spend any more time in this section of town and couldn't imagine being stuck here until nightfall. If she called Shane right away, she could wait inside McDonald's until he picked her up.

If he wasn't home … well, she'd leave a message. Tell him where to pick her up. Simple, really. Now all she had to do was make the call.

Maggie walked outside and pulled out her cell phone. Damn, no bars. Why didn't she have reception here? Her service was supposed to work anywhere in the freakin' state.

A jackhammer ravaged the sidewalk a few blocks up the street. The cars rushed by so fast she was afraid they didn't notice her. An uncomfortable feeling nagged at her as she half walked, half ran across the street and headed for an old-style phone booth.

Two scraggly haired white men stood several yards away, cigarettes hanging out the side of their mouths as they exchanged money and a small package.

One of them looked at her like what the hell are you doing here? She pretended not to notice as she opened the door to the booth and slammed it shut. She pulled Shane's number out of the side zipper, grabbed several quarters out of her wallet, and placed the wallet on the ground next to her backpack.

Maggie had looked at the number a zillion times and dialed it from memory. She held the receiver so tight her fingers hurt as she entered each number carefully. She listened as the phone rang on the other end.

Please answer.

A click, then a pause, and Maggie was connected to a female voice on the other end of the line.

"We're sorry. The number you have reached is no longer in service. If you feel …"

Maggie dropped the phone and sank to the ground. It felt like someone had kicked her in the stomach, and it took a moment to catch her breath.

Okay, maybe she dialed the number wrong. She grabbed more change, deposited it, and dialed the number again.

A man suddenly appeared next to the phone booth. When he smiled at Maggie, she noticed one of his front teeth was missing.

"You almost done in there, doll face?" The words spit out the gap, and he yelled so loud a couple more bums joined him.

"Hey, cutie," another sneered. Maggie turned her back on them and shoved another quarter into the slot. Maybe she needed to enter the area code as well.

Sweat formed on the nape of her neck, and her finger shook as she punched in each number.

503-555-3584

She repeated the number over and over in her head as the phone rang.

She heard a click. The same pause. The same stupid woman shouted the same absurd message she didn't want to hear.

Her quarter dropped into the coin return on top of the others.

"Need any help in there?" The man with the missing tooth licked his lips and grabbed his crotch.

Maggie threw her backpack over her shoulders and hurried out the booth. She used her sleeping bag as a barricade between her and the bums and moved sideways past them.

"Need a ride anywhere, doll cakes?"

Maggie pretended she didn't hear the slime ball's remark or the cackle of laughter from his dirty and disgusting friends.

She walked as fast as she could without looking scared and made the crosswalk just when the walk light came on. She hit a dead run and sprinted the entire two blocks back to the bus depot. She practically pushed an old man over as she rushed beyond the doors.

It was quiet when she walked inside. She was so afraid that every bus going anywhere was already gone. She'd be stuck right here. With those dirt wads. Just waiting for her to go back outside again.

She was tired and thirsty and wanted to cry.

I have to think, she told herself. Get a grip. Figure out what to do.

She reached inside her purse to grab change for a Diet Coke.

Her wallet was missing. Shit.

Maggie sat down on a bench in the middle of the station and looked around. A group of students wearing Catholic uniforms sat quietly in a row. Maggie wished there was a Catholic school in Rockaway Beach. If there was, she'd have gone there for sure. She could slip into her own uniform right now. And blend right in with them.

Maybe if she told the head nun her plight, she could whisk her back …

Home.

She couldn't go back. Not now. Not yet. She stood up and walked past the Catholic group and paced the inside perimeter of the station. The front entrance bordered the main street. The side exit opened to a parking lot. It stretched out toward a deserted road. A wooded area linked the parking area on the left.

Maggie took the side exit and looked around. Three teenagers were sharing a cigarette on the edge of the road. Other than the parked cars, the parking lot was empty.

She slipped behind the car closest to the building and crouched down as she headed toward the woods. If she walked the perimeter of the woodlands and back down toward the highway, she would eventually hit the Columbia River. And the Columbia River emptied into the Pacific Ocean. So if she followed the river toward the ocean, she could hitch a ride to North Beach. Maybe she just might hit the beach when Henry was out there clam digging. And maybe he would finally admit the truth and tell her which way her dad had headed that day.

She crept past the second to the last car and tightened her backpack before she started to run. Just as she increased her speed, she tripped forward with a thud and her sleeping bag rolled under a car.

A tall man in a light-blue-and-navy pinstriped shirt stared down at her. His smile made her stomach turn as he rubbed his chin with his hand. Dirt caked under his fingernails, and Maggie could smell his foul body odor as he knelt down beside her.

"And where are you going, pretty thing?" His rancid breath made her wince.

"Practicing my sprint. I'm on the … Catholic girls' track team. We're heading to a meet." She inched backward and then stood up as fast as she could. She frantically looked around and was relieved when she saw the girls in uniform walking toward a van. A huge semi-truck was parked behind it, and the van blocked the truck from leaving the parking lot.

The man stood and looked over at the group of girls and then back at Maggie.

"Yeah, well, you don't have a uniform on—"

"So what. I spilled ketchup all over it and had to change." She backed away from him. "I have to go, mister. I can't miss my ride."

"Yeah, well, if you don't want to go with them, you can ride in my big rig. I'm a fun guy to be with …"

He reached over and tried to grab Maggie's shoulder, but Maggie ducked just in time. He slammed his hand into a car's side-view mirror, and he buckled with pain.

"You fucking little bitch … get back here."

His words echoed behind her as she raced around the van and straight into Mother Superior.

The woman flew back into the van driver's arms and when Maggie realized what she'd done, she reached over and took hold of the nun's hand.

"Sister, Mother, I'm so sorry. Are you all right?"

The nun's look of surprise turned to concern as she held Maggie's trembling hand.

"My child … are *you* all right? And what are you doing alone in this parking lot?"

"My mom," Maggie had to scramble fast. "She just bought my ticket, and then I walked to the parking lot with her to see her off. I know I shouldn't have stayed out here by myself and …"

"What time does your bus leave, dear?"

Maggie looked at the bold face on the nun's watch. It was 3:12.

"At 3:15. I'd better hurry. I'm so sorry I ran into you like that. Thanks for your help."

"But I didn't do anything, dear. And you're white as a ghost."

"I'm fine, really. I can't miss my bus."

Maggie darted back inside the bus station and spotted the bathroom sign across the lobby.

She knew she couldn't go back outside because the truck driver was probably waiting for her. And if he already found her wallet, then he knew where she lived and would probably try to find her. Going home now was completely out of the question. She'd have to wait inside the bathroom until it was safe. Then head for the woods again.

Maggie sat sideways on the toilet, tucked her backpack behind her, and braced her feet against the wall. She pulled her purse against her chest as tight as she could.

The sudden flow of adrenalin dissipated, and she went limp with exhaustion. She closed her eyes and thought about Becca and the warm cozy comforter on her bed at home.

She buried her head into her purse and dozed off. The sudden boom of a man's voice startled her awake.

"Bus 241, now boarding for Portland."

Maggie teetered sideways and almost fell. She threw her legs in front of the toilet and wobbled to a standing position.

She was hungry. And thirsty. And she missed her father. And if it wasn't for that damn truck driver, she could just call her mom.

"No point in prime-time drama," she whispered to herself. "Like Mom could help me with anything right now anyway."

Maggie hung her backpack on the stall door hook, sat down, and went to the bathroom.

She flushed the toilet and started to walk out of the stall when she heard the main door swing open automatically, like someone had pressed the handicap button.

She threw her backpack over her shoulders and waited for the sound of wheels skimming across the floor. Instead, she heard hard, steady footsteps walk inside the stall right next to her.

Maggie waited for the stranger to lock the door and sit down. Then she eased over to the wall opposite the newly occupied stall. She held her breath and bent down to get a look at the intruder's shoes.

A pair of grayish white women's underwear rested on top of brown worn-out sandals, and Maggie winced as the woman released a huge stream of gas. She pinched her nose with one hand and hurried out the rest room, dragging her backpack behind her.

The bus station was crowded when she walked into the lobby. Every traveler seemed preoccupied as each rifled through his or her belongings and readied for the bus to depart.

She looked up at the huge clock on the wall and was frightened when she saw it was 3:25. She couldn't waste any more time if she wanted to reach the beach before it was totally dark.

Maggie slipped unnoticed toward the side exit. She followed an overweight woman out the door and peered over to the spot where the truck driver's rig had been sitting earlier.

It was gone.

The air was cold, and the floodlights were already lit in the parking lot. Maggie pulled the zipper up on her jacket as she headed toward the rear of the lot. This time she stood tall and waved and acted like she just saw the person she was going to meet.

She spotted her sleeping bag next to the building and bent down just long enough to grab it. When she reached the end of the lot, she looked back to see if anyone was watching. Several people were busy talking, and she knew they didn't even notice her as they walked to their cars. She heard a baby crying and wondered if it was the same child she saw at the Rockaway Beach station.

Maggie scanned the lot one last time and then slipped behind the bus station. There was a trail behind the building, and the floodlights provided a steady source of light. She'd stick to the woods until she was sure the truck driver was gone for good.

She followed the passageway into the forest, and when she felt dirt underneath her heels, she took off running.

TWENTY-FIVE

S hadows danced across the living room and cast eerie figures on the walls. Nora shivered and fumbled for the afghan. When she discovered it wasn't within her reach, she remembered what had happened.

She turned on the lamp. Everything looked the same as it had when she had walked into the living room just hours earlier.

Her coffee cup sat in the exact spot she'd left it—on the coffee table where, where ...

Jesus. It was just a dream. If it were real, there would be bits and pieces of shredded newspaper everywhere. And the magazine would be lying on the floor.

Nora switched the lamp on high and bent down to examine the rug. Nothing, not a spec of paper. Nothing out of place. Except for her coffee mug. And she had brought that in herself.

Nora picked up the cup. She leaned down and the smell of bourbon hit her nose. She'd been drinking. And mixing meds. And must have fallen asleep.

It was all just a crazy dream.

Nora walked over to the bar, fumbled with the pack of cigarettes, and then shook them out on the counter. She grabbed one, lit it, and inhaled deeply.

There was one thing she knew for sure. If she didn't get rid of John's things, she would lapse into insanity—John's insanity—and she couldn't let that happen.

Nora could reason with Maggie when she came home from Becca's. She would convince her that John was never coming back. They could pick up the pieces. Find some sort of normal in their lives.

What pieces? Nora had done everything but tell Maggie all this was her fault. Okay, so she strongly insinuated it, but that was in the heat of the moment and … and she had pushed her only child so far it might be impossible to get her back.

Nora ran her hand over the bar. She crushed out her cigarette and grabbed another one. She looked at the clock. It was four forty-five.

She couldn't think about Maggie now. She'd mix a drink. Get John's things packed and figure out how she'd make everything okay once Maggie got home.

Nora went to the kitchen and grabbed a glass from the cupboard. She filled it with ice and then poured in two shots of bourbon with a chase of water. She took several drags off her cigarette and then put it out and headed for the bedroom.

* * *

Maggie watched the sky darken overhead, and the cold evening air made her shiver. Her clothes felt so damp that even her down jacket couldn't keep the chill from penetrating her body.

She sat down on a tree stump and listened to the murmur of each car that drove past. She checked her watch. It was five fifteen. She hadn't made as much progress as she'd hoped. She was far enough into the woods to feel safe, yet close enough to hear the constant hum of tires on pavement.

If she slept until the sun came up, she could use the daylight to move across the edge of the woods and stick near the highway and not get lost. And once it was light, it would be safe to hitchhike. Maybe a family with kids and a dog would be heading for the ocean, and they'd offer her a ride.

Maggie unrolled her sleeping bag behind a fallen tree. She looked over at the highway. The headlights of a truck moving much slower than any of the cars caught her attention. It crept past her, and she watched its taillights until the big rig came to a sudden stop.

Maggie scooped up her sleeping bag and backpack and ran deeper into the woods. She heard a branch break behind her. She scrambled around a fallen tree, tripped, and tumbled backward down a deep hole lined in mud. She landed in a pile of soft dirt.

She climbed inside her sleeping bag and burrowed her way backward and then pulled the bag over her head. She held her breath and hoped the pounding in her chest wouldn't shake the ground and give her away. She listened for the crackle of a twig. Or leaves rustling under someone's feet. All she heard was the sound of her own fear ringing in her ears. And a constant growling in her stomach.

Maybe she was just hearing things. Or maybe what she'd heard was the wind picking up and breaking branches off the trees.

The hiding place felt warm against her cold body. Her sleeping bag smelled like home, and she felt homesick without even trying. As hard as she tried to keep her eyes opened, she gave in to exhaustion and drifted off to sleep.

* * *

Nora teetered back into the bedroom with a full bottle of wine. She steadied herself against the door and tried to make out the time on the alarm clock, but the numbers blurred together.

She'd stick with the light stuff until she was done packing. Then she'd have just one drink and head to bed. Even if she slept until five on Sunday, she'd be up before Maggie got home. And she'd have this mess cleaned up and her head clear enough to reason with her daughter.

It had to be close to morning because Nora could see the faint outline of trees against the horizon. But maybe that was just the street lamp outside.

She couldn't go to bed until all of John's clothes were packed and any memory of him safely locked in his studio. Maybe Steve could take over from there. Get rid of them. Burn them maybe.

Nora staggered over to the pile of shirts she'd thrown off the hangers. She picked one up and pressed it against her face. She tried to find a hint of cherry tobacco.

But John's scent wasn't there. She rolled the shirt into a ball and tossed it in the packing box and then picked up another.

The collar was frayed, and there were holes in the sleeves. Another painting shirt. She opened the bottle of wine and took a drink before wadding the shirt into a ball and throwing it inside the box.

Nora gathered several shirts into her arms and buried her head in them. She could smell the lavender scent from the detergent and a hint of Outdoor Spring from the dryer sheets. She sat for a moment, head buried as she tried to cry. But the tears wouldn't fall. And the irony of wanting to cry over someone she wanted to rid herself of made her angry.

She recalled her first glimpse of him and their immediate connection when the first date turned into eight hours of animated conversation. It had felt right. Meant to be. And now, twenty years later, here she was alone. Anger coursed through her body again.

She was so angry. Angry that he wouldn't follow the doctor's orders. Or take his meds. Why had he done this to them? Why didn't he want to stay alive just to be with her because she didn't care if he was crazy or not. She loved him. Wanted him even more now that he was gone.

"Oh God!" Nora stood up and shook her fists at the ceiling. "You did this to me. Why? Why? Why, John?" She picked up a vase from an end table and threw it as hard as she could, shattering it against a wall.

She knelt down and spilled the bottle of red wine. It soaked into the pile of John's shirts.

It looked like blood as it oozed into the carpet.

TWENTY-SIX

A shimmering cascade of morning sunlight made its way down the hole. Each knoll of fresh mud it touched turned into a mound of warm dirt. The air felt as warm as the middle of July. As Maggie emerged from her hiding place, she heard the sound of running water and a woman singing.

"Where have all the flowers gone? Long time passing ..."

"What kind of song is that?" Maggie inched around the tree's trunk and peered up into the clear blue sky.

The singing stopped, and she thought maybe she was dreaming. She walked away from the fallen log and heard something behind her. When she turned around, she touched noses with a woman whose steel-blue eyes sparkled with laughter.

"Boo!"

Blond hair fell in front of the woman's face. Before Maggie could back away, the person snapped forward and knocked Maggie in the forehead. Maggie tumbled back onto a blanket of pine needles and dried maple leaves.

"Ahhhhhh!" Maggie screamed and tried to get a good look at her attacker.

Pine needles swirled everywhere, and dirt flew into her eyes. She squinted with pain. She crouched on her knees and raised her arms as she crossed her hands in front of her body.

"I have a black belt ... don't come any closer." Maggie waved her hands in the air and tried to blink the dirt out of her eyes.

"Get away from me!" The screaming voice was the same one Maggie heard singing just moments earlier.

The dust settled, and Maggie saw a girl, no, young woman actually, cowering in front of her. When Maggie got up, the young woman fell backward and screamed again.

Maggie stood over her, hands on hips, sending a stern look downward. "What's your problem? First, you scare the hell out of me, and now you act like you're scared to death. Who are you, and what do you want?"

"You can see me?" The young woman sat up and straightened the ring of daisies that sat lopsided on her head and then brushed the loose leaves off her dress.

"Of course I can. Why did you get all weirded out like that? I wasn't the one trying to scare you." Maggie allowed her shoulders to relax and rubbed her forehead as she looked the woman up and down.

She wore a flower-print empire-waist dress that gathered at the shoulders, and the hem barely covered her butt. She had at large copper peace sign and at least a dozen beaded necklaces hanging around her neck. Maggie covered her mouth and tried not to laugh.

"Well, I'm just so sorry if I hacked you off. I just don't dig why you think this is so funny. And anyway, you just totally freaked me out, that's all." The young woman scowled as she talked.

"Well, it's not like I couldn't see you … what did you expect me to do?"

"Hey, it's cool. I just didn't have my groove on."

"What kind of talk is that?" Maggie said as she glanced over the girl's retro look again. "What's with the outfit? Is it a hippie costume? You going to a party or something? Because Halloween isn't until *next* weekend, or don't you have a calendar?"

The young woman gave Maggie an indignant glare. "Just because I freaked you out doesn't mean you have the right to drag me down with you. And for your information, these rags happen to be—"

"Okay. Let me guess. You're some kind of weird, overgrown forest elf?"

The girl stopped talking suddenly and covered her mouth with both hands. She giggled and bounced in the air like a loose spring. She swooped down, grabbed a handful of leaves, threw them in the air, and started singing. "I'm gonna be FREE ... and freedom's gonna be so groovy for me ..."

"What group sings that? Never heard it before." Maggie backed away from her, and she stopped singing and grabbed hold of Maggie's wrist.

"The Who."

"Who?"

"Yeah, you got it. Now come on. You don't have to jam out on me like this. We just met."

Maggie barely felt the light touch of the woman's hand. "Okay, so what's with you anyway?"

"I just figured out what the long hair was talking about."

"What??" The lady's double talk was really starting to bug Maggie.

"Never mind. It's all good. Hey, what's your name? I'm Star Dust."

"Star Dust? What kind of a name is that?"

"Well, okay. So my for-real name is Jane. But I changed it down at the Hemp Fest. We all got stoned and did the whole rebirth thing and ..."

When Maggie's mouth dropped open, Star Dust quickly changed her direction. "Anyway, what's your name?"

Maggie's stomach rumbled so loud it hurt, and she suddenly didn't care who this Star Dust person was. She had to find something to eat.

"My name is Maggie, and if you don't mind, I was just leaving."

"Maggie, cool name. What's it short for, Margaret? You look like you could scarf down an elephant. Have you been on the road long?"

"Scarf?"

"Yeah, you know, eat."

"Yes, I am hungry." She could stay maybe for a little while if Star Dust could feed her. "Do you have anything to eat?"

"Of course, well, not exactly. There's an apple tree over there on the other side of the waterfall."

"So I did hear water falling. And it was definitely you I heard singing."

Star Dust blushed. "Yes, I love to sing. I just can't help myself."

"Yeah, you sound more like an off-key elephant trampling through the woods," Maggie mumbled to herself.

"What'd you say?"

"Nothing. Never mind."

"Far out. Come, sit with me."

Maggie sat down and studied Star Dust's face. If she stared too long at this strange woman, she had a difficult time focusing. But when Star Dust smiled, everything turned crystal clear, and Maggie felt safe. And it had been almost twenty-four hours since Maggie had had a conversation with a real person.

"Are you running away from—or to—something?" Star Dust smiled and Maggie decided she liked her.

"Both."

"Far out. I'm hip with that. Let's walk. And you can lay it on me."

Finally. Someone who'd listen. Even if Star Dust was a bit strange, she definitely wasn't a serial killer, or terrorist for that matter. Besides, she was so tiny she almost floated when she walked. Well, Maggie wasn't totally sure if she actually touched the ground. It was her lightness that calmed Maggie. And she could definitely use some light in her life right about now.

"I have to grab my things first." Maggie scurried down the hole and came back with her sleeping bag and backpack.

Star Dust was twirling around next to a log; the dirt and leaves danced off her with each turn. When Maggie surfaced, Star Dust stopped and blushed but said, "I dig dancing, too."

"So do I. My dad and I, we used to dance sometimes in his studio. Usually after he finished a long painting session. I paint, too." It hurt to talk about him.

"Where's your old man now?"

"Well, there was an accident. He saved me from drowning, but then he disappeared."

"So you're on the road to find him."

When Star Dust took hold of Maggie's hand, Maggie avoided eye contact.

"Yes. That's right. I'm going to find him."

"But first, you must pig out." Star Dust grabbed hold of the sleeping bag and flung it over her shoulders.

"Last one to the waterfall is a candy ass!"

Star Dust ran ahead of Maggie. The sleeping bag flew behind her like Aladdin's magic carpet, and Maggie tangoed after her.

Star Dust ran into a meadow filled with gerbera daisies in beds of baby's breath and butterflies so big they could serve as an umbrella.

The air was as warm as a summer's day, and the possibility of any other season had been swept away. The maple leaves rustled in the wind, and each falling leaf danced on its way to the earth's floor.

"How could this be happening?" Maggie breathed in the warm air and welcomed the sunshine as it flushed her cheeks. "Those flowers couldn't possibly be real, and besides, it's way too late for anything to be in bloom. And those butterflies—they're ginormous and—"

"Are you talking about these?" Star Dust touched the wing of a butterfly, and Maggie thought for sure it winked at her before it flew away.

"Yes, I mean, no. The daisies."

Star Dust picked a handful of daisies and wove them into a crown. "These? Well, they're always in bloom here."

"But how could they be?" Maggie felt as if she'd just walked into a dream.

Star Dust smiled, and when she walked toward Maggie, she was actually floating. "I dunno. They just grow here. And they're my favorite." She placed the crown on Maggie's head. "Groovy—you're one of us now."

"One of who?" Maggie reached up, touched the crown, and was surprised when she discovered the flowers were real.

"Doesn't matter—just go with the flow, Maggie. Waterfall is this way."

Star Dust ran down a steep hill, covered in wild ferns, and around a corner, hugged tightly with huckleberry bushes, each bush so full it looked like it would burst.

Maggie flew after her, and when she saw the waterfall, she stopped so suddenly she tripped and almost collided with Star Dust again.

Long sprays of bubbling white foam sparkled as it flew into the air. The stream thundered down and crashed into a pond so deep the center turned midnight blue.

Clusters of rocks capped with patches of emerald-green moss lined the edges of the pool. A cedar had fallen, broken in two, and then sunk in the middle of the pond. Each end of the tree fanned up and out of the water, and the spray from the waterfall cast the illusion of wings.

"Wow, it looks like an angel's flying right out of the middle of that pond," Maggie whispered, afraid the sound of her own voice might shatter the extraordinary image.

"And that's why they named it Angel Falls," Star Dust replied as she directed Maggie to her campsite.

A broken down Volkswagen van with a peace sign painted on the side in a kaleidoscope of colors sat several hundred feet from the deep pond. When Maggie walked closer, a mother rabbit ran out from under it with her babies trailing behind.

"Welcome to my pad. That's Fluffy. She's been my friend ever since I got here. We don't actually see, I mean get, many visitors, so she stays on the down low."

Maggie dropped her backpack and sat down on a rock. She was so tired she forgot she was hungry. All she wanted to do was take a nap with someone around her so she could finally sleep without being scared.

"Apple tree's this way. There's still some choice fruit left. At least enough for you to chow down on."

Star Dust's feet brushed across the grass, and Maggie wondered if Star Dust had painted this entire scene in her head. Maggie took deliberate steps and watched each foot land in front of the other as she headed toward the lowest branch on the apple tree.

Maggie reached up and took a firm hold on a striped apple. The fruit's skin was warm, and the feeling of the morning sun on the back of Maggie's hand was real. She plucked the apple off and took a huge bite. Juice ran down her chin and the sweetness of the apple tickled her mouth.

"Wow, you're, like, really hungry."

"Like, like, wow." Maggie giggled and then picked several more apples and tucked them inside her jacket. She thought about asking for salt but couldn't figure out where Star Dust slept, let alone kept supplies.

"Are you going to eat?"

"Nah. I'm cool right now." Star Dust smiled at Maggie, then walked over to a huge rock hanging over the pond, and dangled her feet in the water. "Wow, this is so chill."

Star Dust didn't wait for Maggie to reply; she just splashed her feet like she'd never felt water before and started humming.

Maggie ate two more apples and then walked over to the pond. She leaned back against a huge rock and looked over at Star Dust.

"How old are you anyway?"

"Well, how old are *you*?" Star Dust splashed her feet in the water and started humming another weird tune.

"I just turned fifteen."

"Hummm, let's just say I'm older than you. What's your sign?"

"Virgo, with a Libra rising."

"Groovy, you know your astrology. What's your birth date?"

"September 24, 1991."

"What?" Star Dust bolted to her feet. "No way. Did you say 1991?"

"Yeah, I told you I'm fifteen."

"So that means this year is … it can't be. It isn't, is it? 2006?"

Star Dust stood up and paced back and forth. She hurried over to the van and opened the side door and rummaged around inside.

Maggie followed and peered over Star Dust's shoulder as far as she could. "So you been hiding under a rock or something?"

"No. I mean no sweat. I've just been trippin' a lot longer than I thought." Star Dust shoved a pile of papers under a box and shut the side door.

She looked puzzled and then muttered something about this was her mission. She turned and smiled at Maggie, and Maggie knew she was trying to hide something.

"So, what's your sign, Star Dust?" Maggie strolled back to the edge of the pond and sat down.

"Umm … I'm a Gemini."

Maggie laughed. "Well, that explains a lot. When's your birthday?"

Star Dust turned her back to Maggie before answering.

"June fourth."

"That's nice. What year?"

When Star Dust turned around, she had a weird look on her face.

"It doesn't matter," Star Dust answered slowly. "Anyway, if I told you, you'd just trip out on me."

"No, I wouldn't. Try me."

Star Dust stared at Maggie like she was trying to figure out what to say. Star Dust stood there for a moment then took a deep breath and blurted it out. "1949."

Maggie could feel her mouth fall open. "Wow! Are you kidding me?"

Star Dust blushed. "No, actually, I'm not."

"Wow, lady, then you've had some major work done, haven't you?"

"What?"

"You know. Face lift, eye job." Maggie walked a full circle around Star Dust. "You definitely had a tummy tuck and breast implants. Maybe some lypo too."

"What are you talking about?"

"I watch *Drastic Plastic Surgery* on the Oxygen Channel, and nobody your age can look as young as you do without having a bunch of work. Take Joan Rivers. She looks young. But she's a walking plastic-surgery factory."

Star Dust moved away from Maggie and looked up toward the sky. "Why didn't someone tell me this wasn't going to be easy?"

"That what wasn't going to be easy? Are you for real, Star Dust?" Maggie walked over and sat down next to her.

"Yeah, right on. Of course I'm for real. Let's just say I'm radically preserved for my age. You dig?"

Maggie laughed and didn't care if Star Dust was slightly stretching the truth or not.

"I dig. And I really don't care how old you are, Star Dust. You're weird, but I like you."

The water bubbled and churned at the base of the waterfall and splashed lightly as it hit the pond. Maggie yawned. Star Dust wrapped her arm around Maggie's shoulder, and Maggie closed her eyes.

"If you want to crash for a while, that's cool with me."

Maggie opened one eye and yawned again. "Will you be here when I wake up?"

"No sweat, chickie-do."

Maggie checked the time before she gave Star Dust her watch.

"It's ten o'clock. Will you wake me at around two? I have to get back on the road way before it gets dark."

Star Dust smiled. "Of course, sleepy head. Now catch some good z's."

Maggie laid her sleeping bag under a tree, and Star Dust covered her with a soft knit blanket from the back of the VW and tucked it around her.

"Sweet dreams, young lady."

Maggie flashed Star Dust the peace sign and then closed her eyes.

TWENTY-SEVEN

Nora stumbled as she pushed the last box toward the stairs. She'd been too drunk to carry any of them down, but it had been hours since she'd spilled the wine.

Sometime during the night, between the time she was drunk and almost clear-headed, she'd filled the boxes with all John's clothes. His JC Penney's shirts and Dockers tennis shoes. Old Navy jeans and Ralph Lauren underwear. All of it. Every last piece of John would be gone from her room. And finally, she'd be ready to get on with her life.

She heard the grandfather clock chime ten times.

Good God. She'd been up all night.

She couldn't have a drink at ten o'clock in the morning. Only alcoholics drank in the morning. But then again, she hadn't even been to sleep, so it wasn't really morning to her. It was … sort of an extended evening. And since she was still, well, in night mode, she really wasn't drinking in the morning. After all, her evening hadn't even ended yet.

Nora walked into the kitchen. She pulled a clean tumbler out of the cupboard and poured in two shots of bourbon, then ice and water. She opened the kitchen curtains and was surprised once again at how long the grass had grown. But it was almost Halloween. Too late to worry about it now. Maybe in the spring. She could mow it then. Maybe even weed the flower beds and plant annuals and refill the bird feeder.

She walked over to the bar and lit a cigarette. Nora shivered as she gulped her drink and allowed the alcohol to warm her belly. The room seemed different, almost surreal. She glanced out the picture window and watched the sun peek in the trees and bounce across the front yard. She finished the drink, and the alcohol rushed her veins like anesthesia through an IV. The inside of the house grayed as fast as the sun brightened the outside.

No, it couldn't hit that fast. This was the first drink she'd had in hours. And it was just a couple of shots, not enough to give her even the slightest buzz.

"Just one more."

The sound of her own voice came out of nowhere and echoed across the empty living room. When she turned to walk back into the kitchen, everything went black.

*   *   *

The darkness faded, and a fine mist swirled around John, and he could hear water thunder and crash below him.

Brilliant streaks of orange speckled with browns and gold crystallized into fall leaves clinging to tree branches in a grove of maple and alder. An umbrella of blue sky shielded the trees from the heavens as clouds floated aimlessly across the horizon.

A young woman sat next to an adolescent sleeping under a nearby tree. She hummed a tune straight out of John's childhood as she stroked the child's forehead.

The child—a girl—stirred in her sleep and turned toward John. He thought he recognized her, and his heart stopped as he walked toward them.

John sat down, and the woman didn't move. She stared straight ahead, as if he wasn't there.

John took a closer look at the sleeping child and gasped when he realized it was Maggie. Her blond hair had been cut short, the top spiked and matted with black hairspray.

Maggie's face looked thin, and the deep circles etched under her eyes made her look like a frightened old woman trapped in a child's body.

John's grief overwhelmed him as he listened to Maggie's breathing. He watched the water plunge down the rocks, and the relief of finding her safe in the forest overpowered the questions that raced through his mind.

The young woman stood and then walked over to the waterfall and started singing.

"In the village, the peaceful village …"

Her voice so low, so soft, John was drawn into the song. He stood next to her and hummed while she sang the next refrain. She swayed back and forth, and when she started the last chorus, he sang with her.

Once they finished singing, she turned to John and smiled.

"Hey, man, that was some nice vocals. I'm Star Dust. You must be Maggie's missing old man."

John was so surprised he lost his footing and tumbled toward the pond. Star Dust grabbed hold of his arm and steadied him.

"What the hell? Why didn't you say something, let me know you knew I was here?"

"Yeah, I should have. I figured you hadn't been dead long enough to catch the vibe. I saw you as soon as you walked up so I played my little game of hide and seek with you."

"You know I'm dead? Can Maggie see you?"

"Yeah, but she doesn't know I'm dead."

"I don't understand …"

"I didn't either at first. But I always play games with the mortals that happen to find my pad. Sometimes I play this little game with myself. I pretend I can freak them out because I know they can't see me. Then I walk right through them and feel what's in their heart. With Maggie, it was different. *She* scared *me*. And when I realized she could see me, I knew she was the one I was supposed to help. Like, you know, release me from here so I can do the whole transcend trip like everyone else."

John thought for a moment and then blurted out. "Then we're supposed to join forces, transcend this place together."

"Negative. The way I see it, you're stuck in-between for an entirely different trip from mine. I'm getting the vibe you won't beat feet until you hang loose with that."

Star Dust motioned John to sit next to her. She stiffened, sat perfectly still and then turned and looked at him.

"Wow, these messages are trippin' through my head like I'm a defunct shrink or some kind of tripped-out psychic."

"What? Yeah, right. Like a dead person has clairvoyant power." John could feel the frustration in his voice.

"Oh shut up for a minute." Star Dust closed her eyes and took a long deep breath. Her face turned pale, and she grabbed John's hand. She sat for a moment and then opened her eyes.

"We think the only lessons we learn are when we have human form. That's not true. Sometimes there's business that needs completion after death, before we can move on."

Her words came from outside her, and when she finished, the color returned to her cheeks. She let go of John's hand and smiled. Star Dust dropped her feet in the pond, and John watched her swirl them in the water.

"I guess we're both caught in this world of still feeling, wanting to be human, John. We can feel our bodies and the pain ... but the pain is really coming from the ones we left behind."

John looked over and watched Maggie sleep peacefully under the tree. "So I'm stuck here because of Maggie. Just like the weirdo said. Feel the love or never leave."

"Shaggy haired dude with a beard and sandals?"

"Yeah, that's him. Acted like a third-rate magician stuck in the sixties." John was about to apologize when Star Dust interrupted him.

"F**kin' A, man. Your daughter already lip-flapped me enough about my rags, so don't be downplaying the messenger too."

"So why the sixties look?"

"That was my time, man. And that bearded dude. Well, I've never been able to figure him out."

"Okay, I'll go with that. So why are you still here?"

"The last thing I remember before I died was sitting right here on this rock with my boyfriend, Bennie. It was so, like, steaming hot that day. We were gonna skinny-dip, then eat the Cheese Whiz and French bread we kiped from a ma-and-pop store we hit before heading up here to this spot by the falls. We drank a couple bottles of Tyrolia wine, and I took a triple hit of acid. Everything was copasetic until I flipped out and jumped in the pond. Bennie jumped in after me."

Star Dust took a deep breath, and John watched the tears well up in her eyes.

"Heavy, man," she said. "I can, like, feel real tears."

John knew exactly what she meant. Every physical sensation he experienced made him feel as if he was still alive.

"What happened next?"

"I sank to the bottom of the pond, and my feet got tangled up in some gnarly weeds down there. Every time Bennie grabbed hold of me, I thought he was an octopus with a million tentacles and was trying to eat me alive."

Star Dust wiped her eyes and laughed. "It sounds so far out. But he tried to save me. And I killed us both."

The wind picked up and swirled a spray of scarlet and gold maple leaves past them. John watched the leaves glide over the surface of the pond before the wind dashed them under. The waterfall hammered against the rocks, and he was afraid the pounding uproar would wake Maggie. He looked over at his daughter, and she was still sleeping.

Star Dust stood up and continued talking. "It was crazy, man. And the real bummer is I'm saner dead than I was alive."

The air filled with the crispness of fall. The red and orange leaves on the trees looked more vibrant than John ever remembered.

"Wow, Star Dust, I know exactly what you mean."

She walked back over to him and sat down.

"Do you remember the date, Star Dust?"

"What date?"

"The day you died."

"Yeah, it was June 22, 1967."

John gasped and clamped both hands over his mouth.

"What's the matter, John?"

John lowered his hands. "That's my birthday."

"Groovy, man. So you're a Cancer?"

"No, that's not what I meant. June 22, 1967, is the day I was born."

John watched Star Dust's mouth fall open. She grabbed both of his arms and her eyes danced with excitement.

"You know what this means, don't you, John?"

"No, but you're really freakin' me out."

"It means I'm supposed to help you, too."

John took a deep breath and talked in a whisper.

"Then you *can* make it possible." John twirled around in a circle and planted a kiss on Star Dust's forehead.

"What are you talking about, John?"

"You can make Maggie see me."

The doubt on Star Dust's face took the wind out of him. He sat back down on the rock facing her.

"I don't think that's possible, John. If Maggie can see you—then she'd know you're really dead. And she's too bummed out to hang with that right now."

"But sometimes, I know she can feel me."

"Love is so strong it trips the boundaries between life and death. Feeling you gives her the comfort she needs and the strength to continue her search. But she can't search forever for something she won't ever find."

Star Dust pulled a cluster of daisies out of the grass. "Look at these, John. Each petal is so, like, perfect. I never noticed that when I was alive. It's amazing how flowers are born. Their seeds spread over the universe without ever knowing where they came from—they just *are*. And that's how your life was, John. You just *were* and really didn't need to know who Shane was because he couldn't have changed the course of your life, even if he had wanted to."

Star Dust shook her head and rubbed her eyes. "Wow, this stuff is trippin' through me like an opium-laced joint."

John gritted his teeth, and his words hissed as he spoke. "How do you know about Shane?"

"Chill out, John. I just know he's your old man."

"But how can you know that?"

"Hey man, remember? I'm dead. And once you get the right vibe, there isn't anything you can't know. It just trips right out of your head."

Star Dust handed the flowers to John. He examined each one in the palm of his hand and then arranged them one by one in the grass, forming a heart.

"But what if he, Shane, is just like me?"

"What's the matter with being like you?" Star Dust brushed her hand across John's cheek, and he blushed.

"No, what I mean is, the moods, feeling so hopeless, as if there is no way out. I don't want Maggie to go through that again."

"Let me ask you this. Did you have that downer feeling the last time you were with Shane? Because you know, emotion is the one thing we hang with best."

John laughed, and the lightness of Star Dust's spirit loosened the tightness around his heart. "Shane was so calm. I knew he was my father when I watched him paint. The moves, each stroke so in tune, so free, as if he was born to do it. It was how I always wanted to feel when I painted. Confident. At peace in my own skin. It was like watching my highs and lows meet in the middle. A place I always wanted to be but was never able to maintain long enough to talk myself out of the next up or down."

"Sort of like a bad acid trip?"

"Exactly, and in Technicolor."

Star Dust splashed her feet in the pond one more time. "So Shane has the groove you always wanted. But you never found the right vibe."

"Yes, I guess you could say that." John reached down and touched each daisy that graced the outline of his heart in the grass. "But he stole my home. He took the willow, the tree house, my mother—everything that was important. He took it all away from me."

"It's not too late." Star Dust's voice was as light as a cloud floating across the sky on a warm summer day. When John looked into her eyes, he saw the confidence of a mountain lioness protecting her young.

John got up and walked over to where Maggie still slept. He sat down and watched a strand of hair dance across her forehead.

Maggie stirred and whispered in her sleep. "Paint the sunset, Daddy." He longed to paint with her in the willow. If only he'd kept his promise.

"I told Maggie I wanted him to pay for what he'd done."

"What do you mean—pay?"

"I don't know. I was angry. Hurt. And I wanted to get even. That's why I never took her to the tree house."

John had painted alone as a child, scaling the willow and retreating into his art in the same way he had retreated from his life.

The man who raised him had no artistic talents. His mother was too delicate to try. *My mother, her mind so fragile, just like mine.*

But Shane. John's talents challenged his. And even though Shane stayed silent, he came forward to comfort Maggie when John died.

John stood up and paced under the tree where Maggie lay sleeping. Shane's silence had made John's entire life a lie. Yet … his mother was the one who had sworn Shane to secrecy.

John sat down next to Maggie and watched the gentle rise and fall of her breathing. She was such a strong child. She had chosen to leave the craziness of the world he had left her in and find a way to fill the void in her heart. She had taken a chance because she didn't have his unhinged behaviors or his mother's fractured mind.

Maggie was like Shane. Artistic. Loyal. Full of life. She was her grandfather's child now. Shane could help her mend her relationship with Nora. And only Shane could provide her with the artistic connection John's selfish act had taken away.

Star Dust walked over and sat next to John. "Forgiveness is what life and death are all about."

John hadn't noticed the crickets until now. Their song drifted inside the silence and blended with the water falling gently down the rocks.

"I was just like my mother."

Star Dust took hold of John's hand. "And now, you can make a difference. Go back to him, John, one more time."

John sat up and could feel the resistance building in the pit of his stomach. "By not telling me, Shane made my entire life a lie. Why would I want Maggie to be around him after he betrayed me like that?"

"Get real, John. Maybe your life was a lie. But do you want Maggie's to be one also?"

John's resistance melted, and he felt a flood of sadness wash over him.

"Give him one more chance, John. Their day—well, it isn't over yet."

"What do you mean?"

"Our days, they're gone. We won't ever get them back."

John looked over at Maggie and watched the steady rhythm of her breath.

"Just go, John. Once you see Shane again—you might not be so hacked off at him. See if he's hip to what's happening with Maggie. And for real, you can't give back what you've taken from your kid, so you owe her this."

John scooped up the daisies and pressed them against his heart. He knew Star Dust was right. Maggie needed a father figure.

And maybe Shane *was* the only person left in Maggie's world who could—and really would—give her what she needed.

TWENTY-EIGHT

I t had been unusually cold that afternoon, so cold Shane planned to sit in front of the fireplace and lose himself in the pages of a good book. He was willing to do anything that would silence the nagging feeling he had.

Shane paced back and forth in the kitchen as a second pot of coffee finished brewing. He looked at the clock. Damn, it was already three o'clock. He walked over to the window and looked out at the valley below.

Fall had turned the willow's leaves to a gentle gold, and the branches had thinned just enough for Shane to detect movement in the tree.

He leaned closer to the window and squinted. He saw it again. A slight mist whispered in-between the tree's branches, undetectable if he'd merely given it a quick glance.

Yet it was movement just the same.

The kitchen chilled, and Shane gave an involuntary shudder, keeping his sight fixed on the tree. There was no wind breezing around the willow. Everything—even the clock above the sink—was completely still.

Maybe he was seeing things. God knew he was hearing things. Like the other day up in the attic. And his sense of smell was kaput too—there was no way Genevieve's fresh powder scent could fill the house the way it did that morning. And yet he had felt someone there.

He squinted out at the tree again. The clock ticked so loudly that it shook the room. The sound startled him, and he jumped backward and sank into a kitchen chair.

"Jesus, enough already! I'll go take a look," he muttered. "Great, now I'm talking out loud as if there's someone here to hear me."

He pulled his thermos out of the pantry and filled it with steaming coffee.

"May as well dabble while I'm out there if the paint isn't too cold." Shane laughed as he continued talking aloud. "If I can't beat 'em, may as well go out and join 'em."

Shane walked over to the mudroom and slipped into his ski parka and cowboy boots.

"Coffee. Almost forgot. Damn …"

He tiptoed across the kitchen floor and made sure he didn't leave a trail of dried mud. Genevieve always scolded him when he made a mess in the kitchen.

Genevieve.

Shane hurried over and grabbed the thermos and then walked out the back door into the crisp fall air.

He looked up at the sky. Not a single cloud to be found as he hurried off the deck and down to the willow.

The grass was slick under his feet, and the air so chilly he knew it would be as cold as hell in the tree house. When he climbed up the ladder and shoved his thermos up on the floor, the small space seemed unusually warm.

Shane peeled off his jacket and ran his hand over the back of his neck. His hair was already damp with perspiration. He surveyed the perimeter of the tree house. Nothing out of place since the last time he painted. But why was it so damn hot?

He picked up his brush and a tube of paint and started to dab oil paint on his palette. A sudden cold swirled inside the tree house and knocked the brush out of his hand. Shane laid the palette down on the floor and leaned against the wall.

He closed his eyes. A vision of orange blended with burnt umber turned into fall leaves on a grove of maple and alder. The scene was so vivid he knew he had to paint it.

He opened his eyes and exhaled. His breath hit the cold air and hung right in front of him. Before he could logically figure out why, he realized John was right there with him. In their tree house.

"Getting pretty damn clumsy in my old age. Can't even hang on to a paintbrush."

Shane felt the warmth return. He laid his brush on his palette and watched a series of heat waves move from the window and into the corner next to his easel.

He sketched the mental image onto the canvas. Each stroke sent the urgency closer to the surface, and Shane realized this moment might be the only one he would ever have to be a father to John.

And even if John wasn't really there, Shane knew he had to speak the words he promised had Genevieve he would never say.

"Love's an oddity, son."

Tiny heat waves arched from the corner and then dissolved. Shane took it as a sign of agreement as he finished the rough sketch.

"You can feel as if everything you're doing is out of love. Then realize it's nothing more than the demons that kept all the guilt bottled up inside."

Shane picked up a tube of cadmium yellow and laughed.

"Damn demons." He put the yellow in the center of the canvas and highlighted with white as he created the horizon. "It took bottle after bottle to keep them demons buried. At least that's what I did when I got back from Vietnam."

Shane mixed ultramarine blue with a touch of dioxazine purple and spread it across the top of the canvas and then delicately blended it into the horizon.

"And it's not as if I drank because I didn't want to live or the war screwed me up. Hell, the war and POW camp were nothing compared to what was waiting for me. Hell was what I walked into when I came home."

He mixed white with the dioxazine and a touch of Hooker's green and then picked up a clean brush and dabbed the color into a formation of distant trees.

"I couldn't wait to see your mother. And you … well, I knew you were six years old and there was so much I wanted to teach you—so much time to make up."

Shane stared down at the tubes of paint. His eyes watered, and he couldn't read any of the fine print.

"The army got hold of her somehow, and when I came home—right here to this house—she was living here with Rex, and she was a mess. The doctor had given her a couple of new meds, and all that did was screw her further into isolation."

Shane rubbed his eyes and started talking again.

"She wouldn't—or I should say Rex wouldn't—let me see you. He said having Genevieve upset was enough. He asked me politely, okay, harshly, to leave."

Shane blended carbon black with burnt umber, stroked tree trunks onto the canvas, and when he was done, stood back and looked at the picture.

"Genevieve ran after me and pleaded with me to remain silent—to keep the secret. I swear to God—if I didn't think it would have killed her—I would have told you I was your father. And I would have insisted I be part of your life."

He choked back a sob and squeezed dollops of Ruby red, canary yellow, and burnt umber on his palette. He made soft, irregular strokes, and the brilliance in the maple trees he created quelled his anger.

"I so wanted to be your father, John. Rex was a good man and a good father. My options were stolen moments with your mother, filled with reports on your childhood, or else nothing. Those secret meetings with her were all I had. And watching you grow up from a distance was my only choice if I was to remain in your and Genevieve's lives."

Shane mixed blue with white and used straight downward strokes as he painted a waterfall peeking out of the right side of the picture.

"When Rex died, it was too late. You had grown into a young man."

The wall in the corner of the room quivered. He walked over to the single window in the tree house and peered out. The valley looked as if it was covered with a thin frost, but the warmth generated from the corner of the tree house made the possibility of winter seem out of the question. Shane kept his gaze on the valley and continued talking.

"So I kept my hair long and my beard full so no one could see the strong resemblance between us, John. Looked like a damn hippie most of my life because I thought it was the right thing to do. And your mother—well, I thought she wanted me to keep quiet, even after we got married. All she did was obsess about how much you would hate her, and I knew that would kill her for sure. There was no going back."

The wind picked up and hummed around the willow. Shane stood transfixed as he listened to each rustling leaf strike a unique chord. He thought about Genevieve, how she loved listening to the wind compose music in the willow's branches.

"I didn't mean to alienate you, John, before your mother died. After Genevieve and I married, she didn't want to—she couldn't—leave this house."

Shane stared out at the valley for several minutes before talking.

"She wanted to be a grandma to Maggie. But she just wasn't strong enough to live."

Shane bit his lip and tried to back pedal. "What I meant, son, is your mother was manic—she had severe mood swings. Not the violent type, she'd just close up tighter than a clam. And it didn't matter what meds those quacks gave her—nothing helped. That's why they suggested the shock treatments."

Shane tightened his fists as the memory flooded back. "And she was so afraid of the treatments. Afraid of what they'd do—but more afraid of not having them. Now I wish you would have known how it was with her. Maybe if you'd known, things could have turned out differently."

The wind blew, and tiny streams of sunlight flooded the room.

"And when I called you that day, son, I didn't know what to say. Except that I was sorry. So sorry that I was never a father to you. And sorry that your mother took the secret to her grave."

Shane stopped talking and turned his attention to his easel. He moved away from the window and stood in front of the picture, gasping at the single word scrawled across the freshly painted sky.

forgiven

Shane felt something touch his shoulder as the warmth left the tree house. He took a deep breath and whispered, "Thank you," and then picked up his brush and applied the final touches to their work of art.

TWENTY-NINE

John emerged into the grove of maple and alder and compared his surroundings to the scene Shane was painting. They were identical, down to the path moving off the right side of the canvas leading to the waterfall.

He hurried down the trail and was relieved to see Maggie still sleeping. Star Dust turned and smiled at him.

"So?"

"So he was painting the grove of trees right next to the waterfall. It was as if he read my mind. The colors—the oranges and hints of red on the maple leaves—I ached to paint them myself. After I knocked his paintbrush out of his hand, he knew I was there and knew I wanted to see it on canvas … so he painted it for me." It was the first time passion felt good and didn't make John want to die all over again.

"I believe I detect a wicked *feeling* in your voice, John. Was it …"

"Forgiveness. That's all I could paint on the picture. Shane was looking out the window in the tree house, and I felt it so strong I was able to pick up the brush and sketch it across the sky."

"Like a banner?"

"Well no. All I could write was the word 'forgiven.'" John looked at Star Dust, and she had a playful smile on her face. "Fine. Make fun of me. I didn't know I was capable of doing that—picking up a paintbrush and actually using it."

Star Dust motioned John to sit down. "No silly. I'm feeling the love—the healing, you know, the vibes that everything is cool."

John sat down and clasped his hands under his chin. "You're right. Maggie—Shane ... Shane can help her get through this. And maybe even help Nora as well."

"Whoa, one at a time, John. Besides, Nora has her own hell to hang in. And it's her trip—not yours."

"But I didn't help," John stammered.

"You're right. You didn't. But it was her choice to trip out on prescription meds and alcohol."

"How'd you know that?"

"Like, remember ..."

"Yeah, yeah. I know, but aren't you being just a bit hippie-critical—having done the whole drug thing yourself?"

"I was too far out to reel myself in. Nora, well, she still has choices. And the most important thing right now is to connect Maggie with Shane."

John nodded in agreement. "Because if Nora falls off the deep end, Maggie is going to need someone."

"You got the vibe, daddy-o."

It all sounded so simple, yet John had no idea where to start or how to make it happen.

"But how can I help her, Star Dust? How can I tell Maggie what to do?"

"Well, you born-again badass, why don't you talk to her in a dream?"

John brushed a kiss across Maggie's cheek, and she smiled in her sleep.

"Butterfly kisses, Daddy." Her voice was a whisper, and it startled him so much he kissed her again. "Love you." Maggie turned on her side, and John watched as she fell into a deeper sleep.

The wind picked up, and John felt himself drift above the group of trees sheltering his daughter. He could see Maggie's dream floating just ahead of him and closed his eyes as he flowed through its gentle boundary.

Giant ferns nestled amongst mushrooms as big as boulders, and tiny birds sung so sweetly it brought tears to John's eyes. The sky welcomed a group of small, fluffy clouds as they marched across the horizon. The sun's rays produced an innocent glow around Maggie's face.

"Can you help me finish this picture, Daddy?" Maggie was perched on a large brown mushroom, paintbrush in hand with her palette resting across her knees as she examined the picture on her easel.

John walked over to her. His hand trembled as he gently touched his daughter's shoulder.

"Sadness not allowed here, Daddy. Now, what did you do with your paints?" She gave him a scolding look and then laughed.

"I have to talk to you, Magpie. No time for painting now."

"But this is what we always do here, Daddy. I don't want to talk."

She rubbed her cheek against his hand and began mixing a soft shade of green.

"Magpie, you have to find Shane."

"I'm painting; no time for anything else." She stroked her brush on the canvas and added highlight to a cluster of leaves.

"He lives right here. In the house with the willow tree. Where I wanted to take you, where you can paint with Shane."

"I can paint right here, thank you." Maggie stirred a deeper shade of green on the palette and looked back at the painting.

"He's your grandfather, Maggie."

"Silly Daddy. I don't have any grandfathers. They're dead. In heaven. Now where are your paints?"

"Maggie, you have to find Shane."

The sky dimmed, and John panicked. He wasn't ready for the dream to end. Everything melted around him, and all he could hear was her voice.

"Silly Daddy. In heaven."

"No, Maggie, listen." He struggled to finish.

Find Shane Find Shane Find Shane

The fog surrounding him swallowed his final words and echoed them inside his mind.

Darkness took over, and John found himself circling above the cluster of trees. Maggie bolted to a sitting position, and John moved in as close as he could. She pulled the knit blanket around her shoulders and whispered as she rocked back and forth.

"Daddy, please help me. I have to find Shane."

Star Dust walked over and pulled Maggie into her arms. "What's the matter, hon? Have a bad trip?"

"No, I just need to find someone, that's all. I need to go now."

"Look, Maggie. It's already 3:30." Star Dust handed Maggie her watch. "By the time you trip out of these woods and hit the highway, it's gonna be dark. And I can't let you creep around in the woods all by yourself. And you don't want to hitch at night. It could be a bad scene."

"Well …" Maggie hesitated for a moment. "It just felt so real. But I guess dreams do that, don't they?"

"Ah yes, they do." Star Dust smiled in John's direction, and John gave Star Dust a stern look. "But, maybe you do need to find this Shane guy. It's safer to travel in the morning. After a good night's sleep."

"All right. I do like being here with you, Star Dust. And I should get a good night's sleep before I hit the road tomorrow."

"Groovy. Leave in the morning. I'll build a fire. And we can sing. We'll sing and dance the night away, and then you can leave once the sun comes up."

John sat next to the pond and watched Star Dust usher Maggie over to a bowl of apples. Maggie sat down and picked out the biggest one. When she bit into it, he heard the crunch and almost felt the juice running down her chin as she ate.

Star Dust rummaged around in the back of the VW and emerged with some clothing and gave them to Maggie.

"What are these for?"

"Dress up. We're going to dance and you need the right digs. Cool?"

"Whatever Star Dust." Maggie grinned and disappeared into the back of the van to change.

Star Dust sat down next to John and whispered in his ear. "Your wish is my command."

"What?"

"Just follow my clues."

Star Dust walked over to the fire pit and finished building a fire. When Maggie emerged from the van, her hair was adorned with a crown of daisies. She wore a purple gypsy skirt with beads and sequins rolled up and tied at the waist. A white peasant blouse was capped loosely on her shoulders. Her eyes twinkled as she waited for Star Dust's response.

"Close your eyes, Maggie. Imagine it's nightfall and you're inside the most beautiful painting you've ever created."

Maggie giggled. "Oh, I love this, Star Dust. Dad and I used to go to imaginary places together when I was little."

"Groovy. Then do it, Maggie. Make it happen."

John watched Maggie close her eyes. The sky above melted into a deep azure blue, and the stars that appeared were even brighter than the fluorescent stars on Maggie's bedroom walls. Fireflies hovered overhead and then draped themselves around the surrounding trees like giant strings of Christmas lights. Birds appeared everywhere. Yellow warblers, red-breasted robins, goldfinches, and exotic lovebirds with peach faces or black wings. Like a tiny orchestra finely tuned, their voices united and whispered in the bushes and harmonized from the top of every tree.

Maggie opened her eyes and squealed with delight.

"How did you do all this, Star Dust?"

"I didn't do anything, Maggie. This is your trip. Now come over here; let's get our groove on."

Maggie curtsied, and her gypsy skirt flowed freely in the wind. She danced around the campfire and stopped between John and Star Dust.

John held his breath as Star Dust reached over and took hold of Maggie's hands, sandwiching John between them.

Star Dust looked up at John.

"Now I want the wind on my back."

"Me?" John was confused.

"Yes. The wind please."

"What?" Maggie looked up at Star Dust. "I don't get what you mean."

"Never mind. You don't have to."

Star Dust tilted her head to one side, motioning to John. He walked behind her, turned, and faced Star Dust's back.

"Closer. And take hold of my hands."

"Me?" he whispered in Star Dust's ear.

"Yes, you," she whispered back.

"What?" Maggie asked. "I couldn't hear you."

"Sorry, kiddo, just move closer to me."

Maggie moved in as close as she could. As John moved closer to Star Dust, he blended into her body.

"I smell cherry tobacco." Maggie said as she sniffed the air.

"Just concentrate, Maggie."

John couldn't tell if he'd just heard his voice or Star Dust's and then suddenly, he felt the softness of Maggie's hands.

"Hey, Star Dust, your hands just got warm."

"That's right, honey. Now close your eyes, and dance with me, Magpie."

"What?" There was a look of surprise on Maggie's face when she replied. "Your voice sounds weird, Star Dust."

John moved away and waited for Star Dust's direction.

"Sorry, honey. Must have been a bubble in my throat."

"Or something." Maggie giggled. She stood tall and threw her shoulders back as she positioned herself to begin dancing.

John blended with Star Dust again and squeezed Maggie's hand to reassure her. "Just keep your eyes closed, Maggie. And dance."

John felt the smallness of his daughter's hands. He looked down, and her eyes were shut tight, and her smile lit up her face.

John stumbled at first and then stood tall and floated around the campfire as Star Dust sang.

"If you're going to San Francisco, be sure to wear some flowers in your hair …"

The moon's beams were so brilliant they transformed the maple leaves into a carpet of gold. The wind strummed the tree branches like strings on a guitar. Every bird harmonized as the crickets sang background. The waterfall thundered the chorus as the love between father and daughter filled the air and whirled them around the campfire.

THIRTY

The air turned cold, and Maggie woke up shivering. She reached over to pull Star Dust's blanket back over her shoulders. But the blanket was gone.

She sat abruptly and bumped her head on the dirt above her. Maggie inched out of her sleeping bag and moved to the top of the hole. She peered up into the pale morning light. Everywhere she looked was gray and covered in a thin mist.

She rushed down and grabbed her sleeping bag and backpack and then dragged them behind her as she ran down the hill toward the waterfall.

The thick blanket of trees blocked the sun, and shadows lurked everywhere. Maggie rushed over to the fire. The once hot coals had turned to ashes.

She hurried over to the VW to wake Star Dust. There was just enough morning light to see the van was empty.

Maggie panicked when a baby rabbit scurried out from under the vehicle, and her voice was hoarse when she talked. "Fluffy? Where's your mother, little one? Have you seen Star Dust?"

She looked inside the van again. A thick mold covered the newspapers in the back, and the overhead was laced with spider webs.

Maggie tried to shut the sliding door, but when she pulled on the handle, it fell off in her hand. She threw it on the ground and backed away from the vehicle.

"Star Dust, please, where are you?"

The silence scared her even more than the inside of the van. She stumbled back over to the fire pit and sat down. She wrapped her arms around her legs and huddled into a shivering ball. The early morning sun finally broke through the trees. Maggie looked around. The only familiar thing in the campsite was her apple cores stacked next to an old rusted pan.

Maggie looked at her watch. It was ten minutes past five.

An owl let out an eerie hoot, and Maggie jumped. She couldn't wait around to see if Star Dust was going to return. She had to leave *now*.

She rolled her sleeping bag, threw her backpack over her shoulders, and hurried back over the trail leading to the meadow.

The morning air shunned the warmth of the sun. Adrenalin fueled Maggie as she raced back up the hill. It was early enough to get a good start, and she was grateful for the daylight that paved her way.

She walked in the wet underbrush until her feet were so cold she couldn't feel her toes. Her arm ached from carrying her sleeping bag, and her mouth was so dry she couldn't swallow.

She inched along the edge of the highway, staying far enough away that the cars driving by couldn't see her. The highway dipped to the left, and when she crawled over several fallen trees, a side road appeared in front of her.

She walked out of the woods and surveyed both sides of the road. There was an old bus shed directly across from where she was standing. She could hide inside, take her shoes and socks off, and massage her feet until they felt warm again. She had one pair of socks with her. That was it. She'd have to change into them. Maybe tie the wet ones on the back of her pack, and hopefully, they would dry enough for her to wear them again if she had to.

Maggie waited until the adjacent highway was empty and then ran across the road and into the bus shed. She took off her shoes and socks. She had blisters on both her pinkies. She pulled a sweatshirt out of her pack and wrapped her feet in it. It felt good against her aching toes.

She sat down on the bench and leaned against the wall. She pulled her cell out and turned it on. Crap. The battery was dead.

All she wanted to do was cry. Cry because Shane didn't have the common courtesy to have that stupid lady on the recording give out his new phone number. Cry because she was just plain old scared.

Maggie heard a truck backfire and jerked her shoes and socks and sweatshirt off the ground and stuffed them in her backpack. She tossed the pack over her shoulders and jumped into the bushes and hid behind a fallen tree as the truck rolled to a stop.

When the man jumped out of the cab, she gasped.

It was him. The man from the bus station in Angel's Corner.

He walked over to the opposite side of the road and Maggie grabbed for her sleeping bag.

Shit. She left it in the bus shed.

She crept farther into the woods and hid behind a hill covered with ferns. She listened for the sound of branches cracking under the weight of the man's feet.

She heard nothing.

Maggie waited so long and sat so still she fell asleep. When she woke, her feet were throbbing. She looked at her watch. It was almost eight. She slipped back into the woods and looked for the big rig. It was gone.

She tiptoed inside the bus shed to pick up her sleeping bag, but it wasn't there. The emptiness in the shed overwhelmed her, and she rushed back to her hiding spot in the woods.

She rubbed her feet until she could feel them and then pulled on her dry socks. She tied her wet socks together and laced them through the shoulder straps on her back pack before tying the socks again.

She slipped into her wet shoes, and by the time she walked a few hundred yards, her warm wool socks were soaked, and her feet still ached from the cold.

John drifted into the tree house and stood in front of Shane's painting. Shane had completed the waterfall after John had left, and John felt uneasy as he analyzed the image. The water plunged straight down against a rocky hill and bubbled into a small creek below.

It was wrong.

John closed his eyes and pictured the waterfall and the grove of maple and alder. He heard the water thunder down against the rocks and felt the spray against his face. When he opened his eyes, he was standing at the edge of Angel Falls.

"Star Dust?"

John walked over to the van and was surprised to find the inside decomposed and destroyed by the elements of time. The campfire appeared flattened by a multitude of passing storms. The only evidence anyone had been there were the cores left from the apples Maggie had eaten the day before.

He rushed back over to the waterfall and was relieved when he saw Star Dust sitting on a rock. She turned and smiled and motioned for him to join her.

Star Dust took hold of John's hand. It felt light and airy, and her entire being shimmered as she sat next to him. The sensation was so peaceful and perfect that John knew Star Dust's mission had been successful, and everything was going to be fine.

"I was worried. I went back to the tree house and looked at Shane's painting. Then when I came back here, it looked as if no one had ever been here, and it scared me."

"I couldn't let Maggie feel she could stay. I've done my job, and the landscape just naturally returned to its original state. It had to happen this way. It was time for her, for me, to move on."

When John squeezed Star Dust's hand, his fingers drifted through hers, and uneasiness flooded him again.

"What's happening to you, Star Dust?"

"It's time, John."

"Can't you just, like, hang with me?" John hoped his mocking jargon would make her pay attention and listen to him, but Star Dust seemed not even to hear him. "Please stay, just for a few more minutes. I couldn't have done this without you. Maggie's going to be safe now; I just know she is." John tried to believe his own words. Make them filled with hope.

"Don't let go of her just yet, John. Maggie might still need you."

"I'm not—but, I just feel relieved. Shane will—"

"But I feel you letting go, John. Hang with her, or the link will break, and it will go all wrong. Your work is not done."

John scrambled to find words to persuade Star Dust to stay. He couldn't do this without her. He had to convince her before she disappeared. "And Shane, Maggie has to find him. I don't know how to help her. And the message I gave her—"

"John, don't …"

"What do you mean, Star Dust?"

"I don't know. Can't say. I, I see him, John … it's Bennie …"

Star Dust drifted to a standing position, and John tried to pull her back, but the light in front of the waterfall was so bright he couldn't see well enough to grasp hold of her.

"Star Dust, please …"

"It's outta sight, John. So righteous …"

John watched Star Dust float toward the light. He stood up and called her name, but the light extinguished, and she was gone.

THIRTY-ONE

The sun painted a brilliant path across the sand dune. The grass fluttered, and each crisp blade waved and beckoned Nora forward. The beach sparkled like a newly laid carpet of jewels, and Nora was filled with joyful anticipation.

She looked down at her wedding dress and ran her hand lovingly across the beaded bodice. The organza skirt floated on the wind, and the crisp ocean breeze soothed the hot glow on her cheeks as she playfully lifted the hoop under her dress and allowed the wind to lift the skirt even higher.

The breeze swept past her, and when she looked over at the shore, John stood smiling at the water's edge, his bare feet planted firmly in the wet sand, his hand reaching for her as the waves rippled silently against the shore.

A single red rose adorned the lapel on his jacket. His white satin shirt was unbuttoned to his waist. His dark brown hair was much longer than the last time she had seen him. The breeze tossed his shaggy locks, and his smile made Nora's heart flutter.

The wind swirled Nora's veil in front of her face. When she moved it away and looked back at the beach, John was gone. She blinked several times, and John appeared again. He was standing on a sand dune in front of her, but something had happened to his eyes. Gold specks swirled inside the irises until the pupils disappeared. His skin looked like wet cement, and it hardened when he moved his hand.

Nora gasped and stepped backward, and her veil stuck to something gummy. She turned around, and all she could see was a massive web woven together with sticky black wire. There were tiny needles dangling everywhere. The web hung in midair with nothing above it and nothing below it but thick stagnant air.

Nora pulled her veil off and took several steps backward, but her feet sank in the sand. She looked over at John. Dark clouds surrounded him, and the tide had moved in so fast she was afraid that he would be swept away before he could save her.

"Please help me, John."

Nora reached her hand out to him, and all he did was stare at her.

"Help Maggie."

John's mouth opened and closed in slow motion, and Nora tried to scream but nothing came out.

"John, please you have to help me. I'm going to die if you don't …"

Nora fell forward and grabbed onto a clump of dried grass. It sliced her hands. She looked up at John and screamed again.

"Love Maggie." John's voice pulsated, and she pounded her hand against one ear as if she could shake him out of her. Nora leaned back, and the ground turned to quicksand.

"Please, I'm sinking. You have to help me." Nora stretched her arms toward John and tried to grab hold of his hand.

"Love Maggie."

John's voice ricocheted through her head, and she screamed back at him.

"But I do love her, John. Help me, please."

"She's gone, Nora. Find her."

John floated above her. When Nora tried to grab hold of his hand again, she sank deeper into the sand. The sand turned into mud. Every time Nora moved her body, it pulled her deeper into her grave. She held her breath and lay as still as she could. But she couldn't hold her breath any longer.

Nora screamed and opened her eyes. She covered her hands over her mouth and shivered as she looked around the bedroom. The boxes she had filled with John's clothes were gone. The bedspread was crumpled on the floor, and the blankets and sheets were twisted in knots.

The closet door was open. The cabinet containing John's medical records sat in the middle of the floor. The pages were shredded and stacked haphazardly, like a campfire waiting to be ignited. A half-full bottle of bourbon sat on top of the heap, offering the necessary fuel.

Nora couldn't stop trembling. The last thing she remembered was packing the boxes and putting them in the studio. But John's medical records—they were tucked safely in the file cabinet in the closet. What in God's name had she done?

The dream. She remembered the dream. Nora bolted out of bed, and her head throbbed as she fell to the ground.

The phone pierced the silence, and Nora felt sick to her stomach as she crawled across the floor to answer it.

"Hello?"

"Mrs. O'Brien?"

Nora took a deep breath before answering.

"Yes."

"This is Lucy Anderson at Rockaway Beach Middle School. I'm calling to verify Maggie stayed home today. Is she ill?"

What day was it? Nora couldn't think fast enough. Maggie had spent the night last night with Becca. But wasn't that Saturday night?

"There isn't school on Sundays. Who is this, anyway?"

"Mrs. O'Brien. Today is Monday, and it is ten o'clock. This is Lucy Anderson at Rockaway Beach Middle School. Maggie was marked absent in her homeroom. You need to verify she's home with you." The woman was silent and then spoke again. "Is everything all right, Mrs. O'Brien?"

Oh God. An entire day. She had lost an entire day. Nora's stomach churned, and she choked back the urge to puke on the phone.

"Yes. I mean no. We're sick."

"I'm sorry to hear that. I hope that you and Maggie are feeling better soon."

"Yes. Thank you."

Nora slammed the receiver down and ran into the bathroom. She stumbled to the toilet and every time she tried to call out to Maggie, she gagged and threw up. The dream swirled through her head while John's words pounded against the walls in the bathroom.

Help Maggie.

She's gone, Nora. Find her.

Love her Love her Love her

Nora retched until dry heaves took over. When the nausea finally subsided, she stood to walk. Her legs were like a pair of mismatched stilts made of cardboard instead of wood. Each uneven step pushed her forward and back against the wall as she inched toward the bed.

The smell of bourbon hit her as she passed the closet. She doubled over and slammed the door.

Nora clutched her stomach and stumbled into bed and then curled up into a ball.

The blackness enshrouding the previous day prevented a normal replay of events. She shuddered as she tried to piece together the bits that hadn't been wiped clean from her memory.

The boxes she filled with John's clothing … the long haul down the stairs and into the studio … the celebratory drink.

It was all so clear—mixing the drink and looking out the window as the sun signaled morning's arrival.

And then. And then it went gray and fuzzy, and she knew she was there yet somehow felt herself slipping away, and she lost her body—or was it her mind— because all that was left was the pile of shredded paper mounded like a campfire in the closet. If she had set fire to it, they would be dead.

Oh God. Maggie must have witnessed her entire drunken rampage and stayed home from school to make sure Nora survived.

Fear provided the adrenalin Nora needed to move. She raced into Maggie's bedroom and opened the door.

The appliquéd pillows on Maggie's bed rested neatly on top of her pale blue quilt. Nora had promised Maggie right before John died to replace her bedding with a ruffled white comforter and matching pillows. Maggie wanted her bed to look like a huge white cloud. John planned to repaint the walls and splash them with wildflowers and butterflies that turned into stars at night. That never happened. And now, Maggie was …

"Oh dear Jesus, she's gone!"

Nora raced back into her bedroom. She yanked the drawer on the nightstand open and searched for the rosary she kept hidden inside. When she couldn't find it, she flew down the stairs and ran out the front door.

THIRTY-TWO

Rain pounded the sidewalk as Nora ran barefoot to Becca's house. She banged on the front door so hard the windows shook. Kathy answered, and her mouth fell open when she looked at Nora.

"Where is she?" Nora demanded. The high pitch squeak in her voice startled even her. Nora leaned against the doorframe and tried to catch her breath.

"Nora, what's gotten into you? Come in and get out of the rain."

Kathy took hold of Nora's arm and pulled her inside. She grabbed a jacket off the coat rack, draped it over Nora's shoulders, guided her into the kitchen, and sat her down at the table.

"Now what are you talking about, Nora. Where is who?"

"Maggie! For God's sake, Kathy. Isn't she here?"

"Well, no. What are you saying, Nora?"

"She's saying she doesn't even know where her own daughter is, Mom."

Nora turned around. Becca was standing in the doorway. Her eyes were swollen as if she'd cried all night, and her lower lip quivered as she continued talking. "Maybe if you didn't drink so much, you would have noticed Maggie was gone."

"Becca, honey, what's gotten into you? I want you to apologize to Nora. Right now."

Kathy glared at Becca and then turned back to Nora. "I'm so sorry, Nora. Becca stayed home from school today. I'm not sure what's going on, but she's been crying all morning."

Kathy walked over and cradled her arm around Becca. Nora watched as she stroked Becca's hair and gave her a reassuring hug.

God, she couldn't remember what happened yesterday, and worse yet, she couldn't even remember the last time she talked to Maggie without screaming at her.

"Rebecca Marie, did you hear me?" Kathy demanded.

"Fine." Becca glared at Nora as she spoke. "I'm sorry if I had to stay home today because I couldn't stand the thought of walking to school without my best friend."

"Becca, what are you saying?" Kathy grabbed Becca by the shoulders.

"Please, Becca, talk." Nora's voice was filled with the fear building in the pit of her stomach. "Please, honey, will you sit with me and tell me what's going on?"

Becca glared at Nora. "No thank you. I don't want to sit with you."

"Becca!" Kathy almost shook her daughter. "Honey, please, stop this, now."

"It's all right, Kathy. She's angry with me. I don't blame her a bit. Can you tell me where Maggie went? Is she trying to go back to North Beach?"

Becca remained silent.

Please Becca, for God's sake. Tell me where Maggie went! I have to know. We have to find her. I have to call the police, call her Uncle Steve ..."

Nora's hands trembled and she started coughing and didn't know how much longer she could go without a drink.

"Your hands are shaking just like Aunt Cindy's did before she went into rehab."

"Now that's enough, young lady. You'd better tell Nora where Maggie is right now." Kathy's voice resonated Nora's urgency and it made her head throb.

Nora steadied her hands against her cheeks and looked at Becca.

"Kathy, Becca is right. I do need help. But we have to find Maggie first." Nora reached her hand out to Becca. "Please Becca. If you don't tell us where Maggie went, something horrible could happen to her."

Becca clamped her arms over her chest. "I'm sworn to secrecy. I can't tell you."

"But what if something happened to her, Becca? What if she got lost or some pervert picked her up?"

"She said she'd call me when she got there." Becca's whole body shook and her hands fell to her side. "But she hasn't called me yet. Oh Momma, I'm so afraid something horrible happened and I'll never see Maggie again."

Becca buried her face on her mother's shoulder. Kathy lifted Becca's head up and her voice became strong and insistent.

"You have to tell Nora where Maggie was going."

"She, she was go going to find Sha…Shane." Becca sobbed.

Kathy grabbed the phone. She handed it to Nora and Becca ran out of the room. Nora held the receiver tight as she punched in Steve's private number.

"Detective Steve Hanson."

"Steve, Maggie is missing."

"Nora?"

"Just listen. She ran away. She's headed for Shane's house. In Angel's Corner."

"What? Where? Why Shane?"

"Well if I knew that, I'd tell you damn it. Just do something, Steve."

Nora heard Becca walk over to the table and watched her sit down.

"Maggie took the bus, Nora." Becca avoided eye contact as she talked. "That letter from her dad told her to go to the willow tree. She thinks because Shane lives in the house with the willow tree, Shane can help her find her dad."

Nora reached over and squeezed Becca's hand then started talking into the phone. "Becca just said Maggie took the bus. She's going to find Shane."

"I told you, Nora, that man …"

"That man may be my only chance to see my daughter alive. Just stop, Steve, you know how I feel …"

"Okay, fine. I'll have an Amber Alert issued for Oregon and Washington. And we'll contact the police force in Angel's Corner. They can pay Shane a visit and see if Maggie tried to contact him."

"Steve, is that really necessary? Why don't I just call Shane?"

"We have to be safe, Nora, go by the book. Now ask Becca which bus Maggie was supposed to take."

Nora covered the receiver and turned to Becca.

"What bus did Maggie take?"

"She took the eleven thirty … Saturday morning."

"What? When did you say, Becca?"

"Saturday. She left on Saturday." Becca started crying again.

Nora took her hand away from the receiver and screamed at Steve. "Dear God in Heaven, Steve. She left on Saturday."

Nora's hand shook so hard she dropped the phone on the table. Kathy picked it up and started talking to Steve.

"Steve, it's Kathy. Becca said Maggie took the 11:30 on Saturday." Kathy bit her lip. "Yes, that's what I said. I'll stay here with Nora. Let us know when you find out anything at all."

Kathy hung the phone up and Nora stood abruptly.

"I have to go home, Kathy. Maggie might try to call."

Nora ran out the kitchen and front door. She raced back inside her house and checked the answering machine for any new messages. The grandfather clock chimed and Nora looked up. It was eleven o'clock. Maggie had been gone for almost 48 hours.

She picked up the phone and listened to the dial tone. Her hand shook so badly she had to place it back on the receiver. The longer she stared at the phone, the harder her body shook. Her knees finally buckled and she fell to the floor sobbing.

The shaking was almost too much. A good stiff drink would take it away and calm her until … until what? Until she had another drink?

"Dear God, please help me. If I take another drink I … I don't know what will happen. Please, holy Mother of God, I need your help. It's my drinking. My drinking has driven my only child away."

The sobs racked Nora's body and she could no longer feel the shakiness the hangovers always supplied. The only thing she could feel was the pain she should have allowed herself to feel when John died.

Nora heard the front door open but didn't look up. She could feel Kathy kneel down next to her.

"Nora, are you all right? Can I get you something?"

Kathy rubbed Nora's shoulder and Nora leaned into her hand.

"Ironic, isn't it? Me, the believer in God and miracles. And my life is so screwed up that even if there *is* a God, he wouldn't know how to put the pieces back together again."

Nora looked up at Kathy and she knew Kathy didn't know how to respond.

"You don't drink, do you, Kathy?" Nora asked. "In all the years I've known you, I've never seen you drink so much as a glass of wine."

"Well, no. I mean, my mom was drunk most of my childhood. And, well …"

"I never knew that."

"It's not something you tell people. It's one of those embarrassing family…"

"…secrets." Nora finished Kathy's sentence. "So you know what Maggie has been going through."

"Yes, in a way, I do."

Nora buried her head in her hands then looked up at Kathy.

"What's the one thing you wished your mom would have done for you when you were growing up, I mean, when she was drunk all the time?"

"I wished she would have dumped every bottle of vodka in that damn booze cabinet down the sink and never drank again."

Nora felt Kathy's hand tighten on her shoulder and when she looked at Kathy's face, she saw the pain from Kathy's childhood in her eyes.

"All right then." Nora took a deep breath before finishing. "Let's go do it."

"Do what?"

"Go through the damn booze cabinet and all the cupboards in the kitchen and clean them out and dump every bottle of alcohol in this house down the sink."

Kathy started to cry. "Really, Nora, really?"

Nora struggled to stand and Kathy reached down and pulled her to her feet. Nora grabbed hold of Kathy and gave her a quick hug.

"Yes, really, Kathy. I can't do this anymore. I've already lost John. I just can't allow myself to lose Maggie too."

THIRTY-THREE

―――――――――――

When John drifted back inside the tree house, Shane's painting was gone. The easel held a blank canvas and the paint brushes sat clean and ready to produce the next creation.

John sat on the stool perched in front of the canvas then reached down and touched a tube of hooker green. The container felt firm against his fingertips.

He wrapped his fingers around the tube and picked it up. It sat comfortably in his grasp. He took the lid off and squeezed a dab of paint on the palette.

His hand shook and he dropped the lid. It hit a small cup of walnut oil. John watched it tip over and its pungent contents splash down on the floor. He wanted to sweep up his mess but didn't want to waste his newfound strength.

John's heart pounded as he added blues and purples to cadmium yellow and mixed them with a palette knife. The feel of the paint mixing on the palette energized him. He picked up a brush and a sense of astonishment almost brought him to his knees.

Tears streamed down John's face as the colors transformed the canvas into a waterfall. He could feel the pounding water rush over each jagged rock he created and the sound of the falls echoed through the tree house with each new detail he placed on the canvas.

He painted until he could barely keep the brush in his hand then stood back to analyze his work.

The sprawling landscape he was trying to create barely filled the center of the canvas. The harder John tried to focus on his work, the weaker he felt.

He thought about Maggie and Shane and Nora as he mixed the colors on the palette to a deep muddy mass.

He took the color and scrawled two words on the bottom of the canvas. When he finished forming the final letter, the brush fell out of his hand, and he sank into the darkness.

* * *

It was almost noon when Shane felt the urge to paint. The morning breeze nipped his face as he walked down the winding trail to the willow.

He had built the tree house with anticipation of sharing it with his first child. He had carefully constructed each section, making sure the willow would remain strong and healthy. He'd even insulated the walls and added a large window that overlooked the valley below. He had hoped that, someday, he and his child would climb the tree together, set up their easels in the tree house, and find the inspiration to paint.

Shane stood under the willow and looked up at the ladder. A sudden chill urged him to move faster.

The smell of walnut oil greeted him as he climbed inside. He was surprised at first, trying to remember if he'd cleaned up after his last painting session. No, he reasoned, he wasn't senile just yet. He would never leave his supplies scattered around like this.

Several tubes of oil paint lay open on the floor, and his brushes and palette, still thick with fresh paint, sat on the stool facing the easel. The once-blank canvas held an image so small Shane had to squint to see it without his glasses. He rushed over, and it took a moment to decipher the picture.

A cascade of dark blue with long white sprays of foam thundered and crashed into a deep azure pond. It was lined with rocks blended with burnt sienna and black, each one speckled with moss green.

A fallen cedar, broken in two, sank into the middle of the pond. Each end fanned up out of the pond, and the spray from the waterfall cast the illusion of wings. Shane recognized the location immediately.

But the familiar handwriting that scrawled the small letters below the painting startled him the most.

find Maggie

Shane bolted down the ladder and raced back inside the house. He grabbed his cell phone and car keys off the kitchen counter. He started for the front door, and the phone rang.

Shane listened for the answering machine to announce the caller.

"Yeah, Shane, Jeb Reiner. The Rockaway Beach Police Department called and wanted to know if you knew a Maggie O'Brien or if she's called you in the last couple of days. Give me a call when you get this so I can set their mind at ease. And don't forget about our poker game on Thursday."

The recorder clicked off, and the phone rang again.

"Shane, it's Angie. If you're home, turn on the Channel 5 news. There's a special news report on. They're showing a picture of John's daughter, Maggie. She's missing ..."

Shane grabbed the telephone off the cradle and rushed into the living room.

"Angie, I'm turning on the TV right now."

He flipped the television on and listened to the news anchor.

"She was last seen in Rockaway Beach on Saturday, around ten o'clock in the morning."

Shane shuddered—that meant Maggie had been missing for over forty-eight hours. A news anchor on location at the Greyhound station appeared, interviewing the bus driver.

"There weren't any young girls on the bus that match Maggie O'Brien's description or photos. I took over the route just before the bus was scheduled to depart. You should contact the previous driver to see if he recognizes the young woman."

The picture switched back to the reporter in the studio.

"Apparently the bus driver originally assigned to the route was pulled off the bus and handcuffed just before the vehicle left the station. According to our sources, this man was arrested for a warrant in Washington State for alleged rape of a child. He's being held in the Rockaway Beach County jail pending arraignment."

Jesus. Shane cringed at the thought of a pedophile driving Maggie's bus. He prayed John's message meant there was still time. He had to move fast. Shane barked into the receiver. "Listen, Angie—"

"Wait a minute, Shane. Calm down. They aren't finished yet."

Shane trembled as he turned back to the TV.

"An Amber Alert has been issued for Oregon and the state of Washington. If you have seen Maggie O'Brien or have any information regarding her whereabouts, please call your local police agency or dial 911."

Shane flipped off the TV. "I have to do something, Angie."

"But what can you do, Shane?"

"I think I know why she left. At John's memorial, Maggie told me John wasn't dead. And I think I know why she feels that way. I need to help her, Angie."

He knew it wouldn't be long before the police were swarming Angel's Corner. He had to get to Maggie before they did and well … he wasn't sure what he'd do after that. It didn't matter, just as long as she was safe.

"Shane, what on earth are you talking about? I don't understand."

"Angie, just listen up. I'm certain Maggie's up at Angel Falls. Don't ask me a bunch of questions right now, please. But I'll need your help."

Shane waited for Angie's response. He heard her take a deep breath before speaking.

"All right, Shane. But if you find her and don't go to the police, you'll be harboring a runaway."

"I know that, Angie. And I'll take full responsibility. I just know what she's running from. And I need to help her. She's my—"

"Granddaughter. And my great-niece. What do you want me to do?"

"I'll head to Angel Falls and search there."

"I don't understand. Why Angel Falls?"

"It's a hunch. I don't have time to explain right now."

There was a pause before Angie spoke again.

"All right then. Tell me what you want me to do."

"Go down to Angel's Corner and look everywhere. And I mean everywhere. Take your cell phone with you."

Shane looked at his watch.

"It's twelve fifteen. Check back with me in an hour. If you find Maggie, tell her you're my sister. I just pray to God she remembers me from John's funeral."

"And then what am I supposed to do?"

"Take her to my house."

Shane hung up abruptly. He threw the phone on the coffee table, and headed out to the garage. He opened the car door and stopped. Food. Maggie will need food.

Shane ran back inside and came out with another bag and threw it in the trunk. He jumped in the car and headed down the driveway.

The logging roads leading to Angel Falls were full of potholes. The final road leading to the waterfall was barricaded. There was no way Shane could fit his car between the small space on the side of the road and the ditch. He wondered when the last time another human being had come this far.

Everything looked so different now. The last time Shane had set foot near Angel Falls was right after he had returned from Vietnam. He had trampled the woods hoping the forest and a bottle of Jack Daniels would swallow him up and end his pain.

Shane opened the trunk and pulled out a floodlight. He stuck the bag of snacks and large water bottle in his backpack and secured it behind him. He rolled several old blankets together, tied them with twine, and looped them over his shoulder. He looked at his watch. It was twelve forty-five. Angie would be calling in a thirty minutes, and he hoped she was making more progress than he was.

He opened his cell to check for any calls. Shit. No bars—no coverage.

The crisp October breeze burned Shane's cheeks as he walked away from his car. He'd have to make the rest of the trip on foot. When he pictured Maggie running on the overgrown trail, the thought of her out here alone made him quicken his pace.

The progress he made on his uphill climb seemed nonexistent. The side trail he'd taken was much steeper than he remembered. He hoped he was on the right path.

The clouds covered the sun, and a streak of lightning ravaged the trees and brought life to the ferns lining his route. He knew what a fall storm could do to the woods. It was going to get really dark. If he didn't turn around soon, he could easily be stuck in the forest.

Small pellets of hail fell out of the sky as he sat down on a stump. He flipped open his cell again, and the bars flickered. He punched in Angie's number and waited for a ring on the other end. Nothing.

The trails were muddy, and he was thirsty. When he opened his water bottle, he heard a loud rustling noise and then breaking branches.

Shane froze as a black bear emerged from the bushes several hundred feet up the trail in front of him.

THIRTY-FOUR

Maggie took shelter under a fallen tree. Thunder shook the ground so hard the earth seemed to move beneath her. Everything looked the same and different all at once, and she knew she was lost.

She opened her backpack and pulled out her only dry pair of jeans. They weren't as warm as the flannel-lined pants she was wearing, but those were soaked now, and she was cold and shaking so hard she'd do anything to get warm.

She pulled her jeans off and rubbed the stinging rash that had formed in clumps on her thighs. Her hands were so cold when she touched her legs she cringed as she pulled on her jeans. She checked the socks tied to her backpack. They were still wet. She would have to hurry if she was ever going to be warm again.

Maggie threw her flannel jeans underneath a stump. They were too wet to go back inside her backpack. She couldn't risk drenching her remaining clothes. She rubbed her hands together, blew on her fingers, and then threw her backpack over her shoulders and started walking.

She ducked out from under a tree and looked around. Everything behind her looked dark and gloomy. She glanced to her left and saw an opening in the trees. Maybe there was a house built way back here. Maybe someone would be home and would let her use the phone, and she could call her mother.

Even seeing her mother sounded good. All she wanted to do was go home. Crawl under the warm feather comforter on her bed. Feel safe.

Maggie inched her way up over the fallen trees and kept her focus on the clearing ahead. She could smell hamburgers cooking and French fries and even fresh coffee.

She sprinted to a gravel road and then took off running. She hit the backside of a parking lot and the feel of solid pavement almost made her cry. Finally, solid ground, real food, dry clothes and—

A man grabbed her shoulder and slammed her against the side of the building.

"It can get awfully cold sleeping in the woods at night without your sleeping bag, Miss Maggie O'Brien."

It was him. And he was standing there staring at her with his foul mouth hanging open and her sleeping bag unraveled and clamped under his arm.

"How'd you know my name?" Weakness took over, and all Maggie could do was stand there and stare at him.

"Everyone in every county in Washington, Oregon, and California knows who you are. Except your hair's different than the picture they're flashing all over TV. I like it better ... makes you look, well, not so recognizable."

The truck driver reached over and stroked the side of Maggie's face, and she shivered.

"Still cold, sweet thing? Don't you worry. I'll keep you warm. That's what I'm all about, keeping pretty little things like you warm."

He reached over to grab Maggie's shoulder, and she backed away.

"Well, my mom's waiting for me. I'm going inside this Dairy Queen right now to see her, so if you'll excuse me ..."

Maggie turned around and dove behind a dumpster at the edge of the lot and thought she heard the man laugh.

She grabbed a piece of old lumber lying on the ground and positioned it like a sword in front of her. She heard police sirens screaming down the road and sobbed a sigh of relief. Finally, Mom had done something right for a change.

She waited for what felt like an hour and then used the piece of wood as a shield as she peered around the side of the dumpster.

Maggie spotted his big rig in the back of the lot. There was no way she could head out that way. She'd have to go around the side of the building through the blackberry bushes and then down to the road where the police would be waiting for her.

She dropped the wood and scanned the back of the building one more time. She scrambled a few feet down the blackberry-infested hill and realized she'd left her backpack next to the dumpster. When she turned around and strained to reach it, the truck driver reached down and grabbed her hand.

He pulled her up so fast she didn't have time to scream.

"Now you didn't think I'd leave you here wet and cold and all by yourself, did you?"

Maggie opened her mouth and the man clamped his hand over her face as he wrapped her sleeping bag around her.

She struggled and bit his hand. He hit her hard on the side of the head.

"Keep your fucking mouth shut, or I'll kill you right here."

He clenched her face with his hand and pressed his nose against her cheek.

"Now keep quiet, or I'll kill your mother too."

He whipped the bag off and hit Maggie so hard she fell backward on to the ground. The man plunged the sleeping bag over her head and everything went dark. Maggie could feel the zipper pressing into her back as she flew into the air. The bag muffled her weak screams.

The smell of sweat and stale body odor filled the inside of her sleeping bag, and Maggie gagged. Her body bounced against his back as he ran, and she felt dizzy as he raced her away in the darkness.

THIRTY-FIVE

Nora was huddled next to Steve when John drifted into the living room. He wanted to console her and tell her everything would be fine now. Shane was headed for Angel Falls. He would find Maggie. And finally, Nora's life would be normal. Shane would make sure of it.

John floated over to the television. The lightness in his body made it difficult to stay in one place. He heard Nora let out a sob as Steve turned up the volume on the set.

"It's been over forty-eight hours since fifteen-year-old Maggie O'Brien disappeared. The Rockaway Beach police department hasn't released any new information on the case."

The woman newscaster gave the audience a somber smile. "Our hearts go out to Maggie's family. We understand Maggie lost her father just three months ago. What a huge blow." She paused and then continued talking. "Please take a look at the photograph of Maggie O'Brien again. If anyone has any information about her whereabouts, please call 911."

John wanted to tell the woman Maggie was just fine and that it wouldn't be long before she and Shane united. John knew it because he felt so weak. It had to mean it was just minutes before Maggie was safe in Shane's care.

Nora was saying something to Steve when her face suddenly contorted, and Maggie's scream pierced the room.

John watched the windows ripple as flames shot out the back of the TV. Nora and Steve sat motionless, as if nothing had happened.

John heard the scream again and the sudden roar of the ocean shattered the living room window. The waves surged into the room, and all he could see was Maggie struggling against the angry sea screaming, "Dad! Daddy! Dad!"

Nora looked over at the window and turned back to Steve.

"Did you hear something?"

Steve took her hand and held it tight. "No, nothing. Are you all right?"

"It was like the ocean rushed in through the window and disappeared. Oh God, Steve, am I hallucinating?"

Steve pulled Nora close to him and wrapped the afghan around her shoulders.

"You're exhausted, Nora. You were up most of last night."

"Am I? Do you think I'm going …"

"I think you're going to collapse from exhaustion if you don't get some sleep."

Nora looked out the living room window. A faint hint of light outlined the roof on the house across the street. She watched the sky lighten and the horizon turn a blood red as the sun beat against the trees.

"There's something wrong, Steve. Look at the sky. It's turning red—like blood."

"You're exhausted, Nora. The sky isn't red, it's pinkish blue. The rain stopped."

"Then it's going to be really cold tonight, Steve. And what if Maggie isn't … they don't …"

Steve hugged Nora close to him. "They *will* find her before nightfall."

He wrapped the afghan tightly around Nora. "You need rest now, Nora. Please, just lie down on the couch and get some sleep."

* * *

John struggled to keep his balance. The air was thick, the sky molten black. He steadied himself against a dumpster and watched a truck driver throw a sleeping bag inside the back of a trailer. The man jumped inside and slammed the door shut.

Instinctively, John bolted toward the rear of the trailer and tried to get inside. He pushed forward, and each time he did, he fell backward, and the pavement turned to liquid.

He heard a whimper in the back of the truck. And then a cry and his daughter's voice.

"Please, mister, don't hurt me."

John struggled as the pavement hardened around him. Maggie cried again, and the sound of her voice drove him upward, and he flew inside the trailer.

Maggie stood against the back wall, her hands glued over her eyes as her legs buckled and she slid to the floor.

John's hands turned to stone and the blood gushed through every nonexistent vein in his body. He rushed over and wedged himself between Maggie and the truck driver.

STOP, RIGHT NOW.

When John screamed at the man, his saliva spewed all over the truck driver's face.

John watched the expression on the man's face turn from perversion to panic. The veins on the side of John's neck bulged, and his hands felt as if they were on fire. He lunged his head forward and connected to the man's forehead with a thud.

"What the fuck? Jesus, girl, are you possessed?"

The man let go of Maggie's shoulders and stepped away from her. John turned and looked back at his daughter. Maggie's hands were clasped over her mouth and she remained frozen against the back wall of the trailer.

John turned and screamed in the driver's ear.

GET AWAY FROM MY DAUGHTER!

He watched the fury of his words spiral down the man's eardrum, and the lecher winced with pain.

The man looked up. His face turned so white that the dirt caked in the creases around his nose turned thick, black, and crusty.

John grabbed hold of the man's neck with both hands. Cold sweat dripped down the truck driver's collar, and John clamped down with a vengeance.

"Let go of me, you little freak!"

The man looked at Maggie again, and John squeezed harder and harder until warm blood oozed around his fingers.

The man coiled backward, and John kicked him to the ground and then flew to the front of the trailer and unhooked the door. The door snapped upward and John screamed at Maggie. "Run, Maggie, run!"

John heard his voice echo inside the empty trailer and Maggie uncovered her mouth.

"I can hear you, Dad. Where are you?"

"RUN, MAGGIE, RUN!"

Maggie started to sob. John rushed over to the truck driver and wrapped his hands around his neck.

"Somebody help me … this kid's a fucking witch!"

The man tried to loosen John's invisible grip and clutched at the gash on his neck where his necklace dug into his skin.

"NOW, Maggie, GO!" John's voice exploded inside the trailer again and sent Maggie bolting out the rear doors.

The truck driver was sobbing. John let go of his neck and loomed over him.

"If you didn't believe in ghosts before, you will now."

John whirled around, and his rage sent the garbage in the back of the truck spinning.

"You're done, you son of a bitch!" John's words shot out and created a violent wind, and the air circled around inside the trailer, grabbing every piece of garbage and scrap of paper in its path and swirled it at the pervert, pummeling him with the debris.

The man swung at the shooting cans and stumbled backward, out the trailer door and onto the pavement. He jumped to his feet, and John blended into the man's body as he raced into the cab.

"Get the fuck out of me. What the hell is going on?"

The trucker jammed the keys into the ignition, and the big rig burst to life.

John grabbed a rope sitting next to him on the seat. The truck driver watched the rope whip the air. He buckled over the steering wheel, sobbing like a baby.

"I believe in ghosts … I believe in ghosts …," he muttered through the snot running down his lips.

John tied the man's hands securely to the steering wheel then slammed the truck into gear. He pressed his foot on the gas, and the trucker screamed as the vehicle careened across the parking lot and into the street.

THIRTY-SIX

Maggie ran in circles around the back parking lot and then hid behind the dumpster. Her heart beat so fast her eyes felt like they were bulging out of her sockets.

Was it? Could it have been?

She hid behind the dumpster and tried to catch her breath. Her knees locked every time she tried to sit down. When she leaned forward, the words echoed through her mind.

RUN, MAGGIE, RUN!

Of course it was. It had to be. She'd recognize her dad's voice anywhere.

She had to go back. Make sure he was okay. Why didn't he come with her? She inched her way around the dumpster. She heard the truck's engine roar and ran to the front of the building. A group of kids stood under the Dairy Queen sign. They were laughing and pointing in the truck's direction.

She wanted to scream at them, tell them it wasn't funny. That man had tried to kill her.

But all she could do was run past them down the driveway and into the street. A horn honked, and Maggie heard brakes screeching. She covered her ears and collapsed in the middle of the street.

A car door opened, and Maggie felt someone touch her shoulder.

"Are you all right?"

Maggie swung her arms, and when she looked up, a kind face looked down at her. Maggie tried to talk but couldn't find the right words to say.

"Oh honey, I'm so sorry. I scared you. But I didn't even see you. Let me give you a ride home."

The woman helped Maggie into the front seat of the car and then hurried over to the drivers' side. Maggie heard a loud rumbling and looked back at the Dairy Queen. The group of kids started screaming and waving their arms in their direction. Then suddenly, the truck barreled out of the parking lot and almost hit a telephone pole.

The woman jumped into the car and floored it. They swerved to the right and landed on the sidewalk.

The trucker honked, and the rig screamed by. It swayed back and forth as it sped toward the bridge. Just when Maggie thought he was going to cross over, the semi jerked to the right and careened into the river.

Maggie struggled to unbuckle her seat belt. She turned and screamed at the woman next to her.

"I have to get out of here. I need to call my mom ..."

The woman reached over and rested her hand on Maggie's shoulder. The compassion on her face and the warmth of the car made Maggie feel weak. All she could do was lean her head back against the seat.

"Oh honey, I know you're scared. But you're safe now. I promise."

Police sirens screamed past them, and the woman reached over and made sure Maggie's seat belt was secured.

Tears spilled down Maggie's face. She was grateful for the woman's kindness and wanted to throw her arms around her neck, hug her until her weary body stopped shaking.

The woman reached into the glove compartment and pulled out a handful of napkins and handed them to Maggie.

"Your face—you have a bruise. What happened? Are you okay?"

Maggie touched the side of her face where the trucker had slapped her. She wanted to tell her what had happened. But if she started to talk, she'd never stop. She had to leave. Find her father.

"I'm okay. It's a long story. And I—well, I left home on Saturday, and I'm looking for someone and—"

"You must be Maggie."

"What? Well, yes." Maggie blew her nose. "How do you know who I am?"

"I recognized your eyes." The woman told her. "Same color as your father's."

Maggie felt her heart race. She leaned over and took hold of the woman's hand.

"You know my father?"

"Yes, honey. I knew your father. I'm your … I'm related to Shane."

"You know Shane?" Maggie practically jumped into the woman's arms.

"Then you remember him?" The woman smiled as she spoke.

"Of course I do. That's why I'm here." Maggie breathed a sigh of relief. "How do you know him?"

"Well, young lady, Shane is my younger brother."

Maggie held her breath and hoped she'd heard the woman correctly.

"You're Shane's sister?" she said out loud.

"Yes, I am, Maggie. My name is Angie. And Shane and I have been very worried about you."

A patrol car pulled up behind Angie's car, and Maggie watched the officer step out of the vehicle.

"Please, Angie. Don't tell him who I am. I have to talk to Shane. I think he can help me find my father. Please, will you help me?"

The officer tapped on the driver-side window. Angie lowered it without responding. Maggie thought about jumping out of the car. She was so afraid if she ran away again, she'd meet up with another weirdo and …

"Angela O'Shanahan, what in the world are you doing on the sidewalk?"

Maggie watched the policeman give Angie a familiar grin.

"Well, Jeb, that trucker tried to run us over before he plunged into Devil's River. Damn near took out the bridge."

"I'm so sorry, Angie. You must be terrified."

"My hands were shaking so bad I landed right here. Is the man going to be all right?"

"Officers are responding now. Looks as if his cab is nose down in the river."

"Oh good God …"

"Don't be worrying about that son of a B. You just get yourself home, Angela O'Shanahan."

Angie looked over at Maggie and winked and then turned back to the police officer. He peered into the car. When Maggie smiled at him, he squinted his eyes and drew his lips into a thin line.

Maggie reached down on the floor like she was trying to find something in her backpack. She froze. Her backpack. She'd left it next to the dumpster.

"And who is this young person you have with you?"

Maggie's legs started shaking, and her stomach turned flip-flops. She held her breath and waited for Angie's answer.

"You remember Linda, don't you, Jeb? This is her husband's cousin's daughter … Kimberly. She supposedly was going to her friend's house. Wound up right here at the Dairy Queen instead."

Maggie leaned back in the seat and pretended like she was pouting.

Jeb shook his head and leaned in closer to Angie. Maggie knew he was trying to get a better look. "Just what her momma told her *not* to do. Kids," Jeb muttered as he stood up.

"That's right, Jeb. What's a parent supposed to do?" Maggie could hear the relief in Angie's voice.

Jeb leaned back down and, this time, pushed his head all the way inside the window.

"Listen here, young lady. There's a two-state Amber Alert in effect right now for a runaway from Rockaway Beach. You go home right now, and do what your mother tells you to do. God only knows if that poor kid will be dead or alive when she's finally found."

Maggie crossed her hands over her chest and faked a huge sigh.

"Yes sir," she mumbled.

"All right then." Jeb pulled his head back out of the window and lowered his voice. "You have a good afternoon, Angie."

He started to walk away and then came back and leaned close to Angie.

"I've been looking for that brother of yours."

"Me too. Darn guy was supposed to meet me for lunch. Stood me up for sure."

"Figures. I wouldn't have, you know …"

Maggie could see Jeb squeeze Angie's shoulder out of the corner of her eye. Angie's cheeks flushed when she replied.

"Shane called me from his cell and apologized. He's making me dinner tonight to make up for it. I'll tell him to call you."

"All right then. I won't keep you."

Jeb walked back to the patrol car, and Angie navigated her car off the curb and slowly drove away.

Angie didn't say anything until they were on the highway. Maggie was afraid to open the conversation after Angie had rescued her for a second time.

"Nice acting job, kid." She smiled at Maggie.

"Angie, please." Maggie reached for Angie's hand. "I left my backpack behind the Dairy Queen. I have to get it. It has, well, my whole life is in there."

Angie squeezed Maggie's hand and then clicked her left blinker on. "No problem, hon. We'll go pick it up right now."

"And then we're going to Shane's house?"

Angie looked troubled when she answered. "He was supposed to call me, but I haven't heard from him."

"But you just told that policeman you talked to him on the phone."

"I know, Maggie. I had to tell him something."

"Well, where is he then?"

"He headed up to Angel Falls to find you."

"But it's going to be dark soon. And I'm here now. Can't you call him?"

Angie reached over and patted Maggie's leg.

"I'll tell you what, Maggie. Let's go get your backpack and then drive up to his house. Maybe he's sitting there right now, waiting for us."

* * *

The bear swatted the ground, chomped its teeth, and rushed several feet forward and then stopped suddenly and stood on its hind legs.

Shane moved gradually to a standing position. He guessed the bear was a sow with cubs close by. He maintained eye contact with her and spoke in a soft, calm voice.

"Hey there, mamma. No worries with me. I know how much those babies mean to you."

He walked backward and kept his eyes locked on her and started singing.

"Bye baby bunting ... this man isn't hunting ..."

Her cubs could be just about anywhere. Shane knew he had to maintain his distance and knew if he was too close to her babies, well ...

The brush trembled several yards in front of Shane and two cubs scampered up the trail as if he weren't there. The mother stood taller, her lips curled as she let out a fierce growl. The cubs scooted up the trail and cowered behind her.

Mama bear turned and looked at Shane, her black beady eyes enforcing her dominance as she slowly eased back on all fours. He watched her clean each cub behind the ears. She turned and growled one last time before they disappeared in the underbrush.

Shane walked backward down the trail and listened until he could no longer hear any rustling in the bushes and then turned and raced back down the overgrown trail.

The rain stopped, and the clouds were moving rapidly to the east. He knew there was no way he could make it up to the waterfall. Not with active wildlife stalking the woods. And the hailstorm had soaked his clothes through to his skin.

Maybe John's painting didn't mean Angel Falls. Maybe it meant Little Multnomah ... the climb up to that fall was much easier. And God knows the trek up to Angel Falls was just about impossible.

He turned his floodlight on and raced back to his car. Once he had cell service again, he'd call Angie. If she hadn't found Maggie yet, he'd call the state patrol.

Yeah, right. Call the state patrol and tell them your recently deceased son left a picture of a waterfall and a message to find his daughter—your granddaughter—the little girl every cop in two states is looking for.

Shane jumped in his car and started the engine. He drove with his cell phone in one hand, watching the bars flicker up and down. He stopped the car when the service returned and redialed Angie's number.

She picked up on the first ring.

"Thank God you're safe, Shane."

"Have you—"

"She's with me, Shane. We're at your house. She wanted to see the willow and the tree house. She's down there right now."

"Is she—"

"She's fine. A bit tired and scared. Shane ..." Angie hesitated.

"What? Are the police there? You didn't call them, did you?"

"No, no, nothing like that. It's just that ... well, she ran away so she could find you."

Relief and disbelief flooded Shane, and he waited a minute before he could answer.

"Does she know?"

"I don't think so. But she thinks you can help her find John."

"She's right, Angie. I think I can help her. I'll be home as soon as I can."

Shane closed his cell phone and stepped on the gas, driving as fast as the abandoned road allowed.

THIRTY-SEVEN

———————————

Maggie rounded the corner of Shane's house and headed down the path leading into the backyard. When she turned the corner, the willow tree came into full view.

The low hanging branches danced over the ground at the tree's base. The sun setting above the willow turned its top spindles into gold. Maggie wished she could mount a canvas on her easel right where she stood and capture this first glimpse with paint so she could remember it forever.

Maggie tried not to run as she moved further down the path. When she reached the willow, she immersed herself in its spindly branches.

She dropped her backpack on the ground and swayed with the cool fall breeze. She closed her eyes and pretended the limbs were feather boas. She twisted and turned around the tree's perimeter, wrapping the thin vines around her. The leaves tickled her skin and made her giggle as she waltzed beneath them.

Maggie threw her arms up and leaped just the way a ballerina jumps when lifted into the air. The wind whispered through her hair, and she felt like a feather as she swirled back down to earth. But when her feet connected to the ground, she stumbled, shrieked and rolled down a hill.

* * *

When Shane pulled into the driveway, Angie was waiting on the front porch.

"Where's Maggie?"

"She's out back. Surprisingly calm for all she's been through. Then to top it off, a big rig tried to run me off the road and ended up in Devil's River."

"Sounds like a good place for the bastard. But Maggie's safe, right?"

"Yes, she's fine. Do you want me to stay?"

"No, I can handle it from here."

Shane started to leave but then turned back to his sister.

"You won't tell anyone yet?"

"Of course I won't. But you can expect a visit from Jeb Reiner any time now. I saw him, and he's looking for you."

"Jeb called a few minutes ago. Decided it was a waste of his time to drive all the way out here. Thank God he can't see my poker face over the phone."

Angie laughed. "Now go take care of your granddaughter."

Shane smiled, waved her off to her car, and then hurried into the backyard, down the path, and under the willow's branches.

The bushes rustled behind the limbs in front of him. He stopped for a moment and heard a branch snap and then a thud.

"Shit. Ouch …"

The words sounded half-hurt and half-angry. Shane took several steps forward. A young girl emerged from behind the bushes, cradling her left hand. He could see blood trickling between her fingers, and her familiar face was twisted with pain.

"Margaret, Maggie? Is that you?"

"Shane? I had to find you. And I wanted to make sure the willow tree was back here. My dad promised to take me here. And then I got a letter from him last week, and he said for me to climb the willow tree. And, well, I wanted to make sure this is the exact willow he was talking about."

"All right, Maggie, I'm glad you're here. Come now; let's go inside the house, and I'll bandage that hand of yours." Shane picked up Maggie's backpack, and she followed him up the trail to the house.

It had been just over three months since he'd seen her last. Her hair was cut short on top and splotched with some sort of black dye. If he didn't know better, Maggie had turned Goth, but she still had an edge of sweetness. She actually looked taller, and the innocence in her brown eyes was replaced with a determination that should have belonged to someone much older.

"Now let's go inside and take care of that hand of yours." Shane led the way back to the house and into the bathroom.

"Thanks. Your sister, Angie, brought me here. She practically saved my life. I haven't seen you since my father disappeared."

"I was at your father's funeral, Maggie. The funeral, do you remember that?"

"Of course I do. It was September 6, 2006. But he isn't really dead; I'm sure of it. There wasn't even a casket. Don't you remember when I saw you that day?"

Shane took a deep breath as he listened. No casket, of course. It was a memorial service.

"Maggie, honey, your mother thought the memorial—"

"I know that whole story, Shane. I don't want to hear it again. My mom's a liar. I don't know how she ever got Dad to take off his necklace, but she did. It doesn't matter now. I just need to find him."

Shane took a clean cloth out of the bathroom cabinet and doused it with rubbing alcohol. Maggie jumped as he dabbed it on the minor cut in her arm.

"I'm sorry, Maggie. I know this hurts. This will only take a minute."

He watched the pain on her face disappear, and the stony cold look that replaced it worried him.

"It's okay if it hurts, Maggie."

"I'm fine. Really, I'm fine."

Shane watched the determination fade, and her eyes watered as she reached over and gave his hand a tight squeeze.

"I'm fifteen now. Did you know that?"

"Yes, I knew that."

He watched Maggie take a deep breath, and when she looked up at him again, he saw her father in her eyes and her grandmother in the way her lopsided smile tried to suppress her tears.

"Will you help me, Shane? I need to find my dad. And I can't tell anyone. Mom says I'm crazy, and everyone else, even my best friend, Becca, is beginning to think so, too." Maggie let out a big sigh and dropped her head on the edge of the sink. "I just have to find out what really happened. I need to know. Can you? Will you?"

He reached over and pulled Maggie close to him. "Of course I'll help you make sense of it, Maggie. Of course I will."

Maggie surrendered to the security in Shane's arms. It was almost like hugging Dad again. She closed her eyes, and this time, she saw her father's face.

Maggie buried her head in Shane's shoulder and allowed the grief to take over. The real tears she had avoided for so long turned into uncontrollable sobs. The tears melted the fear Maggie carried deep inside. Relief calmed her, and she moved out of Shane's arms.

"Would you like some warm clothes to change into?"

"Sure, but, well, I don't think we're the same size." Maggie smiled sheepishly at him.

"You're right about that. But I think I have something that might fit you."

Shane disappeared and returned with a sweatsuit, wool socks, and a pair of slippers.

"Where'd you get these?"

"Belonged to Angie."

"Wow. That must have been a long time ago. They're really small."

Shane chuckled. "Yes, it was. They've been in the dresser for years."

"No wonder they smell like mothballs." Maggie was sorry as soon as the words came out of her mouth. "But they're great. I'm freezing, and they feel warm."

Maggie shut the bathroom door and changed and then returned to the hall.

"I want to talk now," Maggie told Shane.

"All right, Maggie. Let's go into the kitchen."

Shane offered his hand, and Maggie held it tight. "Can we sit at the kitchen table, Shane? That's where Dad and I had our best talks."

"Of course we can."

Shane dropped Maggie's backpack on the floor. She walked to the window and looked outside. A hummingbird hovered next to a feeder hanging outside the kitchen window. She could almost hear the hum from its teeny wings. It landed on the feeder and tilted its head to one side and looked at Maggie before flying away.

"Hummingbirds don't generally show up this time of year," Shane told her as he sat down at the table.

"Then why do you think it's here?"

"Well, Native American folk say the hummingbird is a symbol of getting to the heart of a matter. Makes sense the little fellah would stop by right now."

Maggie looked over at Shane and watched him tilt his head to one side and smile.

"My Dad does that exact same thing."

"What, Maggie?"

"Tilts his head that way just before he smiles."

She studied Shane's face and realized that without a beard, he looked just as her father would look when he got older.

"You're related to my dad, aren't you?"

"Yes, Maggie, I am."

Maggie stared into Shane's eyes and remembered their eerie counter at the funeral.

"You look like he'd look if he got really old."

She watched Shane try not to smile.

"I didn't mean you're old, just well …"

"Older than your father was."

"Yes, that's what I meant …" Shane's usage of past tense bothered her, and she stiffened in her chair. "Older than he *is*."

Shane didn't respond right away. Maggie watched him walk over to the kitchen counter and make a fresh pot of coffee. He pulled two coffee mugs out of the cupboard and then turned and faced her.

"How about a cup of hot chocolate?"

"That would be great."

"Would you like something to eat? I bet you're starving."

Maggie realized her stomach hadn't growled once since she had arrived at Shane's house.

"Wow, my stomach must have shrunk. I don't even feel hungry right now."

"Let me know if you get hungry. I have plenty of food."

Shane took two packets of instant cocoa out of the cupboard and dumped them both into a single mug. He mixed it with hot water from the dispenser on the sink. A generous splash of cream and huge handful of marshmallows completed Maggie's drink. He poured a cup of coffee and brought both mugs over to the kitchen table.

Maggie bobbed the marshmallows with her fingers before taking several sips. She wrapped her hands around the cup and allowed it to warm her fingers before she started talking.

"He wasn't feeling well the day before. And Mom, well, she just seemed so mad about something. Whenever Dad got in one of his moods, Mom changed, too."

Maggie thought about the distant look on her father's face and the fear in her mother's voice that day.

"I just knew I should do something. So I snuck into the back of his pickup. I decided if I was at the ocean and he got ... well, he needed something, I could help Uncle Steve. Because, well, Uncle Steve just doesn't know how Dad can get sometimes."

The distant roar of the ocean crept into the kitchen. Maggie took a big drink, hoping the warm cocoa would stop the crashing waves.

"Maggie, honey, if you don't want to—"

"I do want to, Shane; I want to tell you what happened."

She dipped the cup just enough to fill her mouth with melted marshmallows and then took another swallow of cocoa and set the mug down on the table. The cocoa warmed her insides, and a relaxed feeling spread over her.

"When I woke up in the back of his pickup, he was already gone. So I ran down to the beach. I saw him just sort of floating on a huge wave."

Maggie looked outside, and the hummingbird was perched on the feeder again. It sat motionless, as if it were waiting for her to finish her story.

"I ran in after him, and the farther I went into the waves, the stronger the current was, and all of a sudden, I was pulled under."

Shane reached over and took hold of Maggie's hand. She placed her other hand on top of his and squeezed.

"Then I saw him again. We were way deep in the water, and he had this peaceful look on his face. I tried to scream at him, but when I opened my mouth, I think I sucked in half the ocean."

This time, Maggie knew she could tell Shane the entire story, that he would believe her and not make her feel crazy as everyone else tried to do.

"I remember how we floated up and out of the water. His arms felt like they always did when he hugged me. But lighter and softer this time. It was like … we were flying, really, up out of those horrible waves and bubbles. And then the next thing I remember I was lying there in the wet sand and coughing up salt water. And Dad, well, he was gone."

Shane stood up, left for a moment, and came back with a handful of tissues. Maggie took one and blew her nose.

"Dad wrote me a letter. I guess he must have lost it in the sand before he went into the water. Henry—he's one of the old guys who found me—he brought it to me right before I ran … left Rockaway Beach. I want you to read it."

Maggie reached down and opened her backpack. She pulled the paintbrushes out of the box and rested them on the table.

"Where did you get that wood case, Maggie?"

"It belonged to my great-grandpa. Dad promised it to me. And the brushes were in the case with Dad's letter."

Shane let out a deep, long sigh.

"What's the matter, Shane?"

"Nothing, I just recognized the case, that's all."

"You look upset. The case upsets you? Or is it the brushes? Are you upset about the brushes?" Maggie's hand shook as she held them tight in her hand.

"No, of course not. I'm fine. Really."

Maggie reached inside the case and pulled out the letter. She studied Shane's face before handing it to him.

"Are you sure you want me to read it?" he asked.

"Yes, I'm positive."

Maggie watched him read, and when he was done, he folded the letter and laid it on the table.

She waited for him to talk. When he didn't say anything, she blurted out the questions she could never verbalize before.

"Do you believe in ghosts?"

"Well, what do you mean?"

"Becca's Aunt Ruth says she can see dead people. And well, do you believe that once we're dead we still hang around?"

"I believe that sometimes a person's spirit will stay here for a while after he or she they physically dies."

"So you believe in spirits then?"

"Yes, Maggie, I do believe in spirits."

"Do you believe my dad knew he was going to die?"

Shane's face looked sad as he talked. "I know your father was ill, Maggie. And yes, I believe he knew he was going to die."

"Do you think he committed suicide?"

Shane struggled to respond.

"You don't have to say anything if you don't want to."

Shane smiled and took a deep breath before he answered.

"Sometimes, when people are sick, they feel death will end their pain. That pain is buried so deep inside they just can't do anything to change it. Your father was depressed—"

"He has schizoaffective bipolar disorder, to be exact. That and post-traumatic stress from the Gulf War."

"Well. You certainly know more about this than I thought you would."

"Mom never told me what was going on. So I always listened when she talked on the phone." Maggie paused. "And, well, at my house, the only way I ever knew what was really going on was by listening in on phone conversations. That and reading the doctor reports in the file cabinet when Mom was at work."

Maggie's eyes welled up, and she grabbed a tissue.

"I hate it when I'm treated like a kid. I'm a lot smarter than people give me credit for, you know."

"Of course you are, Maggie—you're an extremely bright young lady."

She blew her nose again and picked up her father's letter.

"Do you think my dad is dead?"

Maggie didn't look at Shane this time. She knew he was the one person who wouldn't lie to her, and she didn't want to see his face when he answered.

"Yes, Maggie, I believe your father died."

Silence softened the atmosphere in the kitchen, allowing Maggie finally to hear the truth and Shane to feel his own, deep sorrow.

"Do you believe Dad carried me out of the water?"

"Yes, Maggie, I absolutely believe your father's spirit stayed long enough in his body to save you. And I believe his spirit is still here, doing his best to protect you as we speak."

Maggie walked over to the window and stared outside as she fidgeted with her hair. "I saw him at his funeral." Maggie turned around and faced Shane. Her lower lip trembled as she talked. "He was standing right in front of you. That's why I called you Dad." Maggie sniffled and wiped a tear out of the corner of her eye. "I didn't tell anyone because I thought it was a sign."

"What kind of a sign, Maggie?"

"That he was still here."

Maggie choked back a sob. Her body was trembling so hard she had to steady herself against the window sill.

"I thought if I just loved him hard enough, it would bring him back to life."

Shane cradled Maggie in his arms and held her until she stopped shaking.

"And then I saw him again. But I didn't really *see* him. I felt him when that truck driver was going to hurt me in the back of his trailer."

"What?"

The alarm in Shane's voice startled Maggie. "I'm okay, really. That guy ended up cab down in the river."

"Good place for the—"

"Son of a B." Maggie giggled and continued talking. "That's what that cop friend of Angie's called him."

Maggie sat for a moment and studied Shane's warm expression.

"Go ahead, Maggie. I'm listening."

"And then Dad saved me again, but this time, well, I knew it was his spirit."

"Then what happened, Maggie?"

"Dad told me to run. I heard his voice inside my head. The truck driver kept falling backward like someone was hitting him. He called me a witch at the same time. I have no idea how Dad pulled that one off." Maggie laughed nervously. "And that truck driver, what a retard – like a fifteen-year-old girl could punch his lights out. So that's when I knew. Dad was there for me just like he was there for me when I almost drowned."

Maggie leaned over and snuggled into Shane's shoulder. The comfort Shane gave her made her feel drowsy. She almost dozed off in Shane's arms before making the connection.

Maggie sat up and bumped Shane in the chin. "You paint, don't you? I mean, you smell like walnut oil. My dad used it when he'd paint with oils. Sometimes, he used acrylics. Soap-and-water cleanup."

Shane tilted his head to one side and smiled. "Yes, Maggie, I do use oil paints."

She took hold of Shane's hands and inspected each one before looking at him again. She pointed to a small blotch of paint between his thumb and index finger. "That's cadmium yellow, isn't it?"

"You're absolutely right. You certainly know your colors." Shane didn't know if he should laugh or cry. The look on Maggie's face was filled with hope and questions. He wasn't sure how he would handle what he knew must be racing through her mind.

Shane walked over to his desk and came back with an envelope and handed it to Maggie. He watched as Maggie studied the name written on the front of the envelope before she looked up at him.

"This is addressed to my dad."

"That's right, Maggie. I think he would have wanted you to read it."

His attempt at a smile couldn't hide the anxiety on his face, and Maggie quickly opened the letter.

"It's from my Grandma Genevieve."

"Yes, it is, Maggie."

The first time she read it, it didn't make any sense, and she looked to Shane for an explanation.

"Why don't you read it again, honey?" he asked in a low voice. "I know it's a lot to understand the first time."

Maggie nodded and started reading again, whispering at first and then reading snippets aloud.

"Your artistic abilities are a gift … from your biological father." Maggie stared at Shane. "Grandpa Rex wasn't Dad's real dad?"

"No, Maggie, he wasn't." Shane hesitated. "I can explain everything your grandmother didn't include in her letter."

Maggie continued reading aloud. "His name is Jonathan O'Shanahan. That's you, isn't it? You're Dad's real father?"

"Yes, I am, Maggie."

Shane watched as Maggie continued reading. When she looked up at him, she was smiling.

"Wow, Grandma was pregnant before she got married? Wait until Becca hears about that …" Maggie looked at Shane, and his face flushed.

"Yes, we were going to get married, but I was in Vietnam and, well things got complicated."

"I'm sorry, Shane. I guess I'm so tired I forgot to be polite."

Maggie looked down at the letter and read it again. When she looked up, she smiled so wide the dimples on her cheeks brightened her face.

"This means we can paint together."

Maggie wrapped her arms around Shane's neck and rested her head on his shoulder.

Shane wanted to tell Maggie everything was going to be just fine now and, yes, they would paint in the willow and he could teach her …

Maggie moved suddenly and stood squarely in front of Shane.

"You're my grandfather."

"Yes, I'm your grandfather, Maggie."

Maggie sat back down in her chair and folded her arms against her chest. Shane waited for her next question. But Maggie just sat there and stared at him.

"Maggie, honey, your dad was a lot like your grandma."

"You mean depressed?"

"Yes, I believe your grandma suffered from depression."

"Are you depressed?"

"No, Maggie. I've had times in my life when I felt I couldn't handle everything I was facing. But never, ever did I give up."

Maggie tightened her arms against her chest.

"Do you think I'm depressed?"

"No, Maggie, I don't."

"How do you know for sure?"

"Any young lady who has the determination to do what you've done, well, I would say that is a sign of someone so level-headed she isn't afraid to get what she wants in life."

Maggie loosened her arms and stared at Shane again.

"Did Grandma ever get any professional help? I mean, didn't she see a shrink about her depression?"

Shane couldn't help but smile. Maggie's transition from fifteen to thirty all in one sentence made him love her even more.

"Yes, she did. But back then, everything was so different. Treatment for people suffering from depression was so radical. And I never knew how much she suffered. When I came back from Vietnam, she was married to your Grandpa Rex. There was nothing I could do to help her."

"So she married him while you were gone? Why?"

"I was taken prisoner, and the army informed your grandmother that I was dead. It was the only thing she could do to take care of your dad and give him a proper family."

"So why didn't you just tell Grandpa Rex to leave?"

"It's not that simple, Maggie. Your father believed Rex was his father. And your grandmother didn't want to upset his life … or her own. So I made a promise to her."

"But why didn't you just tell Dad after Grandma died?"

"I never told your father because I didn't want to create pain and confusion in his life. He would've felt his mother had lied to him. I couldn't let him think that. Your grandmother loved him too much to have his world turned upside down after she died. And so did I."

Shane could feel Maggie studying him, and he hoped the truth wouldn't push her way.

"So I remained silent, "Shane told her. "Until now. Once I discovered your grandmother really wanted me to be a part of your father's life, I knew she would want me to be a part of yours as well."

"What if you'd never found the letter Grandma wrote?"

"I would have told you the truth, Maggie. I really believe it was what your father would have wanted."

Shane's eyes welled up with tears. His love warmed the cold spot in Maggie's heart. She tilted her head to one side and smiled at Shane.

"I think he would have wanted it too, Shane."

Shane smiled.

"Don't you think it's time we called your mother?"

Maggie cringed.

"She's going to be so mad at me. Do you think you could call and break the ice for me?"

Shane ruffled the spiky top of her hair.

"Yes. Of course I'll do that for you."

THIRTY-EIGHT

The grandfather clock chimed seven times and Nora pulled the afghan tight around her shoulders.

"Why haven't we heard something, Steve? For God's sake, it's been almost eight hours since they started looking for her. And nothing. I'm turning on the news. Maybe the media will be quicker than the damn police force."

She grabbed the remote just as the phone rang. Nora threw it on the floor and grabbed the phone.

"Hello, who is this?"

"It's Shane. Shane O'Shanahan, Genevieve's—"

"Oh God, is Maggie with you? Is she okay? I want to talk to her."

Nora's hand shook as she held the receiver.

"She's doing fine, Nora. Exhausted. Was very hungry. But I made macaroni and cheese, and she gobbled it right down."

"Macaroni and cheese. That was John's favorite."

"Yes. Maggie mentioned that."

An uncomfortable silence fell between them. Nora took a deep breath, and the guilt overwhelmed her as she spoke.

"You must think I'm a horrible mother."

"Not at all. Life hasn't been exactly easy for you."

"No. No, it hasn't." Nora leaned back on the couch. "Does Maggie hate me, Shane? I mean, does she even want to come home?"

"Don't worry, Nora. She's sleeping right now, and I know when she wakes up she's going to want to see her mother."

Shane answered too quickly for Nora to feel any sense of relief.

"I want her to come home tonight, Shane. I know it will be late when I get there but, well, I have to be with her."

"Why don't you plan on staying the night?"

"I don't want to impose on you, Shane."

"Maggie's sound asleep, Nora, and I'm sure she'll sleep until morning. And we could talk. And you could see the tree house I built for John."

"But I thought John's father built the tree house?"

"Oh yes, well, I'd love for you to see it. I'm sure these last days have been exhausting for you. Driving back to Rockaway Beach tonight might be too much."

Nora winced. A few days? It'd only been one day for her.

"All right, Shane. I'd like that. Maybe you can help me decipher all this."

"I think I can, Nora."

"Really?" Nora was almost afraid to believe him.

"We'll talk when you get here. Take it slow, Nora. Maggie will be here when you arrive."

Shane relayed the directions, and Nora wrote them down and then thanked Shane before hanging up the phone.

"I'm going with you Nora." Steve took hold of Nora's hand, and Nora avoided eye contact.

"Steve, I need to do this myself." Nora held her hand out to show Steve the shakiness had diminished.

"But you're still exhausted."

"I was hung over. And the nap helped. Shane asked me to spend the night. And I want to, Steve."

Nora watched Steve fold his hands across his chest. He squinted at her as he talked. "I still don't know how I feel about Shane ..."

"I know, I know. But I already told you I've always liked Shane. And the reason John didn't like him is, once Genevieve married him, John felt that Shane had taken his mother away from him."

Nora took hold of Steve's hand. "You have always been way too suspicious for your own good. That's why you make such a damn good cop."

Steve rolled his eyes at Nora and squeezed her hand. "But it's the cop in me that tells me to go with you."

"Yes, but it's the mother in me that says Shane is taking good care of my daughter." Nora thought for a moment. "Shane was always so calm. And when he came up to me at the funeral, he was so empathic. It was comforting."

"But still …"

"I know how you feel about him, Steve. But the fact that he drove all that way to John's funeral and Maggie thought he was the safest person to be with, well, it just reaffirms what I always thought about him. And anyone who could stay by Genevieve's side tolerating those mood swings of hers …"

"Sounds as if the two of you have a lot in common."

The realization of the bond Nora shared with Shane brought a flood of relief.

"Yes, I guess we do."

"Fine. But you call me as soon as you get there. And don't forget your cell phone. And I'll help you pack a change of clothes for you and Maggie."

Nora smiled at her brother. "Yes, Father Steve. I'll do everything you said."

Steve grinned and wrapped his arms around her. "Thank God Maggie's safe."

Nora looked up at her brother. "I guess there really is a God after all, isn't there, Steve?"

THIRTY-NINE

Nora knelt down next to Maggie and watched her sleep. She almost didn't recognize her with that outrageous hairdo. And what was that black crud matted to her scalp? No wonder the bus driver couldn't identify Maggie from her picture.

It pained Nora to think Maggie would go to such lengths to disguise her appearance. And the way Nora had treated her the morning she ran away … Maggie had almost cried. And all Nora did was tell her to quit biting her lip and then pushed her away. She treated her own child like the devil's progeny. No wonder God couldn't get through to her.

Nora tucked the blanket around Maggie and kissed her forehead. Maggie buried her face under the covers just as Shane walked into the room.

"Made some coffee. Care to join me?"

Shane touched Nora's shoulder. She reached up and took hold of his hand.

"I would love some," she whispered.

Nora followed Shane into the living room and settled into the couch. She took the cup of coffee he offered her and tucked her feet under her legs.

"I'm so sorry about all this, Shane. I have no idea why Maggie ended up here. Or how she could possibly think you could help her find John."

"I think I do." Shane thought about the night when he was up in the tree house and felt John's presence. Maybe, just maybe, he was here with them right now and would finally feel some peace.

"I'm curious, Shane. When did you and Genevieve meet?"

Shane was glad for the opportunity to divert the conversation away from Maggie.

"I was nineteen when I met Genevieve. She was a smidge of a gal, a waist so tiny I could circle my hands around it. She worked at the phone company, had just moved to Portland that spring. There she was, bandana over her sun-bleached hair, boots bigger than she was, standing at the bus stop. *My* bus stop.

"Such a good-natured little thing back then. Walked right up to me and asked me my name. Don't know how I ever got my mouth to spit it out. I do know I must have sounded like Daffy Duck because she laughed before repeating it. She brushed her hand ever so lightly across my face and said, 'Nice name, John O'Shanahan. Mind if I call you Shane?' Been stuck with that nickname ever since." Shane laughed and took a sip of his coffee.

"We spent that whole summer together. I'd just about moved in with her after the first month. And then my mother died. We moved right here after the funeral. Mom left the house to me in her will." Shane stopped for a moment and allowed the memory to replay in his head.

"But I thought the house, it belonged to Rex and Genevieve ..."

"I know, Nora. So did everyone else."

"Please go on, Shane. I want you to tell me every last detail."

Shane shifted on the couch and then continued talking. "Such a childlike presence, Genevieve. We'd just gotten back from Angel Falls when she told me her age. Said she was twenty-nine. I didn't believe her at first. Guess I should have, with her living on her own and all. She was scared. Big ole tears welled up in her eyes."

When Shane looked over at Nora, her eyes were filled with tears. He took her hand and moved closer to her on the couch.

"And you know, Nora. I told her it didn't matter if she was seventeen or twenty-nine or even sixty-five, that I loved her and would until the day I died. I was head over heels in love."

He pulled a handkerchief out of his pocket and handed it to Nora and then used his bare hand to wipe the tears out of his own eyes.

"I'm ten years older than John." Nora choked back the sobs.

Shane looked down at Nora's hands. They were tiny and smooth. He felt as if Genevieve was sitting next to him again.

"I asked her to marry me right then." Shane pictured Genevieve throwing her arms around his neck and kissing his face and whispering yes, yes, over and over again. He tightened his hold on Nora's hand.

"My lottery number was picked, and that changed everything. We were going to get married, but the army shipped me off to Vietnam. Nasty place and just about impossible to get back home once I got there. Genevieve said she'd wait for me."

Shane paused for a moment and then whispered. "Found out later she wasn't as strong as I thought."

He felt Nora squeeze his hand, as if she knew what he was saying.

Nora looked up at him and he saw a determined resolve on her face. "Keep talking, Shane."

Shane leaned back on the couch and sighed.

"I built the tree house in the willow. I had to make sure each board was carefully placed so that the tree house didn't depend on the willow for support and that the integrity of the tree wasn't compromised. I wanted to create a place up high, where I could be surrounded by nature. A place of solitude, where I could let go of everything and just paint. And I dreamed of painting there with my child one day. I spent my last days up there before I shipped out to Vietnam, lost in the colors on my palette as I created one picture after another."

"That's how John was before he died. He'd stay up for days, eyes always brimming red, focusing on nothing but his next creation."

"That is the artist's weakness and also our strength."

Shane stopped and tried to erase the images clouding his thoughts.

"Genevieve sent me a letter and told me she was pregnant. I was on top of the world. Nothing, absolutely nothing, was going to keep me from watching my son—I was sure it was a boy—grow up."

Shane watched a look of surprise spread over Nora's face. He waited for a response, and when she didn't speak, he continued.

"My leave was cancelled twice. And after that, I was knee-deep in Operation Junction City—a massive search-and-destroy mission along the Cambodian border. That's where the Vietcong captured me and four other members of my platoon. Army reported me as MIA. But even before Genevieve heard that, she and Rex married."

Nora bit her lip and nodded for Shane to keep going.

"I don't know. Maybe she was afraid of being an unwed mother—that was a real curse back then. Well, I guess I'll never really know for sure." Shane took a sip of his lukewarm coffee and set the mug back on the table.

"I was in a Vietnamese prison camp for five years. I didn't know she had married Rex until I got home. I wanted to surprise her, didn't want her to receive the news in a telegram or through the army. I wanted to be there to take her in my arms and experience her joy. That didn't happen. Got home to find my best friend had stolen my life."

Shane reached for his coffee mug and then changed his mind. The tepid temperature was too similar to the half-hearted reception he was given when he returned from Vietnam.

"I don't blame her for what she did. She had a baby on the way and fell apart. So I just tucked myself away in Lake Oswego and allowed Jack Daniels to nurse my wounds."

The shock and then disbelief on Nora's face was painfully familiar.

"Oh, it happens to the best of us, Nora. But once you realize the damage alcohol does to your life, well, you can change."

The handkerchief in Nora's hand was soaked. Shane stood up and, without a word, went into the kitchen and returned with a full box of tissues.

"When Rex died, Genevieve came to me, asked me to marry her. I was so surprised we got the marriage license the next day."

Shane stopped and looked down at the floor. He wasn't sure if he should continue. Lord knew he'd disclosed more than his share of secrets. When he looked at Nora, she nodded for him to continue.

"It was good. For a while. But I knew it couldn't—wouldn't—last forever. Then the mood swings got so bad all she did was curl up in a ball on the bottom of the closet. The doctor suggested shock treatments—either that or have her committed for good."

"So that's why she had the treatments."

"Well, no. That's not exactly what happened. The night before she was scheduled to go in, I woke up around four o'clock in a cold sweat—

and could smell exhaust fumes all the way up stairs."

"Oh God, Shane, no. I had no idea. I thought—John thought—she died from the shock treatments."

"I know. And I didn't want John to know differently. I knew he blamed me—and I was fine with that. I didn't want him ever to know that his mother took her own life."

"I understand completely. Thank you, Shane. You've reaffirmed a lot of things for me tonight."

"You're welcome, Nora. It's getting late, and I'm sure you must be exhausted."

"Yes. This ... there's just so much to process right now."

"Then a good night's rest will do you good. You can sleep in the bedroom next to Maggie."

When Nora looked at Shane, he felt her sadness and sat down next to her on the couch. "Maggie is a resilient young woman, Nora. You can mend what's been broken."

"You think so, Shane?"

Shane didn't hesitate this time. "Absolutely, Nora, absolutely."

FOURTY

M aggie snuggled into the warmth of the down comforter.
"Thanks, Star Dust." She pulled the blanket up around
her neck and nestled into the flannel pillowcase.

Wait a minute.

Maggie opened her eyes and bolted upright and looked cautiously around.

Her next-to-favorite burgundy sweatpants and sweatshirt were folded neatly on a chair. A bottle of Bumble and Bumble hairspray sat next to her shampoo and super-rich conditioner on the dresser.

Skechers tennies sat below the rocker with socks stuffed inside one of the shoes. And not just any socks—*the* socks that matched the hot-pink stripes on her sweatpants.

Maggie grabbed the shampoo and cream rinse and tiptoed into the bathroom. Two clean towels and a washcloth sat on the counter next to a bottle of Jergens lotion and her Olay cleanser and face cream. Maggie turned the shower on and then looked in the mirror. Her hair was matted to her head and her teeth felt like she'd been eating sandpaper-coated cotton balls.

She grabbed the toothpaste and toothbrush off the counter and brushed her teeth until her gums bled.

Maggie jumped into the shower. The sound of the water spewing from the showerhead reminded her of Angel Falls. She wondered if Star Dust ever went back to their campsite … and thought how mad her mom was going to be when Maggie saw her for the first time.

She shampooed her hair three times and scrubbed her face twice. Each time she scrubbed her body, it took a layer of anxiety away. After she rinsed the conditioner from her hair, she was ready to talk to her mom.

Maggie towel-dried her short blond locks and then lathered her skin with lotion. Her face looked soft and pink and new, and the scent of Jergens smelled like she was home again.

Maggie dressed and then headed for the kitchen. The aroma of fresh coffee greeted her as she peeked around the entry.

Nora stood in front of the kitchen window, coffee cup cradled in her hands as she watched a hummingbird drink from the feeder.

Maggie took a deep breath before walking into the room. "Mother?"

Nora turned, and Maggie watched her eyes well up with tears.

"Oh Maggie, honey. I've missed you so much."

Nora sat the coffee cup on the table, and Maggie rushed into her outstretched arms.

"When did you get here?" Maggie buried her head in Nora's chest, and the mom fragrance Maggie loved so much made her cry.

"It's okay, Maggie." Nora pulled her closer and stroked her hair until her daughter's tears subsided. When Maggie looked up into her mother's eyes, Nora smiled at her.

"Then you're not mad at me, Mom?" Maggie's voice faltered, and Nora hugged her again and laughed and cried at the same time.

"No, young lady, I'm not mad at you—I'm mad at myself for being … being such a bitch of a drunken mother to you."

Maggie giggled. She wasn't used to her mom swearing, and Nora's honesty freed the lump in Maggie's throat.

"Well, that's true, Mom. You were drinking way too much, and those meds, well—"

"Were dumped down the toilet. Along with every bottle of alcohol in the house."

Maggie stood back and stared at her mother.

"Wow, you got clean? I mean, you didn't have to go to treatment or anything?"

Nora hugged Maggie again.

"Dr. Roberts suggested I go to outpatient treatment. It's in the evenings, so you would have to stay with Becca while I'm gone."

"Oh my God, Mom! Becca—I was supposed to call her. She must be just worried sick and madder than anything at me right now."

Maggie plopped down on a chair, and Nora sat next to her.

"But I need to say one more thing before I call Becca, Mom."

"All right, Maggie. I'm listening."

Maggie took hold of Nora's hands.

"I know Dad's dead—"

"I know you do, Maggie."

"Wait a minute. I'm not finished. The reason I didn't believe it is because I felt him carry me out of the water. And well, when I was at the funeral, Shane walked up to me, and I thought he was Dad." Maggie squeezed Nora's hands. "And Dad saved me from the truck driver, and I heard his voice in my head, and nobody can or will ever convince me that I didn't."

"Truck driver? What are you talking about, Maggie?"

Maggie's words flooded from her mouth. "Well, I saw him when I went outside the bus station. After I found out Shane's number was disconnected. I was going to follow the highway to North Beach. You know, stay in the woods so nobody could report me. Well, he tried to grab me then. But I ran away from him. I smashed into this nun, and I think she was a mother superior. After that, I hid in the woods. And this hippie chick, Star Dust, took care of me, and then she was gone, and …" Maggie took a deep breath when she saw her mother's mouth drop open in disbelief. "And well, all I'm really trying to say, Mom, is I'm so glad you're here."

Maggie felt a tear spill down her cheek, and Nora reached up and wiped it away.

"And I know Dad saved me. Well, maybe the spiritual Dad or something—but he did, and I'll never believe he didn't."

Nora's smile softened Maggie's anxiety.

"I believe you, Maggie, because I felt him, too. And I think … I think your dad was just so worried about you—us—that he wanted to make sure we were okay before, well, before he left for good."

Maggie looked up at her mother, and for the first time, she knew Nora believed her.

"Thanks, Mom. I believe that, too."

Nora wiped the tears from Maggie's eyes. "You're welcome, honey. Now, I brought my cell with me. You can call Becca right now if you want."

"But today's Tuesday. She'll be in school."

"I talked to Kathy an hour ago. Becca stayed home today. And she's waiting for your call."

Nora walked over to the counter. She pulled her cell phone from her purse and handed it to Maggie as Shane walked into the kitchen.

"Sleep well, Maggie?" Shane winked at her and smiled.

"Oh yes, thanks, Shane. I'm going to call my best friend, Becca. Did I tell you about her last night?"

"Yes, you did mention her."

"And I'm sorry I didn't shower before I went to bed, Shane. There's probably half a forest between the sheets."

"That's why washing machines were invented, Maggie." Shane laughed and then turned to Nora. "Care to join me in the living room for another cup of coffee?"

"I was just going to suggest that myself."

Nora smiled brighter than Maggie had seen in months. Shane picked up her mother's mug, refilled it, and then topped off his own.

"There's fresh juice in the fridge, Maggie. And chocolate chip muffins on the counter. Help yourself."

Maggie watched them walk into the living room and then poured a glass of apple juice. She picked up a muffin, balanced it on top of her glass, and grabbed Nora's cell as she walked out on the back deck.

The autumn sun warmed Maggie's face, and the coolness of the breeze made her sweats feel all snuggly and warm. She watched the wind ruffle the willow's branches and was trying to decide how she'd start her conversation with Becca when the cell phone rang.

"Hello?"

"Can you understand how … how super pissed off I am at you right now, Maggie O'Brien?"

Maggie detected a sense of relief in her best friend's voice.

"Well, can you imagine how mad I was when I had no cell service? And I had to call Shane's phone number from this ancient phone booth? And then a stupid lady on the recording said the number was disconnected?"

"Shut up, Maggie."

"And then I lost my wallet and almost mowed down a mother superior. That was before I met this hippie chick who called herself Star Dust after I ran into the woods and tried to hide from this truck driver—"

"The one who drove his truck into Devil's River? I heard about him in the news."

"Yep, that's him. He was so gross. There were fish eating the gunk off his teeth when they pulled him out of the river."

"Shut up, Maggie." Becca giggled. "I'm just so glad you're alive. And well, when your mom finally sobered up enough to realize you were gone ..."

"Yeah, I know, well, she might do the outpatient treatment thing when we get back."

"That's great, and we're going to have so much to talk about, Maggie. It feels like you've been gone a hundred years."

Maggie heard Becca take a deep breath and used the opportunity to down her apple juice.

"Want to know the best part, Becca?" Maggie picked a chocolate chip out of her muffin and waited for Becca's response.

"Come on already, Maggie. Tell me. We don't have all day."

"Sure we do."

"Stop it, Maggie."

"Fine. You remember your mom saying there was something she never understood about Shane?"

"Yeah, so ..."

"So Shane's my grandfather."

"Shut up!"

"That's what I said, Becca. Shane's my grandpa!"

Maggie popped another chocolate chip in her mouth and waited for Becca's response.

"Well, you know what that means don't you, Maggie?"

"Of course I do, nerd. It means Rex wasn't really my dad's dad."

"No, stupid—it means your grandma had sex with Shane before she ever married anyone."

"You are such a retard, Becca."

Maggie chuckled as she pulled the top off her muffin and took a bite.

"Well, it's true, Maggie."

Maggie laughed even harder. "I miss you so much, Becca."

"Yeah, well, when are you coming home? I mean, you're not going to, like, live with Shane now, are you?"

"No. I found what I was looking for. I'm ready to go home."

"For sure? Then you're coming home, Mag, I mean *for sure*?"

"Yes, Becca, for sure, I'm coming home."

FOURTY-ONE

A band of clouds floated casually across the heavens. The wind shifted suddenly, and a steady rain began working its way from the northeast, threatening to take the warmth from the Indian summer afternoon.

The willow tree's branches began their dance as Nora and Shane lounged on the outdoor swing. Maggie ran off the back porch and down the hill, John's paintbrushes held tightly in her hand. The old swing crooned with satisfaction as Maggie sat next to Shane.

John sat in the grass several feet from the swing and took in the tranquility of the moment. A warm breeze ruffled John's hair, and a hand gently touched his shoulder. He looked up, and Star Dust smiled down at him.

"I'll never have that."

"Have what, John?"

"That solid connection with Maggie."

"You made a choice, John."

"Yes. I did."

Star Dust sat down next to John and held his hand. "Shane has aged gracefully. He looks even better than … than when we were young."

John couldn't believe what Star Dust had just said. "What are you talking about?"

"Genevieve. Your mother. She was my best friend."

"But how? Then you knew all along."

"No. Maybe at first I thought it was possible. But it was just too trippy to be coincidence. But once I saw Shane, well, then I knew."

"And Shane. What do you make of him now?"

"He's still the most remarkable man I ever encountered."

"Shane is the missing piece in all my paintings." John watched Maggie unclasp the gold chain he'd given her. "The part I thought was missing was here; he was right here all along. And I didn't even know it."

"This locket belonged to my dad, Shane." Maggie's words floated on the wind as she took the locket off the chain. John watched Shane turn the locket over in his hand.

"It's beautiful, Maggie." Shane's voice bounced above the breeze, and the lightness of his words surrounded John.

"Open it, Shane."

Shane unclasped the locket and paused before speaking. "It has your picture inside and one of your father."

Maggie opened her locket and revealed its contents.

"Mine has a picture of Dad." Maggie ran her finger across the tiny portrait of her father and then looked up and smiled. "And there's room for a picture of you on the other side, Shane."

"Yes, Maggie, there is." Shane closed John's locket and tried to hand it back to Maggie, but she quickly clasped Shane's hand around it and shook her head.

"No. Keep it. You should have Dad's locket, Shane."

"Are you sure, Maggie? It belonged to your father and well …"

"He would want you to have it, Shane. I can feel it in my heart."

A sudden gust of cool air swirled around them, and Maggie jumped out of the swing and headed toward the willow.

"Maggie, there's a storm coming. Stay here on the covered swing with us, or you're going to get drenched."

Nora's voice sounded soft, the way it used to, and when Maggie turned back to answer, Shane was holding Nora's hand.

"Let her go, Nora. It's just wind. She'll be fine."

Shane tilted his head to one side and smiled. Maggie raced back to his side and whispered in his ear.

"I love you, Shane."

Each deep breath of clean air made Maggie feel so alive her feet tingled as she soared over the grass. She practically flew up the ladder, and when she arrived safely inside the tree house, she laughed a huge belly laugh, and it started to rain.

Maggie's laugh resonated through John's soul. He cried tears of joy with each of Maggie's uncontrollable giggles. The clouds gathering above the willow thickened, and the pain of living was replaced with a vast love. John could feel himself growing smaller as he floated skyward.

Maggie's laughter turned into uncontrollable weeping as she placed a canvas on the easel. A bolt of lightning flashed across the horizon, and seconds later, thunder roared.

Maggie grabbed a brush and a tube of white paint. She applied it directly to the center of the blank canvas in front of her. The outer edges were splashed with a mixture of cobalt and ultramarine blue. She mixed dollops of white with a touch of lemon yellow. A circular motion lightened and blended the blues together until they muted to the palest blue and harmonized with the white in the center of the canvas.

The air crackled, and the willow's branches came to life. They swayed with the breeze, and the tree house moved beneath her feet. When the wind kicked up again, Maggie connected to the melody playing.

Each brushstroke felt orchestrated by something much larger than herself. She allowed the vibration of the storm to dictate each move. The branches sang in unison with the wind. She felt the music surround her as she transformed the center of the painting into the shape of a dove.

A dab of Payne's gray blended with burnt umber formed the bird's beak. A touch of black and a drop of ultramarine defined the dove's eyes. A final blending of gray provided it with wings.

With each stroke of Maggie's paintbrush, John felt her letting him go. A flock of white birds surrounded him, and he allowed the gentle swoop of their wings to encircle and guide him skyward. As he floated up, the intensity of his love for Maggie drifted down. The relief he felt made him lighter and smaller as he traveled effortlessly toward the heavens.

Maggie stood back and looked at her final work. She placed the brush on the easel and sat down on the tree house floor. She closed her eyes and swayed with the rhythm of the storm. The willow's branches danced to the next refrain, and when she opened her eyes, she looked out at the sky. The upper limbs of the tree parted just enough for her to see a flock of doves flying toward the heavens.

"Dad?"

The willow swayed, and Maggie moved to the window, remembering her father's final words.

Never forget that I will always be with you. Climb the willow tree and listen to the song the wind has to sing, for it is my song to you. Always remember, Magpie, that up there, you will find my love and it will fill your heart.

A mist of tiny raindrops fell from the clouds, and each drop felt like a butterfly kiss as it touched her cheek.

The birds shimmered in the sunlight and their wings blended with the clouds and highlighted the patches of blue sky.

"I'm right here, Daddy."

John watched his daughter's life unfold before him.

Her birth. First steps. Creating the castle on her bedroom walls. The times filled with laughter and tears. All so intense and beautiful, as though he was experiencing them for the first time.

John felt comfort in knowing there would be new memories for her, even stronger than the ones they shared.

His heart soared, and the upward motion of the doves faded into small, white fluffy clouds. John took one final deep breath before allowing all his love for Maggie to drift downward.

Maggie scrutinized the dove she'd painted and then highlighted its wings with white, giving the bird a translucent glow.

The tree house felt warm and cold all at once, and the branches on the tree sang louder with each gust of warm air, whispering assurance that Maggie would never be alone again.

She allowed a shift deep inside, down where it hurt the most when her father died. She knew now he would always be with her, and she wanted him to know that.

She moved to the window, leaned out as far as she could, and looked up toward the sky. Raindrops fluttered across her face as she whispered one final message to her father.

"Can you hear it, Dad? Can you hear the weeping willow sing?"